D0561786

BETTER LUCK NEXT TIME

ALSO BY KATE HILTON

The Hole in the Middle
Just Like Family

BETTER LUCK NEXT TIME

A NOVEL

Kate Hilton

HARPER**AVENUE**

Better Luck Next Time
Copyright © 2020 by Kate Hilton.
All rights reserved.

Published by Harper Avenue, an imprint of HarperCollins Publishers Ltd

First edition

No part of this book may be used or reproduced in any manner whatsoever
without the prior written permission of the publisher, except in the case of brief
quotations embodied in reviews.

HarperCollins books may be purchased for educational, business or
sales promotional use through our Special Markets Department.

HarperCollins Publishers Ltd
Bay Adelaide Centre, East Tower
22 Adelaide Street West, 41st Floor
Toronto, Ontario, Canada
M5H 4E3

www.harpercollins.ca

Library and Archives Canada Cataloguing in Publication

Title: Better luck next time : a novel / Kate Hilton.
Names: Hilton, Kate, 1972- author.
Identifiers: Canadiana (print) 20200188739 | Canadiana (ebook) 20200188747
ISBN 9781443451482 (softcover) | ISBN 9781443451505 (ebook)
Classification: LCC PS8615.I48 B48 2020 | DDC C813/.6—dc23

Printed and bound in the United States of America

LSC/H 9 8 7 6 5 4 3 2 1

For Sasha,
my better luck next time,

and for Heanda and Laurie,
guardian angels and wise women

THE GOLDSTEIN-HENNESSEY FAMILY

The Hennessey Branch

ZOE HENNESSEY (42), advertising executive, sister to Zack, cousin to Mariana, Nina, and Beata

ZACK HENNESSEY (33), scriptwriter, brother to Zoe, cousin to Mariana, Nina, and Beata

LARRY HENNESSEY (72), investment banker (retired), father to Zoe and Zack, brother to Lydia Hennessey

JUDY HENNESSEY (69), homemaker, mother to Zoe and Zack

The Goldstein-Hennessey Branch

MARIANA GOLDSTEIN-HENNESSEY (44), journalist, mother to Siobhan and Iona, sister to Nina and Beata, cousin to Zoe and Zack

NINA GOLDSTEIN-HENNESSEY (39), doctor, sister to Mariana and Beata, cousin to Zoe and Zack

BEATA GOLDSTEIN-HENNESSEY (35), craniosacral therapist and Reiki practitioner, mother to Oscar, sister to Mariana and Nina, cousin to Zoe and Zack

LYDIA HENNESSEY (70), activist, writer, feminist icon, mother to Mariana, Nina, and Beata, sister to Larry Hennessey

MARVIN GOLDSTEIN (73), dentist (retired), father to Mariana, Nina, and Beata

SIOBHAN AND IONA KELLEY (both 4), Mariana's daughters

OSCAR GOLDSTEIN-HENNESSEY (15), Beata's son

THE SUPPORTING CAST

DEVLIN KELLEY (41), Mariana's husband

ELOISE EMBREE (40), a divorce lawyer

WILL SHANNON (44), Zoe's friend from university

DECEMBER

CHAPTER I

Zoe

It isn't Zoe Hennessey's usual habit to stop in for a double espresso shot on the way to Christmas dinner at her mother's house, but this year she feels the need to fortify herself. Her local café is open: Thank you, baby Jesus! It's the only Christmas gift she needs, and she's grateful for this slight but welcome evidence of civilization's progress. There are few others to be found these days, as far as she can tell.

Her favourite barista is behind the bar today, heavily tattooed, delicious. She is objectifying him. She knows this. She's been on the receiving end often enough. He graces her with an easy smile, and she thinks it might be fun to take him home some night. She's had her share of lovers, but no one with tattoos. They weren't that fashionable last time she was on the market.

"Hey there," he says. "You're . . ." He stops. A frown drifts across his lovely face.

"I'm Zoe." He recognizes her. It's a sign.

"Sorry," he says.

"No problem. You see a lot of faces every day. And I don't think I've ever told you my name, anyway."

"It's not that. I was confused for a minute. I thought you were someone else."

Encouraging indeed, she thinks. She reminds him of someone in his orbit, an orbit full of hip young people with tattoos and piercings, doing whatever such people do for fun. She doesn't yet know what those things are, but she intends to use her unexpected freedom to find out.

He says, "I thought you were my buddy's stepmom. It's funny, you really look like her."

This is when the realization comes crashing down: her life is over.

She is not, as she has been persuading herself in the mirror with daily affirmations, a young, soon-to-be divorced woman with an insignificant starter marriage behind her and a horizon littered with choices ahead. She is, rather, a middle-aged castoff who looks like someone's stepmom. Merry Christmas.

Zoe takes a cab to her mother's house. She slouches in the back seat, working on her public message. She could keep this to herself, she understands that, but she's learned often enough in the advertising business that winning is about controlling the story. And she needs a win today. She opens Facebook and posts: *The hunky barista at MainLine just mistook me for his buddy's stepmom. Thanks, Santa!*

She's late, and she can feel the vibration of chaos behind the door to her mother's house. The door swings open before she can ring the bell, revealing her brother, Zack, wearing a parka.

"Tag," he says. "You're it. I'm going for a smoke."

"Zoe!" Judy Hennessey pulls her daughter into her arms. "Where's Richard?"

"He's at his mother's," says Zoe. It has taken thirty seconds for her to start lying, which, while not unprecedented, gives her a sense of foreboding.

"See you soon," says Zack, heading down the front steps.

"Don't be long!" Judy calls after Zack's retreating figure, and then closes the door, trapping Zoe in a building with all the rest of her living blood relatives.

"I thought Richard was coming here this year," says Judy.

"He wanted to."

"If he'd wanted to, he would have. I have to say, Zoe, I think it's hurtful that Richard always prioritizes his own family. He knows how much I love Christmas."

"Everyone knows how much you love Christmas," says Zoe's father, Larry. He gives Zoe a kiss on the cheek.

"Or," suggests Zoe, as she does every time this topic comes up, "let's consider the possibility that it's not about you."

Her mother pretends not to hear her.

"What can I get you to drink, Zoe?" asks Uncle Marvin.

"I'll have what you're having."

"He's having double Scotches," says Lydia, Zoe's aunt.

"I'm down with that," says Zoe.

"Why don't you sit down and relax, honey?" says Larry. "You've been working so hard."

"We've barely seen you," says Judy.

Zoe does not rise to this bait. She is trying to live in the here and now, but in the here and now, her mother has already started to annoy her. She chooses a seat in the corner of the living room, away from the madness under the tree, where her cousin Mariana's four-year-old twin daughters are pulling wrapping paper out of a garbage bag and tearing it into confetti. She contemplates the future, an imaginary future where she spends Christmas on a beach with someone who looks like the barista at MainLine.

She ignores Mariana's husband, Devlin, which is easy to do since he is ignoring everyone else, addressing himself to his iPhone with fervour, facing away from his children in a pose that says, unmistakably, *Not my problem.*

Uncle Marvin appears with her drink. "Merry Merry," he says, clinking his glass against Zoe's. He is sweating profusely.

"Are you feeling okay, Marv?"

"Oh, sure," he says. "If you don't mind it being a million degrees in the house."

"I'm cooking a turkey, Marvin," says Judy. "If you're planning on eating it, you can stop complaining."

"Don't mind me," says Marvin. "I'm only dying of heat prostration."

"Have a drink," says Lydia. "Oh wait, you already are."

"Give it a rest, Mom," says Mariana, Zoe's oldest cousin. "It's Christmas."

"That's entirely my point," says Lydia.

"Mom, do you need help in the kitchen?" asks Zoe. The energy in the room is rising, and not in an uplifting way. She feels the need to chop something, carve something.

"Yes, I certainly do," says Judy. "Lydia, I'm delegating the living room to you." Her tone suggests that she's not sure Lydia is up to the job. In the early days of Larry and Judy's courtship, Lydia expressed disappointment that her brother had fallen for a woman without professional ambitions or feminist convictions. Judy's quiet fury still burns after almost fifty years.

Zoe stands. There's a knock at the door. "I'll get it," she says. "And I'll be right with you, Mom."

She opens the door for Zack. "You came back," she says. "Not sure I would have made the same choice."

"How's Richard?" he says, removing his coat.

"He's fine. He went to his cousin's for dinner."

"You said he went to his mother's."

"He drove his mother to his cousin's house."

"You might want to get your story straight."

"You might want to mind your own business."

"Then again, I might not," says Zack.

Zoe reaches out and pinches her pain-in-the-ass baby brother hard, and he punches back harder. "Ow," she says.

"I've been working out. It's my new drug of choice."

"That's good, Zack," says Zoe. "Really good." She pauses. "Are you writing?" Can she ask? Should she?

"That depends on what you mean by writing," he says.

Zoe hopes it doesn't mean mining the family album

for inspiration. Zack enjoys a certain amount of fame in the entertainment world as the screenwriter behind *After the Revolution*, a critically acclaimed television dramedy that ran for three decreasingly popular seasons. It was fresh and funny and, in the view of all branches of the Hennessey family, insufficiently loosely based on Lydia and her children.

Zoe understands how temptation overwhelmed whatever common sense Zack possesses. Lydia is a feminist icon. She's marched and lectured and sat in everywhere that matters. Her face is on buttons and posters and television screens. She's a compelling character, as Zack demonstrated rather too successfully. Zack's life changed overnight, from pounding out pilots in a shitty apartment to seeing and being seen with his posse of famous friends. There were award nominations, glamorous vacations, a celebrity girlfriend, and party drugs. And then there was a series cancellation, a tabloid break-up, a stay at some kind of rehab centre, and a move home with promises to regain trust and mend relationships.

"Weren't you telling me about an idea you had for a new pilot? Something about art students? Or film students?"

"I threw it out. It's been done before."

"Everything's been done before. Your talent is in finding a fresh way to tell an old story."

"I'm not fresh anymore," says Zack. "I'm frozen."

Zoe rubs her eyes to prevent herself from rolling them. Zack's millennial angst can be irritating. Now thirty-three, he was the long-awaited golden child born nine years after Zoe, and there are moments when the generational difference is striking.

"Is anyone going to help with this dinner?" Judy shouts from the kitchen.

"She means you," says Zack.

Zoe doesn't bother to disagree with him. Producing festive meals is a form of martyrdom reserved for the women in her family. Her father, at least, has his own version; Larry has been known to mow the lawn at high noon in July, and he's burned, sliced, and impaled himself doing home repairs that no one of his age and skill level should attempt alone. Judy's suffering waxes and wanes with the seasons, reaching peak intensity around holiday meals, particularly those with too many guests and too many courses. It is a tribulation that cannot, evidently, be borne alone: it is to be shared, ideally with a daughter.

"I'm not done discussing this with you," Zoe says to her brother.

"My suggestion? Focus on your own problems," says Zack. "And have a drink. I would, if I weren't trying to 'resist numbing behaviours.'" Zack has taken to using air quotes around mantras from his stint in rehab. Zoe wonders if this demonstrates less buy-in to the message than might be desirable. But she's finished worrying about Zack today. It is her Christmas present to herself. And her mother clearly needs some attention.

"How are we doing?" Zoe asks, entering the maternal sanctuary.

"It will be a miracle if this meal hits the table before nine," says Judy. "A miracle!"

"'Tis the season."

Her mother glares at her. "I've been in here since seven o'clock this morning, without one iota of useful help from anyone. Can you pick up where Lydia left off on the salad?"

"Lydia and Mariana stand ready to assist, my dear," says Larry, passing through to get more ice from the back porch. "And I did offer to help myself, numerous times. You kicked us all out. In the sweetest possible way, of course." He drops a kiss on his wife's cheek.

"Lydia may have been on the front page of *The New York Times*," says Judy, not bothering to lower her voice, "but she couldn't make a ham sandwich if her life depended on it. Mariana has her hands full with those twins. And you, darling, are the love of my life, but keep walking."

"Your wish is my command," says Larry.

Zoe attempts to resuscitate Lydia's mangled cucumbers. "Lydia is obviously a special case. But Dad's not that useless, surely."

"Your father worked his fingers to the bone his whole life. The least I can do is give him a lovely Christmas dinner." Zoe and her mother have this conversation every year; it is their Nativity pageant.

"Zack's fingers work fine, too," Zoe says, reciting her lines by rote.

"Zachary has been working himself into a state of exhaustion for months. He needs some peace and quiet."

"Zack's been in rehab."

"It was a wellness retreat. And why would you bring that up on Christmas?"

"Do we have a moratorium on the truth at Christmas?"

"Is it so much to ask that we could *have a nice time*?"

"A nice time," as defined by Judy Hennessey, is a period in which the entire family jettisons reality and pretends that everyone is doing as well as Judy has told her friends they're doing. Zoe wonders if perhaps her mother is onto something. What if she and Zack aren't trying hard enough to imagine their perfect lives into being? What if their personal catastrophes are fundamental failures of imagination? Or maybe everyone is this screwed up, but better than they are at staying on message.

"No," says Zoe. "It's not so much to ask." She puts her head down, and an hour passes in chopping and basting and stirring and seasoning. Her mind wanders to Richard.

She doesn't miss him, exactly. It's impossible to miss Richard at Christmas, because Richard has always been a complete pill about family holidays, and if he were here, Zoe knows, she would be in the kitchen worrying about whether he was enjoying himself in the living room (where Mariana's children are now engaged in timed sprints to resolve an argument over which one of them is the faster runner), or else she'd be in the living room trying to pacify him while worrying about her mother working unassisted in the kitchen. No, she doesn't miss those Christmases. She misses the Christmases she's never had. She's homesick for a life that has never existed, a life where she is married to a man who buys her stupid gifts that reference charming in-jokes between them. Who wears ugly Christmas sweaters and passes the hors d'oeuvres and helps Mariana's kids assemble their ear-splittingly loud plastic toys and watches stupid YouTube videos with her nephew, Oscar. Who says *all I want for Christmas is you*, and means it.

Zoe misses the Christmases when she doesn't have to tell her mother that she's getting a divorce, which represents every Christmas, real or imagined, except this very one, right here and now.

"How are we coming along there?" asks Judy. "Keep stirring!"

"I've got this," says Zoe.

"We're ten minutes away. Don't let the sauce curdle!"

"Not on my watch," she says.

Although the truth is that bad things do tend to happen on her watch: for example, Richard's affair with the woman-child who sold them the kayak at Hiker's Haven, the very kayak that Zoe bought for Richard's birthday, so that he could get closer to nature. Zoe encouraged Richard to expand his horizons; up to that point, his relationship to nature had been one of appreciating its fruits, notably artisanal cheese and Barolo, and (not unrelated to that fact) she thought he could use some exercise. Expand his horizons he did, well beyond monogamy, and she forgave him—accepting "mid-life crisis" as an excuse—only to discover, after six months of therapy and self-flagellation, that the girlfriend was still in the picture. All of which was awful enough without having supported his career shift from a decent-paying job in banking to a fledging home-based consulting gig, which, she now realizes, both reduced his income dramatically and gave him daily opportunities to cheat on her.

Her own idiocy mortifies her. Her life is a catastrophe of her own making. But she won't let the sauce curdle. You have to draw the line somewhere.

"Are you and Richard having problems?" Judy asks.

"Why would you ask that?" Why would she? Zoe has been careful to tell only her closest friends, a group that does not include any family members other than Mariana, about the ongoing saga of her marriage. Has Mariana been indiscreet?

"You are, aren't you?"

"Why are we talking about this now? Isn't the turkey ready?"

"Forget the turkey," says Judy.

It is a statement with the force of an explosion. Judy Hennessey has never, in her entire life, uttered the words *forget the turkey.* "Mom," says Zoe, "this isn't the time. People are waiting."

"That's not an answer."

"Things with Richard are not ideal, but let's focus on dinner right now, okay?"

"How close are we?" says Larry, coming into the kitchen. "Mariana's kids may turn feral if we don't get some food on the table, pronto."

"Then grab an oar," says Judy, in a tone that is more

than slightly hysterical. "Do you think this dinner will get on the table all by itself?"

Larry looks surprised—justifiably, in Zoe's opinion—and begins backing out of the room. "I'll get your brother," he says to Zoe, disappearing through the archway as she says, "Please don't."

"What's going on in here?" says Zack, materializing instantly. Zack has an obvious talent for generating and participating in scenes of family dysfunction. It's tempting to blame this propensity on his recent immersion in the television industry, but he's been stirring the Hennessey pot since childhood.

"Absolutely nothing," says Zoe, filling his arms with serving bowls. "Make yourself useful. Take these out to the table."

"Zoe and Richard are having problems," says Judy.

"You don't say," says Zack, putting the bowls down on the kitchen counter.

"You don't say what?" says Larry, coming back in.

"Dad," says Zoe urgently, "we need to carve the turkey. The carving set is over there, along with the platter."

"On it," he says, removing his suit jacket and rolling up his sleeves.

"Mariana's kids are going to lose it if we don't get some food into them ASAP," says Lydia, whose specialties, in addition to baiting her sister-in-law and bungling culinary assignments, include barging into rooms and making unwelcome pronouncements.

"We're nearly ready. Could you put the cranberry sauce in this bowl?" asks Judy. "I'll heat it up."

"Oh, I should have mentioned it earlier," says Lydia. "I didn't bring any. The store was sold out."

"Why didn't you call? I would have made some from scratch."

"With all the other dishes you've made? Don't be silly. It won't be missed. No one eats cranberry anyway."

"I do," says Judy. "As you know."

"We're five minutes away, Lydia," Zoe says. "Why don't you call everyone to the table and get them seated?"

"Isn't Richard coming?" asks Lydia.

"He's at his cousin's house," says Zoe.

"I thought he was at his mother's house," says Zack, in an extraordinarily loud stage whisper.

It is pure instinct that drives her arm up and behind her shoulder and then forward with velocity, the instinct of a natural athlete, or an animal under attack. The ladle is an extension of her arm until she releases it, and then it is an entity unto itself, hurtling through space, no longer obeying the commands of whatever primitive part of Zoe's brain has set this scene in motion. The ladle spirals up through the air, ascending to a point well above Zack's head, and then begins a spectacular arc downwards that terminates abruptly in the middle of Marvin's forehead.

"Fuck!" yells Marvin.

"Marvin!" shrieks Lydia. "Language!"

"Zoe!" says Judy, rushing over to Marvin. "How old are you? For god's sake."

Zack's laugh rises over the general din.

"Better luck next time," he says.

CHAPTER 2

Mariana

Has a woman of sound mind and independent finances ever made a poorer choice in a husband than she has made in Devlin Kelley? Mariana Goldstein-Hennessey wants to know. It is not an idle question. She has pondered it, at length. She would ask others, even, but it would hurt to reveal her own awareness of how utterly foolish she has been, how plainly misguided, in her selection.

Women throughout history have made terrible marriages, of course. She's hardly the first. But to have been given what so few women have had, what her own mother spent a lifetime fighting for—the right to choose with no constraint other than her own preferences—and to spend it on a man with so little claim to suitability? Her own recklessness astonishes her.

Here they are, with their four-year-old twins at their feet, and she is spending Christmas daydreaming about his future death. It could happen at any time, although it's unlikely. Dev could smash the car after a few too many beers, because he does that; he gets into the car after a gig where he's been drinking steadily all night. He could fall off the roof, doing one of the ineffective repairs that he refuses to hire someone to do properly. He could smash his head at the skate park, where he rarely wears a helmet. How did she marry someone who hangs out at a skate park? It boggles the mind.

He was Irish, for starters, and a musician: a rom-com personified. He was easygoing, like a Labrador retriever in human form. It was the least demanding relationship imaginable, and it freed up all the space in her brain that had hitherto been devoted to Finding Someone. Her career caught fire. She was nominated for a major award for her investigative series on city hall corruption. She appeared as an expert on the evening news. She took a beach vacation with Dev where they barely saw the beach because they were having so much sex.

And then they had twins, and everything went to shit.

Siobhan and Iona have been cranky since they arrived at Aunt Judy's house. They missed their naps today. "Can we have one blessed day without a military schedule in force?" Dev had asked, and Mariana hadn't fought him, despite her legitimate reservations.

And now the children are fighting over a piece of plastic, while Devlin pointedly ignores them. She wants to murder him, but not, she tells herself, in any real sense. No, she'll outlive him the old-fashioned way. She made a deal and she'll keep her word. She'll do what is expected of her. She has enough to keep her going. She has meaningful work (mostly), and friends (she should make more of an effort to see them), and interests (that could be reignited if she had a moment to herself).

"I have to go pee," says Iona.

"Dev, could you take her please?"

"Why me?"

"Because I want to catch up with my parents," she says, which isn't entirely true. What's true is that she wants Dev to make himself fucking useful. It's Christmas, after all. Dev sighs, and so she says, "Take Siobhan, too, if you wouldn't mind." She angles herself towards her progenitors, pretending not to see her husband's scowl. "What's new with you guys?"

"Not much," says Marvin. His cheeks are flushed.

"Speak for yourself, Marvin," says Lydia. "Some of us do more than sit around the house all day."

"Are you still going to the gym, Dad?" asks Mariana. Retirement has been hard on her father. He lacks purpose, and seems unwilling to seek it.

"You sound like your mother."

"That was not my objective," she says.

"It's a good question," says Lydia. "And the answer is no. Your father is not taking care of himself the way he should."

"As fun as this is," says Marvin, "I'm going to change the subject. Let's talk about your feature on the politics of garbage, Mariana. Very smart writing, I thought."

"Thanks, Dad."

"When are you going back to chasing dirty money and embarrassing politicians? Someone with your talent for investigative journalism can have a real impact in the world."

"I know," says Mariana. "But when you do that kind of work, you have to be willing to drop everything at a moment's notice and chase the story. I couldn't be on call like that after I had the girls." With Devlin, she thinks.

"Family first," says her father. "That's how we raised you."

"Exactly," says Lydia.

Mariana makes a concerted effort not to raise her eyebrows. She remembers a lot of TV dinners prepared by a lot of babysitters, while her dad put in extra hours at his dental practice and her mom attended conferences and rallies across the country. Sometimes, Lydia had dragged Mariana and her sisters along, insisting that revolution was the best teacher and mortifying them by being the opposite of what they understood a normal mom to be. Mariana sees now that this was her mother's point, and she doesn't judge Lydia and Marvin as she once did, at least not for their parenting failures. She sincerely believes that they did the best they could with the tools they had. Dev is another story entirely.

"It's too bad that book didn't work out," says Marvin.

Not the book again. "Yes," she says. "But it was a few years ago now, so I'm over it. You should get over it too."

She'd been in negotiations with a major publisher for a book about a government scandal that unseated several politicians. But it was a time-limited opportunity. She would have had to write it over a few short months, when the girls were barely one. Dev was auditioning with a new band and he wanted to have weekends and evenings free in case they booked a gig and needed him to fill in. And there was an opening at the newspaper for a features writer, with regular hours and stories planned in advance. Her partner in the investigation, a male journalist with less seniority, had written the book with her blessing, and it had been a huge bestseller. It is a significant regret, and she tries to think about it as infrequently as possible.

"Touchy," says her father, rising. "I'm ready for a refill. Anyone else?"

"No, thanks." She watches her father walk towards the kitchen. His diminishment alarms her. She wonders if he's shrinking, literally.

"Mommy!" The twins run back into the living room and leap on top of her. "Fix it!" Iona waves a piece of coloured plastic in Mariana's face. Her face is wet with tears. "Siobhan broke it!"

"*You* broke it!" yells Siobhan.

There's a knock at the door. "Could you get that?" she asks Devlin.

"It must be nice to have a manservant," he says.

"I wouldn't know," she says, shaking her children off her and trying to stand. "Calm down, girls. I'll look at it in a second. *Stop yelling.*" She stands and walks over to the door herself. It's Nina, the middle sister.

"Merry Christmas," says Nina, giving Mariana a hug. "Why are the girls crying?"

"They broke a toy."

"Oh, dear. That's a shame."

"Not really," says Mariana. It doesn't bother her, to have one toy down before they even leave. She has learned from experience that they'll go home with a car full of plastic garbage and she'll spend the next week trying to find a spot somewhere in the house for all of it. It's revolting how much *stuff* the children have. It makes her want to move to a desert island where the girls can learn how to play with rocks and sticks and dirt and their imaginations.

"I have something that might help." Nina produces a pair of lollipops from her pocket and unwraps them, handing one to each child. The shrieking ceases, instantly.

"You're an angel," says Mariana. "It must be Christmas."

"Tools of the trade," says Nina. "They come in handy when kids need stitches. I've been covering some holiday hours at a friend's walk-in clinic this week."

"Hello, dear," says Lydia, giving Nina a kiss. "It's no wonder these children are losing their minds. They're starving! I'm going to tell Judy that they need to eat *right now*."

"Please don't," says Mariana, but Lydia is on a mission.

The door to the basement flies open, narrowly missing Siobhan, who jumps out of the way. Mariana's nephew, Oscar, bursts into the room, scowling.

"Hi, Oscar," says Nina. "Where's your mom?"

"Downstairs," he says. "Don't tell her where I went."

"Why not?" Mariana asks Oscar's retreating back.

Whatever answer he makes is drowned out by the

sound of her father swearing and a burst of noise from the kitchen. "For god's sake," says Mariana. "This place is a zoo."

Her father staggers into the living room, a red mark in the centre of his forehead. He brushes away the ice pack that her mother is trying to hand to him.

"We've been informed that our help is not needed," says Lydia. "Your aunt is absurdly territorial about her kitchen."

Beata, Mariana's youngest sister, appears in the basement doorway. "Has anyone seen Oscar?"

"I'm sure he's around here somewhere," says Nina, finally removing her coat. "Why don't we take this rare opportunity to have a real family visit?"

"As opposed to a TV family visit?" says Mariana. Mariana, unlike her mother and Beata, is over the shock of *After the Revolution*. Although she has not said so publicly, she both watched and liked the show, and admired the character of Margaret, a tough-talking journalist. But she accepts that she was portrayed in a more flattering light than either Lydia's Lindy or Beata's Bethany. Nina was erased altogether, replaced with a Zack-inspired brother named Nick.

"Beata told me I got cut from the TV family," says Nina, "so I think I'll stick with this one." She sits down, and pats the seat next to her.

Mariana joins her. "You really haven't seen it?" Mariana wonders if Nina feels slighted by her omission, or fortunate.

Nina shrugs. "I'm out of the pop culture loop," she says. "Occupational hazard."

Beata stands behind their father's chair and massages his neck. "Do you think he's all right?" Mariana asks Nina, softly.

"For the moment," says Nina. "I'm keeping an eye on him, though."

"That's good. How long are you home?" Nina is a doctor with Physicians for Peace, and she's been on three consecutive missions in Syria. Mariana wishes that they were closer these days, as they'd been when they were younger. But Nina seems more remote since her last stint abroad. Mariana would like to know what her sister has seen overseas, and how it's changed her, but she's never found the right time to broach that conversation, and she isn't sure that Nina would welcome it.

"I'm not sure," says Nina. "I haven't accepted a new mission yet. I'm waiting for the right opportunity. I might take a contract at a hospital here while I figure it out. The walk-in clinic isn't a long-term strategy."

"You're not going back to Syria?"

Nina shakes her head. "I'm done there."

Mariana wants to probe further, but her mother interrupts them. She's working up another head of steam about the timing of dinner, when—mercifully—Judy calls them to the table.

They troop into the dining room, where the games begin. Judy is attached to a tradition of going around the table and asking everyone to share their feelings of gratitude, one at a time. It is cloying and irritating. Mariana despises false sentiment.

She tunes the exercise out while she cuts up turkey for the twins. She should be bathed in gratitude for her two healthy girls; she knows this. She is fortunate in family and education and real human freedom beyond the reach of most inhabitants of the planet. But she feels pickled in resentment instead. A woman raising twins more or less alone is a woman constrained.

Mariana believed once that she could have all of it—marriage and children and professional success and choice, choice, choice as far as the eye could see. Marriage, she now sees, is a trap designed to strip women of their freedom. It has been this way since humans invented wedlock, and women throughout history have understood this. Only her generation has managed to convince itself that marriage is whatever you want it to be, and if you aren't having a good time at the party, you can make a polite exit. How is it that the most educated generation in history can't see the bars on the windows until they're inside and the door swings shut behind them?

"Mariana?" Aunt Judy is ready for her gratitude contribution. This, at least, she has the freedom to refuse.

"Pass," says Mariana.

"What about you, Devlin?"

"Sorry?" Devlin glances up from his lap. "What's that?"

"He'll pass," says Mariana. "He's very busy on his phone right now."

"No phones at the table!" says Aunt Judy, and Mariana

holds out her hand for the contraband phone, like a fussy schoolmistress. She accepts that she is responsible for her children's behaviour, but she refuses to be judged for Dev's conduct around the dinner table. She'll be judged for her own.

She closes her hand around the phone and rises from her seat. She hears Aunt Judy thank her as she strides into the kitchen, and then she's opening drawers and pawing through ladles and spatulas and pancake flippers until she finds what she wants. She puts a cutting board on the counter and places the device on top of the plastic. And then she raises the meat tenderizer above her head like a horror-movie villain and pulverizes Devlin's phone with one blow.

CHAPTER 3

Beata

Beata Goldstein-Hennessey lies on the floor of her aunt's basement and reflects on how this day has turned into her worst-ever Christmas.

Pain, she knows, often flows from unhealthy attachments, or expectations. Fifteen years ago, she'd been so sure that her baby was a girl that she'd declined the tests to confirm her intuition. The single parenthood of her imagination had been filled with art and dance lessons, and tea parties, and feminist music festivals. It was a shock to hold her baby and realize she knew nothing whatsoever about raising a boy. She rallied quickly; Oscar was her child, and bound, she thought, to share some of her interests. Beata put a lot of stock in the power of nurture. And wasn't gender fluid, anyway?

Oscar, though, seemed to fall on the nature side of the nature-or-nurture debate. He disrupted dance recitals, and smeared paint on his unisex overalls with embroidered flowers, and, in one heart-stopping episode, disappeared at a summer festival, only to be located at the edge of the field, sitting on a tractor and pretending to drive it.

"Let the boy be himself, Beata," said her mother. It was easy for her mother to say, since she'd been blessed with three daughters. "Give him some space. Stop projecting."

Beata's mother had views, and few qualms about sharing them. She disapproved of attachment parenting, despite the articles Beata shared with her. "Oscar should be sleeping in his own bed. Independence is healthy for him and healthy for you. If you don't give him room to breathe now, he'll be hell on wheels when he's a teenager."

"I'm the parent, Mom," said Beata. "I have a right to make my own mistakes." Her mother had made plenty. Beata could have listed the most egregious ones, and so, probably, could her therapist(s).

Lying on the floor now, she can see everything she's done wrong, and how all of her mistakes are coming home to roost. It's hard to keep up with the pace of her lowered expectations now that she has a teenager. Today, for example, all she wanted was for Oscar to participate in the Christmas celebration with her family. She even agreed to let him bring his Xbox in exchange for his promise to interact cheerfully with his relatives. But he made a bee-line down to the basement when they arrived, and refused to hold up his end of the bargain.

"It's Christmas," she told him.

"It's my Christmas too, not only yours. And this is how I want to spend it."

"That's not a choice that's available to you," she said, in her most calming tone.

"That's because you're basically a totalitarian dictator," said Oscar.

"If I were a totalitarian dictator, you wouldn't have an Xbox at all."

"I paid for this Xbox with my own money," said Oscar. "You can't touch it."

"Watch me," said Beata, grabbing for the controller and wrestling with him.

"Dictator!" yelled Oscar. "Control freak!"

"Grounded!" shouted Beata.

Oscar released his grip on the controller, and she fell backwards, clutching it. He stepped around her, stomped upstairs, and slammed the basement door, leaving her alone in the semi-dark.

And here she lies.

Her baby has turned into someone she barely recognizes. She misses him and continues to look for signs of her lost child in this creature who has burst, Hulk-like, from Oscar's body. His face, shrouded perpetually by a hoodie, has broadened and coarsened, and broken out. He smells. Every morning, the walls shake when he launches himself out of bed, late, and storms through the house.

Is his volatility normal? She remembers feeling angry at his age, furious at her mother and misunderstood by the world, but his fury seems more sustained than her own ever was, and she fears it's getting worse. She isn't naive, despite having that reputation in her immediate family. She knows that anger is a natural part of the separation process. She's read a number of books about how to raise spirited children, and she both respects and values Oscar's right to chart his own path. Still, it would be nice, she thinks, if spiritedness were more than a euphemism for rage and unwillingness to conform.

There are so many avenues for failure as a parent, so many crossroads with multiple paths branching out. Should she have offered him a stronger cultural or religious identity, for example? Beata herself, like the other Goldstein-Hennessey children, grew up in a home where multiple traditions were recognized but none were practised. In recent years, she's taken comfort from various Eastern religions and philosophies, or at least from practices adjacent to them, and she's tried to encourage Oscar in the direction of mindfulness. He is resistant, to say the least. As far as Beata can tell, her son venerates YouTubers and snarky exit lines, and not much else.

Beata rises from the floor and goes upstairs, carrying the Xbox with her. She steps into a family drama: her mother carrying on about Aunt Judy and her father holding an ice pack to his forehead. "What happened?" she asks, sitting down next to him.

"Wrong place at the wrong time," he says, wincing. "It's only a headache. No need to fuss."

She stands and puts her hands on the back of his neck. "Let me take the tension out, at least." She kneads the muscles at the base of his skull.

He sighs with pleasure. "You're not doing that Reiki stuff on me, are you?"

"Of course not," she says, moving her hands to his temples and restoring balance to the flow of energy pulsing beneath his skin. What he doesn't know can only help him.

"Much better," he says. "Thank you, sweetheart. You have magic hands."

"True," she says, kissing the top of his head and sitting down next to him again. Of all the children, she is the one closest to her father. When she found herself pregnant at twenty, still a child herself really, it was her father who insisted that she move home, who gave her money to pay for her RMT training, and who hired a babysitter so that she could attend classes. She shudders to think where she'd be now without his intervention. In recent years, she's evolved her practice away from traditional massage and into craniosacral therapy and Reiki healing, much to her father's dismay.

"What's happening with your blog?" he asks. "I haven't seen a post in months."

"It's on hiatus," she says. "I've been taking some extra hours at the clinic to put money away for Oscar's college fund." This is true, but it's not the only reason. *Mindful Mothering*, named one of the Top 50 Mom Blogs of 2010, made Beata a major influencer in the authentic parenting movement, but lately she's been feeling like a fake. Why should anyone take her advice about raising kids?

"I support that," says Lydia. "Mindfulness is all the rage, but it's a fad, in my opinion. Stress management is valuable, sure, but why promote wholesale self-acceptance? Is it wise? Take the goal of social change. How do you provoke revolution in a climate of complacency and self-congratulation?"

"There's a solid scientific basis for mindfulness," says Nina. "And speaking as someone who's lived in war zones for the last few years, revolution is overrated."

"I was speaking of intellectual revolution," says Lydia. "We can all improve ourselves, and we should try. Speaking of which, Marvin, pace yourself."

Marvin pretends not to hear her.

"I don't know why Judy can't get dinner on the table at a reasonable hour," says Lydia, after a pause.

"It's a big job, Mom," says Beata. "Why don't you see if Aunt Judy needs help?"

"Bad idea," says Mariana.

"Dinner!" sings Aunt Judy, coming into the living room. "Sorry it's so late! I had to whip up some cranberry sauce." She looks pointedly at Lydia. "Shall we move to the dining room? Marvin, could you pour the champagne?"

"I'll do it," says Beata. Her dad isn't steady on his feet. How much has he had to drink? She hooks her arm through his and escorts her father to his seat.

"Thank you, Beata," says Aunt Judy, as Beata moves around the table, filling glasses.

Aunt Judy takes her seat at the head of the table. Uncle Larry raises a glass. "I am grateful," he begins.

"Oh, yay," says Oscar, appearing from wherever he's been hiding. "It's the gratitude competition."

"Hush," says Beata. "If you can't say anything nice, don't say anything at all."

"I am grateful for my lovely wife, who always makes me a spectacular holiday meal."

"Thank you, darling," says Aunt Judy. "And I'm grateful for such a generous and thoughtful husband. Who's next? Beata?"

Beata enjoys this tradition of her aunt's. In fact, she incorporated it into one of her most popular blog posts, "Creating Authentic Traditions." She wishes more members of her family would engage thoughtfully in the exercise, instead of sulking and ruining it for those who find it meaningful.

"I'm grateful for my beautiful son," says Beata. She offers a variation on this theme every year. Looking at Oscar's sour expression, she has to admit to herself that it's more of a stretch this Christmas.

"Who's next?" asks Aunt Judy. "Zack?"

"I'm grateful that my nephew brought *Call of Duty* to dinner," says Zack. "Excellent call, Oscar."

Oscar gives Zack a fist bump.

Beata summons gratitude for this moment of manly solidarity, even as it undermines her authority. *Call of Duty*? Really? Couldn't they bond over football, or cars—something boring but harmless, something she hasn't removed from her son's possession in the past hour as a consequence of anti-social behaviour?

"That's not exactly what I had in mind," says Judy.

"All the same," says Zack.

"Marvin?"

"I'm grateful for Larry's excellent taste in Scotch."

"Mariana?"

"Pass," says Mariana, cutting up turkey for the children.

"What about you, Devlin?"

"Sorry?" Devlin glances up from his lap.

"He'll pass," says Mariana. "He's very busy on his phone right now."

"No phones at the table!" says Aunt Judy, smiling brightly.

Mariana holds her hand out for Devlin's phone, and when he surrenders it, she rises from the table and takes it into the kitchen. "Thank you, Mariana! Lydia, would you like to share?"

"I'm grateful that all of my children and grandchildren were healthy and happy this year."

Judy's smile falters. "Nina?"

"Pass," says Nina.

There is a series of bangs from the kitchen and the sound of something breaking. Devlin leaps out of his chair.

"Carry on, Judy," says Lydia, briskly. "it's not our concern."

"Nina, surely you can think of something?" says Judy.

"I'm grateful not to be in a wartorn country, trying to save lives with inadequate equipment and no reliable power," says Nina. "How's that? Could someone pass the wine?"

"Of course," says Larry, eyes wide as he rises and fills her glass.

"Zoe," says Judy, "how about you, sweetie? Do you want to go next?"

"I think I'll pass," says Zoe.

Why are all of Beata's relatives unable to feign happiness even for a brief window of time? How hard is it? Surely her siblings and cousins are able to muster false cheer at their various jobs, so why not here? Why is she the one member of her generation who is prepared to model appropriate behaviour for the children?

"You can't pass," says her mother, stubbornly. "Not without a very good reason."

"I have a good reason," says Zoe. "Richard left me. I'm getting divorced."

Aunt Judy begins crying, and Uncle Larry moves to the end of the table to pat her on the shoulder. "Oh, no!" she says. "I knew it. Oh, how awful."

"I always thought that guy was a douche," says Zack.

"Thank you, Zack," says Zoe. "That makes it so much better."

"I agree with Zack," says Oscar.

"Oscar!" says Beata. "Stay out of it!"

Oscar turns red.

"You know what would be excellent?" says Zoe. "If someone else wanted to do some sharing. Anyone? Oscar?"

"I don't think so," says Oscar.

"C'mon, man," says Zack, as Aunt Judy's sobs grow louder. "Shift the focus. Be a hero."

"Okay," says Oscar. "I'm grateful to know that my

father is not an anonymous sperm donor, like my mother has told me my whole life."

There is a collective intake of breath, and then Zack says, "What do you mean?"

"You have a father?" says Zoe.

"This is not appropriate conversation for the dinner table," says Judy.

"I agree with Judy," says Lydia. "That is enough, Oscar."

"Oscar," says Beata, with some urgency, "let's go upstairs and talk about this privately."

"I don't have anything to say to you," says Oscar. "You're a hypocrite."

"Oscar," says Zack, "I don't know what's going on here, but you need to hear your mom out. This is big stuff."

"Yeah," says Oscar. "It's big stuff when you find out your whole life is a lie."

"Calm down, Oscar," says Beata. "Please. I understand that you're upset, but you don't have all the information."

"Whose fault is that, Mom?" says Oscar.

"I was going to tell you when you were old enough," says Beata.

"That's bullshit," says Oscar. "I don't believe you."

"We're going to sit down and figure this out together," says Beata. "I promise."

"You don't get it," says Oscar. "I've already figured it out, all by myself. I don't need your help. You've done enough."

JANUARY

CHAPTER 4

Eloise

Eloise Embree pushes her chair back from her desk, stands, and stretches. She admires her view, which is, even by downtown standards, impressive. You only get a view like this by billing almost as many hours as there are in a day for most of the weeks of the year, and that's what Eloise has been doing since she graduated from law school. It's a luxury to be able to work as much as she does. She has no dependants, and very few obligations, other than the boards she sits on and her tennis teams (singles, doubles, mixed doubles).

Above all, she owes her success to the human propensity for poor decision-making in marriage. She is a divorce lawyer, one of the best in the city. Her clients tend to be men, the types who hire female lawyers to appear more sympathetic to the judge. Eloise does not tell them that she is tougher than any of the men she faces in court, and that all the judges know it. She provides excellent service, and her clients are as happy as any clients in divorce litigation can be.

"Hey, killer," says a voice from the doorway, and she turns away from her view, smiling.

"So?" she says to Will Shannon, her law and mixed doubles partner. "Who's our competition?"

Will looks momentarily puzzled. He's forgotten, clearly, that he was supposed to find out who else has registered in the mixed doubles tournament at their club. "Don't worry about it," she says. "I'll ask about it tonight at doubles practice."

"Thanks," he says. "Listen, I—"

"Sorry to interrupt," says Tabatha, her assistant. "Eloise, your three-thirty is here in Conference Room C."

Eloise nods. "I'll be right there. Sorry, Will. Catch up with you later?"

"Yeah, sure," he says. "There's something I wanted to ask you about, but it can wait."

"I'm meeting your referral, if you want to say hello." Eloise collects the Hennessey file from her desk and steps into the hallway. "We can talk on the way."

"I'll talk fast," says Will. "A buddy of mine got a weird email yesterday from a kid claiming to be his son. He's not sure what to do. He's wondering if it's some kind of fraud. Have you heard of anything going around like that?"

"Nope. Does he recognize the name?"

"Possibly."

"Is he worried about his financial obligations?"

"No! He's a stand-up guy. He's just . . . surprised."

"I understand," says Eloise. "Why don't you have him come and see me? I'm sure I can give him some reassurance."

"Thanks, Eloise," says Will, as they reach the lobby. "I'll suggest that."

"Mr. Shannon?" says the receptionist. "There's a young man here to see you. He doesn't have an appointment. I tried to reach your assistant."

A teenage boy stands up from one of the armchairs across from the reception desk. "Are you Will Shannon?" he asks. The boy looks somewhat familiar, Eloise thinks, but then most teenagers look the same to her.

"Do you need me to stay?" asks Eloise. She holds his gaze. "Your buddy can consider me retained."

"I . . . no," says Will. "I've got this. You go to your meeting."

She leans in towards him and murmurs, "Hear him out, but admit nothing. Nothing at all, Will. I'll be around after, and we can talk then." He nods and steps forward to greet the boy. Eloise walks through reception and down the corridor to the conference rooms. She knocks on the door of Room C and enters. "Zoe?" she says. "How nice to meet you. I'm sorry it's under these circumstances."

"Not as sorry as I am."

Eloise opens Zoe's file. "I understand that Will Shannon referred you. He was going to say hello, but he got tied up on another matter. How do you two know each other?"

"We were in the same group of friends at university. He dated my roommate, sort of. We've stayed in touch, although lately it's been mostly through social media." Zoe had consulted another lawyer first, an acquaintance

41

with a general law practice who had, upon hearing the facts of Zoe's case, suggested that she spend the money to hire a specialist. Zoe had then abandoned any sense of what her mother would have considered propriety, downed a few glasses of wine, and opened Facebook: *Hive mind! I need a divorce lawyer! Not asking for a friend!* There had been an outpouring of concern and a direct message from Will Shannon offering his condolences and Eloise's contacts. *I know some other good people,* he'd written, *but Eloise is the one I'd trust in a crisis.*

"He said you'd be sensible," says Eloise.

"I'll do my best."

Eloise hopes that this is true. "Zoe, you'll be spending a lot of money on my services and I commit to you that your money will be spent efficiently. There are different approaches to matrimonial law, and I want to be completely straight with you about the kind of lawyer I am. I'm not a therapist. My job is to get you out of a difficult situation as quickly and inexpensively as I can so that you can get on with your life. Does that make sense to you as an approach? If you'd like someone softer or kinder, there are many fine lawyers that I could recommend to you and I won't be offended in the least."

"Are you as good as Will says you are?"

Eloise smiles. "Yes."

"Proceed," Zoe says.

Eloise nods. "I've read all of the notes on your file, and your financial statements, and the preliminary disclosure from your husband."

"Let's not call him that."

"You were always the higher earner, correct?"

"Yes."

"And, with your approval, he left his job a year ago to start a coaching business that has lost money and left him completely financially dependent on you."

"Correct. I was trying to make him happy."

"I understand. The matrimonial home is in his name, yes?"

"I have my own business," Zoe says. "I wanted to protect it in the event of a lawsuit against my company."

"Very sensible," says Eloise. "I'm not judging you. I'm just clarifying facts."

"He's been having an affair for a year," Zoe says. "With someone half his age."

"I'm sorry to hear it," says Eloise. "And that makes him a bad husband, but does not, in this jurisdiction, affect his entitlements in the divorce."

"Which are?" asks Zoe.

Eloise tells her. Zoe puts her head down on the conference table. Eloise moves a box of tissues next to her head. "Take as long as you need," she says. "And then we'll get to work."

Zoe raises her head. Her eyes are dry. Eloise appreciates this lack of drama. "It's worse than I thought," Zoe says.

"That's usually the case."

"But he is such a faithless asshole."

"That's also usually the case. It would be less traumatic

43

for you, in financial terms, if you would consider support payments over a period of time."

"No."

"Be certain that you aren't making an emotional decision about this."

"No," says Zoe. "I want a clean break."

"Based on your financials, Zoe, you are going to have to give him your half of the house and cash out your retirement savings. I'm fairly sure I can protect your business, because—forgive me—it's had a tough couple of years. But that will be a fight, and fights are expensive. I like a fight, but I need to keep your best interests in mind as my client. Trying to get a fair settlement should be the goal here."

"What a mess," says Zoe.

"Oh, this isn't a mess," says Eloise. "You don't have children. This is only money."

"You don't know Richard."

"I don't need to," says Eloise. She settles back in her chair. "I'm going to tell you something that I tell all my clients. None of them believe me on day one. They say they do, but they don't, and some of them never will. Nevertheless, it is a universal truth about divorce."

"I'm ready," says Zoe. "Hit me."

"A divorce isn't a war. It's a funeral. There are no winners, only mourners. Don't get caught up in how the other person is grieving. Focus on what you need for your own process of recovery."

Zoe smiles, very slightly. "I hear what you're saying,"

she says. "Let's offer him the house. I don't want to live there anymore. But he'll have to pry my business out of my cold, dead hands."

"As I said, no one gets there on day one," says Eloise. "Would you mind signing this retainer agreement? We accept all major credit cards."

Eloise escorts Zoe to the elevator and returns to her office. She sees no sign of Will or the boy from reception. Will Shannon with a teenage son? Eloise shakes her head. Will is the one person at the firm that she counts as a real friend, though she likes and respects many others. Even still, they haven't made a habit of sharing the details of their personal lives. They both date women, mostly casually, and spend a lot of time at the office, and play tennis. She's been reluctant to tell him that she's become serious about her current romantic partner; up till now, their lives have been structured along similar lines, and she hasn't wanted to shift the dynamic between them. But if Will's life is about to diverge in a monumental way, and it seems that it is, she might consider telling him about Beata.

There are no secrets in life, she has discovered, and many surprises. Will Shannon with a son. It makes you think. It makes Eloise think about Beata, which is something she tries not to do at the office, where Eloise has a well-deserved reputation for being all business, all the time. She doesn't serve on committees and she doesn't show up at cocktail events. Eloise disapproves of activities that offer no clear benefit and do not further her own identified priorities. She tries to "live authentically," as Beata would say. Eloise, if pressed, would describe her approach as "eliminating as much bullshit as possible," but she interprets the underlying sentiment as at least similar. There is so much nonsense in the world, so much fakery. It seems to her that most people are aware of their own contribution to the aggregate bullshit in the environment but perpetuate the cycle of absurdity anyway. It puzzles her, how time is devalued, even among those who bill by the hour. She is careful, though, not to share her opinions with the vast majority of her colleagues. She has been given to understand that she can sound harsh.

Eloise believes in boundaries, in clean edges. She locks the human wreckage away in her filing cabinets at the end of the day, goes home, and sleeps undisturbed, except by Beata, who dreams aloud.

Will Shannon has a son, and she has . . . what? A problem? At any other time in her life, Beata would have been a complete solution. Beata, who in the two years they've been dating has never asked Eloise to cut back her hours, or shift her schedule around, or complicate her life in any way. Beata, who has never asked Eloise to attend a family function or meet her son, even though Eloise has made it clear that she would do any of these, without hesitation. Beata, who has offered and accepted love without any expectation of, or even expression of interest in, permanence.

Beata, who espouses mindful living and authenticity.

Beata, who literally stops and smells flowers when they walk down the street. Beata, who is generous and sexy and funny. Beata, who has made Eloise want something so urgently and irrationally that she barely recognizes herself.

Eloise wants to get married.

CHAPTER 5

Zoe

January, Zoe thinks, is a nasty month to be going through a divorce: the interminable grey, the perennial chill. Her face feels frozen, as if she's had fillers done. Not that she's opposed to light cosmetic upgrades; it may yet come to that. But in the meantime, she worries that she's forgotten how to smile.

It strikes her that her marriage to Richard is unworthy of her current level of misery. They weren't a grand love story, and their divorce isn't an epic tragedy. It's depressingly ordinary: European art film, not Hollywood blockbuster. The whole enterprise feels slightly antiseptic and misguided in hindsight. She is at least as much responsible for this as he is. There were scenes of great intensity and emotion in the marriage—her intensity, her emotion— and she excised them from the official version. They play out in her mind every night as she waits for the sleeping pill to take effect. Their first sexual encounter, for example, wasn't mind-blowing, but nice enough for an inaugural attempt: that's how she's filed it away in her memory. But now different details are surfacing. Richard, sliding out of bed immediately after a tidy orgasm (his); Richard, climbing back into bed, wishing her a polite goodnight, and passing out; Richard, complaining of the heat and asking her to stay on her side; Richard, up in the morning with his usual alarm, shaking off her efforts to keep him in bed; Richard, mystified by her tears, passing her the sections of newspaper he'd already finished reading.

In the bathroom of the house they once shared, Zoe turns on the hot water. She stands, watching her own reflection as the mirror fogs and she fades and disappears. It is a useful metaphor. There are two people in a divorce, and if both are fifty percent responsible (which Zoe is inclined to dispute), then her fifty percent, the portion of responsibility for the collapse that she is prepared to claim, is the fade-out. She stopped asking herself what she wanted. She stopped being a presence and became an absence. She adapted. She convinced herself that she didn't need outward signs of affection. She learned how to sublimate. She took her frustrated dreams and unmet desires and redirected them into her business.

Zoe lowers herself into the bathtub and slides under the water. The business. That's another problem entirely. If she hasn't demonstrated complete wisdom in marriage, it's hard to fault her business sense. A decade ago, when the market was soft and the neighbourhood unfashionable, Zoe bought a building. Her advertising agency was young but growing, and she wanted to rent an office so that she could hire some staff. But downtown leases were criminally expensive, and the fluorescent lighting and stained wall-to-wall carpeting were depressing. Then one night, at dinner with friends from college, she got some free advice about tax credits for industrial conversions, and almost before she knew what had happened, she had a small business loan, a building, and a bunch of tenants.

Over the years, Zoe has slowly and lovingly renovated the entire building, and while she still has a few tenants, HENNESSEY's motley crew of creative personalities occupies half the space. The agency specializes in advertising for lifestyle brands. She's the CEO, which means that her phone is on twenty-four hours a day, while she plays babysitter/best friend/concierge/therapist to her major clients, all of whom assume her affections are exclusive.

HENNESSEY is Zoe's baby. It was what she gestated while her friends were pregnant, what she stayed up late worrying about while they nursed colicky infants, what she painstakingly built while their kids were learning to walk and talk and eat with their mouths closed. She fended off competitors trying to poach her clients, dipped into her own pockets to make payroll during lean months, and celebrated new contracts with the same pride that her friends described feeling at school concerts and soccer tournaments. There have been some dark days over the past couple of years; while trying to save her marriage, she let her attention wander at work and HENNESSEY lost a huge account. She's had to reduce her permanent staff. She's had to pivot. But she'll survive, as long as she stays focused. Richard will never take her agency. He has taken everything from her that he's going to get.

Aside from the house. And whatever else she needs to pay him to make him go away forever.

Zoe dries off and pulls on a robe. She walks into her bedroom.

"Hi," says Zack. Zoe screams. "Sorry, sorry. I let myself in."

"I see that," she says, grabbing at her robe. "Jesus, Zack. What are you doing here?"

"You invited me for dinner."

"At six!"

"It's after six."

"Oh," she says. "How did that happen?"

"I didn't think dementia showed up this early."

Zoe punches him in the arm.

"Ow. Fuck."

"I need to get dressed."

"You do that." Zack stretches out on her bed.

"Could you get out while I do that?"

"There's a bathroom right there. And I'm comfortable here."

"I thought you were respecting boundaries these days."

"Ouch."

Zoe sighs. "That was unkind. I apologize."

"It's fine," says Zack. "I acknowledge that I may have overstepped."

"Let's try this again. Welcome, little brother, to my home. Please make yourself comfortable."

"Don't mind if I do," says Zack, stretching out.

Zoe grabs yoga pants and a sweatshirt out of the closet and heads into the bathroom. She closes the door most of the way. "So? How are you doing?"

"I'm enjoying a pure and blameless life of eight-hour workdays, sobriety, and personal notoriety that has rendered me untouchable in my former social circles. I'm bored, I'm spending my savings at an alarming rate, I have writer's block, which I don't even believe in, and I'm living with our parents. Perhaps I'll repeat that. *I'm living with our parents.*"

"Sure. But they think the sun rises and sets out of your ass, so how bad could that be?" Zoe comes out of the bathroom to find Zack sitting cross-legged on the bed, his hands folded in prayer position at his chest. "What are you doing?"

Zack opens his eyes. "Rewiring my brain. Unwinding old patterns."

"Such as?"

"Such as falling into childhood patterns of retribution when you suggest that I should be enjoying my current stay at Mom and Dad's."

"I apologize, again."

"I accept. Now. Why don't you tell me how you're doing? The unsanitized version, please."

"I'm not used to you like this," says Zoe. She isn't sure what to make of Zack's newly minted priority on healthy relationships, courtesy of his stay at the rehab centre–slash–wellness retreat. She appreciates the shift away from relentless self-absorption, but Zack's intensity of focus can be wearing.

"You're not used to *you* like this. Cut yourself some slack. You don't have to be perfect."

"Maybe I do. I'm an oldest child."

"You mean a competitive perfectionist?"

Also wearing is his armchair psychoanalysis. "I prefer 'responsible achiever,'" says Zoe. "We can't all be overindulged man-babies."

"You're jealous. And I prefer the term 'creative nonconformist,'" says Zack.

Zoe laughs. "I feel bad about disappointing Mom and Dad."

"By getting divorced?"

"Isn't that enough?"

"Get over it. They're not as upset as you think. They didn't really like Richard."

"No one did."

"No one did," Zack agrees. "They do want grandchildren, though."

"You could get on that project for them," says Zoe. "I'm forty-two. They should move along."

"I'm in the middle of a life transition, and a boyish thirty-three. I have a free pass for now."

"So Mom and Dad can live with disappointment for now."

"Regardless," says Zack, "you should get back out there."

"You mean dating?"

Zack nods.

"No."

"Why not?"

"I'm not ready," says Zoe.

"How do you know?"

Zoe doesn't know for sure. What she does know is that she can't survive another betrayal. She has no words to describe the breathless pain of it. For weeks, it was as if the blood in her veins had turned to acid, corroding her from the inside out. It was as if her organs had burst spontaneously into flames. It was as if her heart had exploded, sending shrapnel through every pore of her skin. She has pushed the anguish down for now, but it could rise again and consume what is left of her. Which isn't much.

"Are you okay?" asks Zack.

"Totally okay," says Zoe. "Yes." She crosses her arms across her chest to keep an ocean of sadness from spilling out. She clears her throat. "When I'm ready, the universe will put the right person in my path." She feels the pain recede slightly, like a tide going out. It's easier to breathe now.

"Trust me on this one. Waiting for the universe is a losing strategy in 2020."

"And how do you know this if you aren't dating?"

"I'm not dating *now*. Unlike you, I have spent much of the past decade dating, and I know that you have to put yourself in the path of a relationship if you want one."

"I believe I said that I didn't want one."

"Yes, but I'm not listening to you."

"Do I have to go online?"

"You do."

Zoe sits down on the bed. "I hate this."

Zack pats her arm. "I'm sorry."

"I'm going to have to give up the house."

"In the divorce? Are you sure?"

"I'm not sure of anything at this point, except that I've been an idiot. I'm going to have to pay Richard a ton of money."

"How much is a ton?"

Zoe sighs. "I don't know yet. The best-case scenario is a huge chunk of the house. He'll want a piece of the business, too."

"What's that worth?"

"Less than it was."

"Why?"

"I've been distracted. I lost a massive client to poaching."

"Can you get the agency back on track?"

"I think so," she says. "I hope so."

"Enough of that for now," says Zack. "I assume from your outfit that we're staying in for dinner?"

"You assume correctly."

"Perfect. We can work while we eat."

"Work on what?"

"Your online profile."

"Do we have to do this now?"

Zack grins. "Yes. Order the food and I'll get started."

"I'll get takeaway from the corner. Be back soon."

The temperature has dropped outside, and it smells like snow. Why would she want to date if it requires leaving the house in winter? She's touched by Zack's determination, and she can humour him for an evening. She reminds herself that she doesn't have to take any steps until she's ready. It's a harmless distraction, nothing more. She's in no danger. She's in control. She breathes frozen air into her lungs, breathes out clouds of mist, in and out.

When she returns, Zack is in the kitchen, tapping away at his computer. He is relentless, she thinks. It is his best and worst quality. "Do you prefer tennis, skiing, or golf?"

"None of the above. Why?"

"Because you need a sport."

"Kickboxing."

"You're doing kickboxing?"

"No, but I'm not playing tennis, skiing, or golfing either."

Zack nods his approval. "Kickboxing is hot. Okay, check this out."

He turns the screen towards her and she sees her own image, along with a few lines of text. "My name is AdventureGal?"

"It's energetic and upbeat," says Zack. "A little bit Wonder Woman, a little bit Girl Next Door. We're creating a character here."

"Isn't the real thing good enough?"

Zack tucks into the butter chicken. "You have to trust me on this. Online dating has a language all its own. We're using that language to let the world know you're ready to rejoin it."

"Why are you being so nice to me?" asks Zoe.

"Aren't I always?"

"It varies," she says, "to be honest with you."

"I was thinking," he says. "Wouldn't it be great to have some more bonding time?"

Zoe laughs. "You can't move in here."

"I can! I would be the best roommate!"

"When is the last time someone said that about you?"

"I've changed."

"I'm selling the house, remember?"

"So I won't be able to overstay my welcome."

"Why do you want to live with me? I'm a total downer right now."

"You aren't our parents."

"So get your own place."

"I don't know where I'm going to be in six months."

"I don't know where I'm going to be either."

"Exactly! Can't you see how perfect this is?"

Zoe sighs. "I have ground rules."

"Hit me."

"You cannot write about me. I will not be research for your next show about a lonely, divorced woman with only her brother and a dog for company."

"You're getting a dog?"

"That's not the point."

"I will not write about you. I promise."

"You have to clean up after yourself. I'm not picking up after you the way Mom does. And you'll pay what I say you owe me for household expenses without a debate."

"Done."

"Fine. When are you moving in?"

"I just did," says Zack. "Now, let's see what's happening in your dating life."

"I don't have a dating life."

"You may not, but AdventureGal does. I've identified a few prospects for her. Oh. Oh, shit."

"What have you done?"

"It's not what I've *done*," says Zack. "It's what I've found."

Zack turns the screen towards her, and Zoe leans in to see Devlin Kelley grinning back at her. "Why are you showing me a picture of Devlin?"

"What I'm showing you," says Zack, "is the dating profile for a gentleman called LuckOfTheIrish."

"Oh, no, no, no. It is not."

"I'm afraid it is."

They stare at each other. "How are we going to tell Mariana?" Zoe asks.

"We could pretend we didn't see it," says Zack.

"We could not," says Zoe.

"Why not?"

"Because solidarity," says Zoe. "Because sisterhood. Because family."

"Well, in that case," says Zack, "this sounds like a job for AdventureGal!"

CHAPTER 6

Mariana

Mariana sits in her cubicle at the newspaper, writing a feature on stress management. Her cubicle is one of four in her pod, two of which have been empty since the last round of layoffs. The third desk is occupied by Farah Khan, her closest friend. So far, they've both managed to avoid a layoff, and neither has opted (yet) for a buyout. They are career journalists. Life in the newsroom is awful, but not yet intolerable, and where would they go anyway? The market is flooded with unemployed writers prepared to work more hours for less money. Mariana knows she has an enviable arrangement, which is why she lives in a state of near-constant paranoia. She's well known, but not untouchable. She can't mail it in.

She reads what she's written so far. *Harmony Delacroix pulls into the parking lot at FairMarket Beauty, the company she started in her basement, on a bespoke bicycle. It's early, but she's been up for several hours already. Her routine—no matter where she is in the world—always includes meditation immediately*

*after she rises. "It's at the heart of my personal wellness strategy,"
she says.*

"Do you meditate?" Mariana asks Farah.

Farah looks up from her screen. "I sleep four hours a night. Does that count?"

"I don't think so," says Mariana. "This woman gets up at five in the morning every day to meditate."

"Good for her. I get up at five in the morning to deal with my kids. Meditation sounds nicer."

"Harmony Delacroix doesn't have kids."

"Then what does she need meditation for?" asks Farah.

"Stress management, apparently."

"Like I said," says Farah.

"Hmm. Do you remember when stress management became a thing? When did we start talking about it as a measure of success?"

"No idea," says Farah. "But I have confidence that you'll crack this one with your in-depth investigative reporting."

"I appreciate it," says Mariana. "How's your story coming?"

"Slowly," says Farah. "I can't get anyone to go on the record. I have a meeting with Chris about it now." Farah pushes her chair away from the desk. "Do you want to get lunch?"

"Sure," says Mariana. "I'll see you later." Mariana's phone rings. It's her cousin Zoe, who is also one of her best friends. She answers. "Hello?"

"Mariana?"

"Hey, Zoe. What's up?"

"Not much," she says. "Listen, I was wondering if you could meet for coffee or a drink. I wanted to talk to you about something."

"Sure," says Mariana. "Is everything okay?"

"Of course," says Zoe. "Do you have any time this week?"

"Is it urgent?"

"No." Zoe's voice sounds strained. "Not urgent."

Mariana doesn't push. She's got too much on her plate to take on whatever is going on with Zoe. "I'm on a deadline this week. If it can wait, can we do it next week?"

"Sure," says Zoe. "I guess so. How's Monday?"

"Monday's fine. Send me a calendar appointment. Oh, and Zoe? Thanks for connecting me with Harmony. You were right; she's the perfect interview for this piece."

Zoe is wildly connected, and she's been an invaluable resource since Mariana started writing lifestyle features. Harmony is one of Zoe's big clients. Mariana wonders how Zoe manages her, if indeed anyone manages Harmony Delacroix.

"No problem. I'm sure she was glad to do it. Self-care is her favourite subject."

"See you Monday." Mariana hangs up and turns her attention back to her feature story. It irritates her, and she has no one to blame but herself. Why did she pitch this series in the first place? She feels like she's participating in the cultural shaming of women who, like herself, are barely holding it together.

She looks back at her life before the twins, when she was covering political scandals, and taking on a mortgage for the first time, and wondering if she'd ever find a man who didn't think she was too much or not enough. She remembers the occasional bout of existential anxiety, unpleasant but generally fleeting. Nowadays, stress rides shotgun on the out-of-control stagecoach of her life, from the moment she opens her eyes to the sound of the twins fussing until she pretends to be asleep when Devlin comes to bed.

And it's boring. Boring to think about. Boring to write about. Stress isn't glamorous. It's the creeping knowledge that the best days of your life are behind you because your ovaries are withering and your career is stalled and you're going to be tired for the next ten years because you had miracle babies at forty, and once you stop being tired, you'll be old. *Meditate on that, Harmony.*

Mariana's phone rings again, her home number. "Hello?"

"It's me," says Devlin.

"I thought you were working today."

"It's nice to hear your voice, too," he says, which is fair, but also not. He *is* supposed to be working today.

"Was the gig cancelled?" She can't help it. She has the uneasy feeling that Devlin's been lying to her about how much he's working. They keep their finances separate, always have, so it's hard to say for sure, but he's been a lot less forthcoming lately than he used to be about the jobs he's booking.

"Yeah."

"That's too bad," she says. "Any idea why?"

"It happens," he says. "It's not a big deal. We can't all have cushy hours and pensions and such. Some of us have to hustle. So I can't pick up the girls today."

"What do you mean?"

"I'm meeting Jared for a drink. He may have something for me."

"Can't you meet him after I get home?"

"Do you want me to work, or not? Make up your mind. You can't give me the gears for being between jobs *and* for trying to land some work."

"I'm sorry," she says. "Good luck with Jared." It strikes her that she hates who she's become in this relationship. She'd never wanted a marriage like her parents': two careerists so determined to fulfill their own ambitions that their relationship became a battleground. Mariana took every step to prevent that result in her own life, marrying a man with no discernable ambition whatsoever. And now she spends her days locked in conflict with her husband over his failure to get or keep a decent job.

She looks at her screen and realizes how late is. It's odd that Farah isn't back from her meeting upstairs. Mariana should be starving by now, but her body clock is off since she began skipping lunch routinely. It's her current strategy for tackling her perimenopausal waistline, since she doesn't have time to exercise and she's not ready to give up alcohol, sugar, or carbs, which are, at present, the three major pleasures of her life.

Her phone rings again. This is why she can't work at the office.

It's her editor, Chris. "Are you free to come up and meet with me for a few minutes?"

"I'll be right there." Mariana takes the internal staircase up one floor—exercise!—to Chris's office. She imagines the luxury of being able to crawl under a desk for an afternoon nap in perfect privacy. She supposes this widely shared fantasy is why no one has an office anymore. Or maybe offices started to seem like useless budgetary frills right around the time large numbers of women got promoted into them. She wonders if there's a story in that.

The door is open partway, but she knocks for the sake of politeness.

"Come on in," says Chris, and when she pushes the door wider, she sees that Reva Tucker, the human resources manager, is in the room as well. Both of these people are friendly colleagues—Chris is even a friend in the broad definition of the word—but neither of them looks remotely comfortable. Mariana tries not to react. Paranoia is unattractive, even if there's a healthy basis for it. She sits and waits.

"I hope you know how much I respect your work," says Chris.

"Thank you," says Mariana.

"You are an excellent journalist and colleague. Absolutely top drawer."

"Chris," says Reva.

Chris looks deflated. "I've been asked to speak to you about your MERLIN scores," he says.

Mariana nods. She's been expecting this since the paper instituted objective performance criteria in the form of a Media Engagement, Reach, and Leverage Index Number (MERLIN) for every reporter. Somewhere in the bowels of the computer system, MERLIN calculates the value of each reporter by measuring the online clicks, comments received, subscriptions generated, and various other kinds of public engagement with individual stories. The effect is an objective measure of worthiness for employment, according to the corporation that owns the newspaper.

Reva clears her throat. "As you know, these are challenging times for our business. We need to stay competitive by responding to consumer interest."

"I still like to think of the people who buy the paper as readers, rather than consumers," says Mariana. "And I still believe that newspapers should do more than cater to what they say they want. We have a duty to educate."

"Yes," says Chris. "We do. But that's an easier case to make for the beat reporters. We aren't reacting to breaking news in features. You're writing lifestyle pieces, Mariana. They're supposed to be fun."

"They can be both. The piece I'm writing right now on FairMarket Beauty is both. We've talked about it. It's a tongue-in-cheek critique of the holistic beauty industry and a glimpse inside Harmony Delacroix's cult of celebrity. It has the potential to go viral. Let's give it a chance to land."

Chris gives Reva a pleading look. She shakes her head. He says, "The thing is, Mariana, FairMarket Beauty is a significant advertiser."

"Don't say it," she says.

He has the expression of a man on the gallows. "The sales department is concerned about the piece."

"You're better than this," she says.

"It isn't his decision," says Reva.

"You're a journalist," she says, ignoring Reva.

"I'm a father of two with a wife who works part-time, and a son with special needs," he says.

"Are you telling me you're killing the story?"

"I'm offering editorial advice about the direction of the story and suggesting that the tongue-in-cheek aspect be toned way down."

"Because it's going to offend an advertiser? Are you kidding me, Chris?"

"Because feminist analysis doesn't do well on MER-LIN. And you can't afford that."

"This might be the most depressing conversation I've had in my entire career," says Mariana.

"I feel you," says Chris.

"And I'll remind you that there are still buyout packages available for staff at your level of seniority," says Reva.

"Do you know how many times a week I get called a stupid cunt by online trolls?" says Mariana. "Do you know how often men write in to tell me I'm too ugly to fuck? There's a reason why there aren't any senior women left at this newspaper. We've lost the courage of our convictions."

"Convictions are expensive," says Reva.

"Let's leave it there," says Chris. "Mariana, I don't want to lose you. Don't make any decisions today, okay? Think it over and we'll talk again."

Mariana walks out of the meeting in a daze. She makes her way back downstairs and finds Farah at her station with a cardboard box. "I was waiting for you," says Farah. "I took the buyout."

"They offered it to me, too."

"I know," says Farah.

Mariana wraps Farah in a hug and feels the tears well up. "How could they do that to you?" she says. "Your work is so important."

"Consumers aren't interested in diversity stories, apparently." Farah's eyes are bright and angry. "I'm going to go out and make some decent money for once and work someplace where strangers don't feel entitled to abuse me every day. What are you going to do?"

Mariana sits down. "I don't know," she says. "I've been a journalist for twenty years, and suddenly it's like I'm making buggy whips. What am I even qualified for?"

Farah pats her shoulder. "Many things. But right now, all you need to decide is whether or not you want to take the buyout. Once you do, you'll make the next decision, and then the next one. When you take responsibility for yourself, the universe comes along to support you."

"Who says that?"

"My therapist," says Farah. "She's very good. You should make an appointment."

67

"Maybe," says Mariana, glancing at her phone. There's a text from Zoe. *Harmony is looking for a communications director. She wants a former journalist. Know anyone good?*

"Do you want to work for Harmony Delacroix?"

"Hard pass," says Farah. "I'm going to the copy room to get another box. Are you sure you don't want one?"

"I'm not sure about anything," says Mariana.

FEBRUARY

CHAPTER 7

Zoe

Forget April. There is no doubt in Zoe's mind that February is the cruellest month. It's outright miserable, and so, for the most part, is she. And the most recent call from Eloise certainly isn't helping.

"Richard won't take your first offer," Eloise says.

"Did you offer him the house?"

"I told his lawyer that you were prepared to settle matters by transferring ownership of the house to him, yes."

"What more could he possibly want?"

"A stake in your business and ongoing payments to supplement what little income he has."

"For how long?"

"Indefinitely."

"He can't have that!"

"Of course he can't," says Eloise. "And he won't. And you won't get exactly what you want, either. That's how divorce works."

"Why is this moving so slowly?" says Zoe.

"As these things go, Zoe, it's moving fairly quickly. I'm sending you his counter-offer, and a bill. We'll schedule a call for next week to go over it. Have a great weekend."

Whenever Zoe speaks to Eloise, she has an unnerving sense that her life has splintered off onto multiple parallel tracks. There must be an alternate version of reality, a fairer one, in which her marriage is successful. Or one in which she's the first to leave. Or both.

Obviously, no one sets out to have a marriage that ends in divorce. She gets that. Who would spend the money or the effort if she didn't intend to go the distance? Who would stand up in front of friends and family and work colleagues and the odd parental acquaintance and the weird date that your brother brought (uninvited) and make those promises? Exactly no one, that's who.

But success, as Zoe has always understood it, is in the execution. And, in her humble estimation, she has been an exemplary wife. She's watched golf; she's cooked dinner for Richard's boring friends and tried to persuade herself to see their good qualities; she's gone to wine tastings and mused about minerality; she's paid a fortune for an opera subscription; she's tailored her interests and downplayed her professional successes and cheered from the sidelines and kept up with current events and appearances. She doesn't deserve a divorce. She deserves a fucking medal.

She checks the time; she's meeting Mariana for a drink late this afternoon. It's hours away, but she has a knot in her stomach already. How should she break the news about Devlin? What if Mariana doesn't believe her?

Should she pull up the dating site and let it speak for itself? And what if Devlin's taken his profile down? If he has, does she still have an obligation to tell Mariana?

Zoe isn't judgmental. She doesn't know what goes on in Mariana's marriage. For all she knows, Mariana and Devlin have an arrangement that permits him to experiment. Maybe Mariana has her own profile on this site. Her own marriage wasn't transparent to anyone outside of it, or to at least one person inside. Really, her humiliation at Richard's rejection is tempered with relief at not having to pretend to be happy with him any longer.

Concealment and truth, she thinks, aren't necessarily at opposite ends of the wellness spectrum. Secrecy can be a useful adaptation at times. And truth can break your heart.

But all of that is immaterial, because if Devlin is prowling around without permission, Zoe can't sit with the knowledge while Mariana is in the dark. End of story. Zoe sighs and logs in to the site to confirm that Devlin's still there. She finds him instantly and swears under her breath.

Zoe has promised herself not to log in to the dating site for her own messages during the workday, but since she's here already, she may as well peek. It's a distraction from the stress of her impending meeting with Mariana. She clicks on her inbox and scrolls through the posts, feeling increasingly dispirited. She wishes more men could spell basic words in English. She wishes fewer of them thought that *u* was an appropriate substitution for *you*. She wishes she could recover the lost time she has already spent pre-dating.

Zoe is becoming concerned that her libido is blown, like a fuse. She's not above having a casual fling, but even that won't happen unless she can sustain some sexual interest in someone who's a legitimate prospect. She needs to reboot the system, but she isn't sure how. What if she is permanently damaged by Richard's perfidy and her own idiocy? She leaves her inbox and wanders over to the system-generated list of matches. The quality here is much higher than what's in her inbox, a fact that is probably salient but not one she wants to contemplate at the moment. She scrolls through the profiles of available men and enjoys a surge of confidence. She could send a message to any of these men: the surgeon who likes rock climbing, the architect who sails competitively, the entrepreneur who speaks four languages fluently. She imagines herself at a fabulous party on Lake Como, telling Amal Clooney, *Yes, we met online, as everyone does these days. We knew immediately.* She wonders what the Italian word is for *destiny*.

Her phone rings, and she starts. Another full half-hour has vanished. "Hello?" She clicks to exit the platform, renewing her vow to restrict her daytime browsing.

"Zoe?"

"Yes."

"It's Will Shannon."

"Hey, Will," says Zoe. "I haven't talked to you in ages. Was it Sophie's Christmas party?"

"I think so. Did you connect with Eloise?"

"I did. She's great."

"She is. I'm very sorry about the circumstances, though. How are you doing?"

"I'm fine." It's not true, but she knows that he knows it, so it isn't exactly a lie. She aspires to be able to say *I'm fine* and to be believed. Or to have it be true. That would also be good.

"Listen, I was hoping that I might be able to meet you for lunch or a drink this week. There's something I want to run by you."

"I'm free for lunch today, if that works. I had a client cancel on me. Otherwise, I'm tied up until Friday."

"Today? Hmm. Give me a minute? I'm going to put you on hold, okay?"

"Sure." Zoe listens to the music on the line, which is a bastardization of one of her favourite party tunes from university. The universe is conspiring to point out that she's past her prime today, it seems. She wonders what Will could want to run by her. She wonders if he's single. What if . . . ? No. She's known Will forever. He dated her best friend. He couldn't possibly be asking her out, could he?

Will comes back on the line. "I'm good. Where and when?"

"Sorry?"

"Lunch. I can do it. Where should we meet?"

"Where are you?"

"The financial district. Do you know Cleaver's?"

"I love that place. Is noon too early? I have an appointment later in the afternoon."

75

"I'll be there," he says.

Zoe grabs her purse and races out of her office, almost knocking Kiki, her assistant, off her feet. "I forgot something at home," she says.

"Are you coming right back?"

"No, I'm going straight to lunch."

"You don't have a lunch."

"I do now."

"Okay," says Kiki. "Am I rescheduling your meeting with Harmony Delacroix?"

"Right. Yes." Zoe pauses, collects herself. She can't afford to offend Harmony. "Could you tell her that I'm running down a lead on her communications director, and I'll know more by the end of the day? And ask her if I can swing by tomorrow instead?"

"Will do," says Kiki.

"Thanks," says Zoe. "You're a lifesaver."

She races home and strips out of her suit. What to wear? She opts for a bodycon wrap dress that could plausibly be office attire and some high-heeled boots. She swaps her puffy coat for a tailored wool trench. She appraises herself in the mirror. Better. What's the expression? Dress for the job you want, not the job you have? She needs to start dressing like an independent woman with a healthy sex life, in the event that an occasion to become one should arise. And who knows? Today could be that day.

She arrives at Cleaver's right at noon and finds Will already seated. "You look fantastic," he says.

"So do you." It's true. Will is as ridiculously handsome

as ever, with only a few laugh lines and some grey at his temples to mark the passage of years. "I'm glad we could make this work."

"I appreciate you fitting me in," he says. "Why don't we order?" They do.

"So," says Zoe. "What did you want to run by me?"

"Let me give you some backstory first," says Will.

Zoe smiles her most encouraging smile. She's never seen Will Shannon flustered before. It's absolutely adorable. Perhaps she's not dead inside after all.

"Do you remember that party you threw for Sophie and Jesse before they got married?"

"It was epic," says Zoe.

"It was," says Will. "I met your cousins there, do you remember?"

"Everyone was there," says Zoe. Has Will had a crush on her since then? It must have been, what, fifteen years ago? If only he'd made a move then! She could have avoided marrying Richard altogether.

"So, anyway, a kid named Oscar came to see me last week."

Zoe has no idea where he's going with this. "Oh? That's my nephew's name. He isn't exactly my nephew, actually, he's my cousin's son, but I think of him as my nephew. Which is beside the point, obviously. Isn't it weird how those old-man names are coming back into fashion?"

Will looks exasperated. "This is awkward," he says.

"It doesn't need to be," says Zoe. "I'm flattered that you called. There shouldn't be any embarrassment in searching your own network for possibilities." She has always thought of Will Shannon as having excellent social skills. It's comforting to know that everyone struggles in the dating arena.

The food arrives, creating a helpful distraction. Zoe picks up her fork and prepares to dig in, but stops when she realizes that Will isn't doing the same.

"I'm not being clear," says Will.

"I'm following you."

"I don't think you are," says Will. "I'm talking about Oscar."

"Okay."

"The same Oscar who's your—relative."

"What about him?"

"He thinks I'm his biological father."

Zoe puts down her fork. "I don't understand."

"I'm with you there."

"Oscar thinks you're his biological father?"

Will runs his hands through his hair. "Yes. That's what he told me when he showed up at my office."

"But that's crazy. You never dated Beata."

"Dated, no." Is Will blushing? "But I met Beata at that party and we spent some time together afterwards."

"Oh," says Zoe. "So you're saying . . ."

"I'm saying it's not exactly impossible, biologically speaking."

"Seriously? You and Beata?"

"It was a one-night, no-strings thing. I didn't misread it, if that's what you're thinking. And if I had, it's not as if

I've been unreachable in the intervening years. I'm still at the same law firm. I have the same email address and phone number. If she'd wanted to contact me, I was easy to find. But she didn't."

"I'm not accusing you of anything, Will."

"Maybe you should." Will's expression hardens. "If I've had a son for fifteen years and I haven't had the opportunity to know him or do anything for him? If he's had no father his whole life when I was here the entire time?"

"It isn't necessarily true that you're his father, is it?"

Will pulls out his wallet and extracts a photo, passing it across to her. "This is my school photo from tenth grade. I dug it out after Oscar came by."

"Oh. I see what you mean." Oscar's face stares up at her.

"Zoe," says Will. "Tell me you didn't know about this."

"I swear I didn't. I thought she'd gone to a sperm bank. That's what she told us." On reflection, Zoe is astonished at her own credulity. What twenty-year-old goes to a sperm bank?

"What was Beata thinking?" asks Will.

"I wish I knew the answer to that. I honestly have no idea why she would have done what she did. How did Oscar find you, anyway?"

"It was a fluke. He was playing detective and he got lucky. According to him, his mother's been having a bunch of closed-door conversations lately, which is unusual for her. He got curious and used the reverse-call function on their phone, which took him to the main reception at my law firm. He couldn't tell the receptionist which lawyer he wanted to speak to, so she told him to check the website. My picture's on the landing page. I guess he saw a resemblance."

"But Beata wasn't calling you?"

"No. She must have been dealing with another lawyer at the firm. There are around a hundred of us. Finding me was a total shot in the dark."

"And he showed up at your office? Just walked right in?"

"To be fair, he emailed me first, but I wasn't sure it was legit and I hadn't figured out how to respond yet. I guess he got impatient." Will smiles. "He's a determined kid."

"Oscar's great," Zoe agrees. "He's not at his most lovable age right now, but even so, I like him a lot. He's been more interested in spending time with my brother, Zack, lately. I think he's been missing having a . . ." She stops.

"Father," says Will.

"Yes."

"I'm sure he does miss having a father. A teenage boy needs a strong male figure to look up to, and to separate from. It's natural to want that relationship. If I'm his father . . ." Will shakes his head. "It's honestly a lot to take in."

"You're angry."

"I'm a lot of things," says Will. "Angry is definitely one of them."

"Where did you leave things with Oscar?"

"We chatted for a few minutes and exchanged numbers, and I told him that I'd call him once I'd had a chance to talk to his mother. And since then I've been trying to figure out how the hell to do that, which is why I called you." Will pauses. "I don't know Beata well, I'm embarrassed to say. Our conversation is bound to be tricky, at the very least, and possibly extremely unpleasant. I wanted your advice about how to approach it."

Zoe sits back in her chair. "This is all quite a shock."

Will laughs. "You think?" he says.

"It might be good if she had a heads-up. She might not react well if you show up out of the blue. She can be pretty protective when it comes to Oscar."

"Is that something you could do?"

"Theoretically yes," says Zoe. "But Beata and I aren't that close. I'm way closer to her sister Mariana. What if I talked to Mariana and asked her to do it? If she won't, I promise I will. Okay?"

"Fine with me, so long as it happens soon. It isn't fair to keep Oscar hanging."

"Understood." The scale of the family drama ahead begins to sink in. "My aunt is going to freak out." But at least, Zoe thinks, it will give Zack something to focus on aside from her dating life.

"I don't want to be responsible for that."

"Oh, don't worry. Lydia freaks out fairly regularly. We all take turns being responsible." Zoe smiles. "Welcome to the family."

CHAPTER 8

Mariana

Mariana is waiting when Zoe rushes into the wine bar. "Sorry," says Zoe. "I had a lunch that ran late and I had to do a few things at the office before I left."

"No problem. I started without you." Mariana lifts her glass and takes a mouthful of Sauvignon Blanc. "Do you want a drink?"

"Sure," says Zoe. "It's been that kind of day."

"So . . . what's going on?"

"It's complicated."

"I expect nothing less from you."

"I choose to take that as a compliment," says Zoe. "Can I run a hypothetical by you?"

"I guess."

"Okay, then. Let's say I was approached by someone I know, who was approached by Oscar about being his biological father."

Mariana's mind races with the implications. She says, carefully, "Our Oscar? Beata's Oscar?"

"Your nephew. My . . . second cousin?"

"First cousin once removed," says Mariana. "Seriously? Oscar found his father? And it's someone you know?"

"Hypothetically, yes."

"Does Beata know that Oscar found him?"

"I don't know. All I'm trying to do is figure out how to help this person I know, who is a well-intentioned and upstanding individual, without alienating Oscar or his mother."

"I wondered when the other shoe was going to drop," Mariana says. "I didn't think Oscar was bluffing at Christmas, but when I asked Beata about it afterwards, she said he was mistaken and clammed up." Mariana takes another drink. She can't believe that Beata managed to keep a secret like this for fifteen years. Mariana had questioned Beata's decision to have a baby at twenty much more than her decision to use a sperm bank; the first decision had struck her as insane, the second as fairly sensible. She and her sisters had been taught from an early age by their mother to exercise control over their reproductive health and sexuality. "So? Who's the baby daddy?"

"Will Shannon."

"That hunky lawyer friend of yours?"

Zoe nods.

"That's random. How does he know Beata?"

"He doesn't, really. They hooked up after one of my parties, roughly sixteen years ago. I don't think they've seen each other since."

Mariana shakes her head. "I didn't know she was ever into men, honestly. This whole thing is crazy."

"I know," says Zoe.

"My mother is going to freak out." Mariana winces. "Zack cannot write about this."

"Why does everyone keep telling me what Zack can and can't do? He's not going to, but I'm not responsible for it either way. What I am responsible for is helping Will."

"What does any of this have to do with you? Personally, I'd stay as far away from it as possible."

"He needs to connect with Beata."

"Sounds like he managed it fine on his own the first time around," says Mariana.

"Gross," says Zoe.

"Now, Zoe," says Mariana, "when two people don't love each other, but are very drunk and horny, and meet at a party . . ."

Zoe covers her ears. "Stop. Seriously."

Mariana laughs. "What does he need help for?"

"It's delicate. He wants to confirm that he's Oscar's father. He doesn't want to get Oscar's hopes up or become too emotionally involved if Oscar's mistaken."

"That makes sense to me," says Mariana.

"So, I thought you could be the one to ask her."

"Why would I do that?"

"You're her sister. You get more biological leeway to offend than I do. She's gone to great lengths to keep this information to herself, and I'm assuming she won't be thrilled by any of this. And she's been pissed at me since Zack's show aired. She thinks I knew about Zack's script and didn't send up a flare when I should have."

"Did you know?"

"I did not, as I've said repeatedly, but I've stopped hoping that anyone will believe me."

"This feels like a dangerous mission," says Mariana. "I'm her sister, sure, but we're talking about her kid. As you said, she kept this secret for a reason. I don't want to get caught in the crossfire and end up paying for it at every family event for the rest of my life."

"If Oscar's right, Will Shannon may be in attendance at every family event for the rest of your life, and he'll owe you one."

"Why can't I have a family less worthy of television treatment?" asks Mariana. She downs her wine and signals to the server to bring her another glass. "Fine. I'll talk to her."

"Thank you."

"Are you sure it's what Oscar wants?"

"He went to Will's workplace and confronted him. It wasn't subtle."

"God." Mariana smiles slightly. "Credit where credit is due, that was a bold move."

Zoe smiles back. "I know, right? I'm proud of him." Their cheese platter arrives, and she takes a bite. "Okay, next topic. Any thoughts on the Harmony Delacroix gig?"

"Is it full-time?"

"Ideally, but it's probably negotiable. The company's

growing and getting a lot of media attention, so there's definitely a strategy element to the role. Do you know someone?"

"Not off the top of my head."

"You must, Mariana. It's an unconventional workplace, mostly women, and fairly flexible in terms of accommodating family commitments. The salary's competitive. Don't you have a bunch of friends who have been taking buyout packages?"

"Yeah, I do, but my friends tend to be . . ."

"Intellectual snobs?"

Mariana grins. "True believers."

"Do me a favour and ask around, okay? Sometimes a true believer decides to take a decent paycheque and save the world on the side."

"Noted," says Mariana.

Zoe pulls out her phone. "I started online dating."

"You're dating? That's fantastic! Any promising candidates?"

"Not exactly promising."

Mariana laughs. "What adjective would you use, then?"

Zoe pauses. "Married," she says.

"The guys on the site are married? That's so nasty."

"It is."

"What if you saw someone you knew? Oh my god, that would be so awkward!"

"Yes," says Zoe. "It *is* extremely awkward."

"Wait a minute. You saw someone you know? Are you going to tell his wife?"

"Do you think I have an obligation?" asks Zoe.

"How well do you know the wife?"

"Extremely well," says Zoe. "She's my cousin."

"Your cousin." Mariana puts her glass down. "What do you mean, your cousin?" Mariana tries to remember which cousins Zoe has on the other side of the family, and whether or not she's met them.

"Mariana." Zoe passes her phone across the table. "Look."

Mariana take the phone, turns it around, and angles the screen. What she sees is a picture of Devlin, bare-chested, on a family holiday in Mexico last winter. "What am I looking at?" she says, although she knows this photo. She took it herself.

"It's a dating profile. I thought I recognized the man in the picture." Zoe sounds unsure of herself. "But he's wearing sunglasses, so maybe I made a mistake."

"No," says Mariana. "You didn't make a mistake. I did." A colossal mistake. She remembers pulling out her phone, telling him to strike a pose, laughing. They were sitting at a swim-up bar, day-drinking, the day as yet untarnished by marital squabbling. Devlin was at his flirty best, and the girls were splashing in the shallow water right next to them. She wanted to capture it for posterity and as insurance against an intemperate exit: *We can be this. Remember.*

But, insurance notwithstanding, she has known for years that this moment would come. She is disturbingly unsurprised. It's appalling, obviously, that Devlin has used this artifact of family life (the girls are playing right outside the edge of the screen, for god's sake!) to deceive and betray. But it isn't deliberate. She isn't making excuses for him. She doesn't need to. She knows he chose this photo because he's half-dressed and looks like a smoking hot fuck, and for no other reason. He has always frustrated her attempts to plumb his psychological depths. Ultimately, he isn't that complicated.

She scrolls down, committing LuckOfTheIrish's vital statistics to memory. She's a quick study, an occupational asset. She notes that Devlin's alter ego is four years younger than the man himself, and makes considerably more money. *Irish gentleman seeks free-spirited companion for friendship and more! Successful musician and entrepreneur, world traveller, lover of all life's pleasures.* A catch indeed. She hands the phone back to Zoe.

"Are you all right?" asks Zoe.

Mariana's mind is racing. There is much to do. Does she need to quit first, or throw him out first? What about the house? Thank god for the prenup. She needs to talk to her insurance agent, get the beneficiary designation changed. And her will. The girls! Can he manage to take care of them? She needs to talk to a lawyer, immediately. Priorities. She needs to prioritize. She needs . . .

"Mariana, please say something. Do you hate me?" Mariana realizes that Zoe is crying.

"I don't hate you," she says. "Why would I hate you? I hate him."

"What can I do?"

"You can give me the contact for your divorce lawyer," says Mariana.

"Are you sure? Do you want to think about it? I mean, you're probably in shock."

"I doubt it," says Mariana. "Disappointed and angry, yes. Shocked? Not really."

"You seem very, uh, together."

"I'm focused," says Mariana. "This is how I solve problems. Devlin just became a problem, and I'm going to solve the shit out of him."

"Okay," says Zoe. "I'm texting you my lawyer's contact. Her name is Eloise Embree. She's not much of a hand-holder, just to warn you."

"Sounds perfect," says Mariana. "What does she charge?"

Zoe tells her.

"Convictions are expensive," says Mariana.

"I'm not following you."

"Tell Harmony Delacroix that I'd like to talk to her about the communications job."

"You? But you love what you do! You're, you know, kind of famous. I wasn't thinking of it for you."

"I love what I used to do," says Mariana. "I'm not famous enough to make decent money at it, and too famous to be left alone by trolls. I have a buyout offer that would cover my legal costs. I'm going to need a decent paycheque for the foreseeable future. I can save the world on the side."

Her cousin reaches across the table and grabs hold of her hand. "If you want the job, I'll tell Harmony to hire you," says Zoe. "She's so excited about the piece you're writing about her. Did you send her a draft? She seems confident that it's going to be absolutely glowing."

"I never send subjects my stories in advance," says Mariana. "Only my editor sees them. But she's right, she'll definitely like it." Mariana manages to keep the bitterness out of her voice, barely.

"If it's what you want, I can make it happen for you."

"I want the job." Mariana stands up. "And now I have to run. I have a lot to do."

"Are you sure you're okay? Do you want me to come with you?"

"No, no. I've got this." Mariana takes in Zoe's expression of alarm. "What?"

"Are you in shock?"

"Am I supposed to collapse in a heap? Do I not seem upset enough to you?"

Zoe holds up her hands. "If there's a right way to do this, I have no idea what it is. Just promise you'll call me if you need backup. I'm so sorry this is happening to you. I wouldn't wish it on anyone, and certainly not on you."

Mariana gives Zoe a swift hug. She needs to leave. She has no time to waste. She stalks out of the restaurant and hails a taxi, punching in the number for Zoe's lawyer while the car is pulling away from the curb. By the time she reaches home, she's retained Eloise, acquired some preliminary advice, and arranged for her mother to pick up the girls from daycare and keep them for dinner. She calls a locksmith and books an emergency appointment. She feels electrified with purpose.

She collects a suitcase from the basement—the one with the wonky wheel—and carries it up to her bedroom.

She throws open the wardrobe doors. All of Devlin's clothes are arrayed on one side of the custom closet. The ability to pack a cheating husband's belongings quickly and efficiently, it strikes her, is an unanticipated benefit of closet organization. She is methodical: shirts, pants, suits, ties, underwear. She runs downstairs for another suitcase. The doorbell rings; it's the locksmith. She provides her instructions, and he gets to work.

Shoes, belts, socks, toiletries. She hauls the suitcases downstairs and into the front hallway. The locksmith shows her the new hardware, hands her the keys and a bill, takes her payment, wishes her good luck.

It's time. She takes out her phone to send a text to Devlin and freezes at the sight of Iona and Siobhan on the lock screen, their arms around each other. Her throat tightens. Can she do this? Should she? Will the girls ever forgive her? Mariana inhales, rolling her shoulders back and straightening her spine. What would she be teaching her girls by staying with a man who doesn't respect her? They deserve more, and so does she.

She types the message. *Call me. It's an emergency.*

Her phone rings immediately. "What's happened? Are the girls okay?"

"The girls are fine," she says. "Where are you?"

"I'm out with Jared."

"Where?"

"For Christ's sake, Mariana. You said it was an emergency."

"It is. More for you than for me. You need to find a

91

new place to live. I had the locks changed."

"You can't do that. I'm coming home."

"You'll find your things on the front porch. I packed them up for you. I'm going to my mom's for dinner so you can come and get them."

"What the hell is going on here, Mariana?"

"I found your dating profile," she says. "I'm not going to do this anymore."

There is a long silence, and she thinks he's hung up. "Are you still there?"

He speaks carefully. "Is there something I could say right now that would make a difference?"

She has to give him credit. He's handling this well. It occurs to her that he's been expecting this call. He's going through the motions of protest, but his heart isn't in it. His heart is elsewhere. "No," she says. "There's nothing. Nothing at all."

CHAPTER 9

Beata

Beata emerges from the treatment room and closes the door behind her. Rina, the receptionist, waves her over. "Your mother called," she says. "Twice. The second time, she made me promise to give you the message."

"Message received," says Beata as the door opens and her client steps into the hallway. Beata looks her over. "That's much better," she says, approvingly. "Your shoulder has dropped nicely, and your posture looks good. How do you feel?"

"You're a miracle worker," the woman says. "I'd heard the stories, but I didn't quite believe it. What's your secret?"

Beata smiles. "No secret," she says. "I pay closer attention than some, I guess."

"But I've had massages for years, and no one ever told me I had a curve in my spine."

"It's a mild one," Beata assures her, "and it's not at all unusual. But we have to start from the spine if you want to keep tension out of your shoulder for more than a day after treatment. Do the exercises I showed you, and you'll have an easier time staying balanced. Rina can book you in next week."

Clarice, a fellow massage therapist, joins her in the hallway. "Another satisfied client?"

Beata shakes her head. "That woman went to the same physiotherapist for two years for pain in her shoulder, and he never figured out that she had scoliosis. Sheer incompetence. One session of craniosacral therapy, and she feels better than she has in months. But we're the ones who can't get any respect from the medical profession."

"The struggle continues," says Clarice. "Keep fighting the good fight."

"Speaking of which," says Beata, "have you given any thought to the blog?" Beata has been trying to get a few of her colleagues at the Holistic Healing Partnership, the ones with young children, to take over the *Mindful Mothering* blog.

"I haven't ruled it out," says Clarice. "Are you sure you don't want to continue with it? It's your baby."

"My baby is a fire-breathing teenager," says Beata. "The blog is just a hobby."

She waits to call her mother until she's home and is settled calmly and comfortably on her bed.

"I'm very worried about your sister," says Lydia.

"Which one?" asks Beata, reasonably.

"Mariana, of course!"

"Why?"

"Because she threw her husband out of the house, and now her poor girls are distraught. It was a very rash decision, if you ask me."

For a lifelong feminist activist, Lydia's views on motherhood and family can be surprisingly unpredictable, as Beata learned early and memorably. "These are Mariana's decisions to make, Mom. You believe that women should be able to make their own choices about marriage, right?"

"I'm speaking as a concerned grandmother," says Lydia.

"Well, if you're worried about the girls, why don't you offer to take them for the weekend? I'm sure Mariana would appreciate the break."

"Have you looked after those girls? It's bedlam when they're in the house. And your father and I have a lot of commitments of our own."

"I know you do. But Mariana needs our support."

"I'm always supportive of my children," says Lydia. "I can be supportive and still have my own priorities. And right now, I have to run and prepare for an interview with *The Guardian*. Speak to you later."

Beata opens her meditation app and opts for twenty minutes of lovingkindness. She realizes, more and more as she ages, how little she controls other than her intentions, her feelings, and her behaviour. She is becoming less ambitious as a result. It is enough of a challenge, most days, to be kind. Especially to her mother. And her son. She hears the door open and the unmistakable banging and thumping that heralds Oscar's arrival: Oscar shucking his gigantic shoes and backpack and throwing them down in the front hall; Oscar banging around in the kitchen, foraging for snacks; Oscar clomping on the stairs. She tunes him out, focuses on Mariana. *May she be happy, may she be healthy, may she be free from suffering, may she be safe. May she be happy, may she be healthy, may she be free from suffering, may she be . . ."*

"Mom!" Oscar is outside the door to her bedroom. "Mom!"

"Coming." Beata closes her practice, rises, and opens the door. "Hi, honey." It's been tense in their house since Christmas. Oscar's anger has been steady, often in the normal range for teenagers deprived of agency, but at other times frighteningly incandescent. She is cautious around him now. She is relearning him.

"Can you come down to the kitchen? I brought a friend home, and he wants to meet you."

"That's very nice. Of course, I'd love to meet your friend." It's been some time since Oscar brought a friend home. He's become cagey about his personal life. He claims—completely unfairly, in Beata's view—that Beata doesn't respect his boundaries. It's true that in the early years of the *Mindful Mothering* blog, she mined, perhaps too deeply, her experiences as a single mother for material. But she prides herself on having heard Oscar's legitimate complaints and responded to them. She no longer shares personal vignettes about Oscar and hasn't for many months now. She appreciates, even admires, that Oscar has learned how to deploy her own vocabulary against her, but it's still an irritating power play.

She walks into the kitchen and hears Oscar say, "This is Will." She feels cold washing through her. She recognizes him easily. He hasn't changed that much, and anyway, she's been reading everything she can about him online since Christmas dinner. How is it that she never expected this day to come? She can see now that it was inevitable, as she stands in her own kitchen, staring at her son's father, feeling Oscar's triumph radiating behind her.

"Did you read the article I sent you?" Oscar had asked, a month or so before Christmas.

"Which article?" she said, although she knew. It was a piece about sperm-bank regulation.

"The one about sperm donors and confidentiality," he said.

"I don't think I saw it," she lied. "What did it say?"

"It said that if you're a biological child, you can call your sperm bank and tell them you want to get in touch with your donor. Most of them will contact the donor now and see if he's willing to meet you. Could we find out if the sperm bank you used for me would do that?"

"I think they might have gone out of business," said Beata.

"Their records have to be stored somewhere," said Oscar. "The article said so."

"Okay," said Beata, trying to keep her voice calm. "I can't remember the name of the company offhand. I'll look in my files, all right?"

Oscar didn't answer, and a week later, she startled him coming out of her home office. She knew there wasn't any documentation to find, but she took the incursion for what it was: a sign that Oscar was taking matters into his own hands. She still had time to figure out the best way to tell him, she thought. What she hadn't anticipated—how could she?—was that he'd manage to do the impossible and find the father no one knew about inside of three months.

With the best of intentions, she has gotten it all hopelessly wrong, from start to finish.

"I'm sorry," she says, and finds that she can't say more. She feels that she might fall, or bolt from the room.

Will's expression is uncertain. "Beata," he says. "It's been a long time. Could we talk?" She nods, and slides into a chair. Will turns to Oscar. "We're going to speak about this later, Oscar. I told you very clearly that I did not want to ambush anyone. Not cool. Not cool at all."

Oscar reddens. "Are you okay, Mom?"

"I'll be fine," says Beata.

"Get her some water, please," says Will. "And some tissues. Would you like anything else, Beata? A drink of something stronger? I brought some wine."

"My mom doesn't drink," says Oscar, filling a glass with water.

"A glass of wine would be good," Beata says. "Thank you." She blows her nose and takes a sip of water. Breathe, she thinks. Breathe. "Oscar, go upstairs. I want to talk to Mr. Shannon privately. No debate, please." Miraculously, Oscar exits without an argument.

Will sits down, facing her. "I take it from your reaction that Oscar hasn't made a mistake? That I'm his biological father?"

"Yes." She could deny it, or pretend confusion, or invent a reason for her silence. But it would only prolong the discomfort. "You're the only person it could have been. I was coming off a dry spell when we . . . If you'd like a test to be sure, I'll consent to it. But there's no question in my mind." She rubs her face with her palm. "How he found out, though, I have no idea. I've never told anyone."

"In a way, I'm glad to hear that," says Will. "It would have been pretty strange if anyone else had known, since I certainly didn't."

"You must be so angry with me." Beata feels ill.

"Yes," he says. "I am. Why the hell didn't you tell me?"

"So many reasons, Will," she says.

"I'd love to hear them."

Beata looks him straight in the eye. "I was twenty. You were a hook-up at a party. We barely knew each other. I didn't have any expectations of you. And I had no idea what I was getting into. Looking back, I wasn't very mature about any of it." Beata pauses, remembering. "And then Oscar was born, and it all got incredibly real, and I was too overwhelmed to cope with much, let alone calling you up and telling you about the baby. It took some time to get myself together, and by then, Oscar and I were a pair, without any sense of someone missing. Honestly? I didn't realize that I was depriving him, or you, until this year. And then I didn't know what to do. I'm sorry, Will. I can't tell you how sorry."

Will clears his throat. "I obviously didn't leave you with the impression that I was someone you could count on back then. I would have liked the opportunity to rise to the occasion. But I'm here now, and Oscar wants me to play some kind of role in his life, and I intend to be here for him."

Beata feels her belly tighten, as if to protect her baby. A mother's body, she thinks, is built for war, in ways no man could ever understand. Will, having arrived fifteen years late, intends to be here for Oscar, as if he knows what that commitment entails. Beata knows. She knows about sitting up for long, quiet hours, rocking Oscar when he wouldn't sleep. She knows about reading *Scoop Saves the Day* twenty-five times in a row. She knows about homework, and soccer games, and birthday parties, and contusions and concussions and stitches. She knows about haircuts, and needles, and fevers.

"I don't doubt your intentions. But what do you know about kids, Will? What do you know about parenting a teenager? What if you find it isn't what you expected? I don't want Oscar to find his father only to be rejected."

Will puts his glass down. "Beata, I'm trying to be fair and constructive. But you're testing me. You have no idea what kind of parent I would be, and that is entirely because you made a decision not to let me be one. I resent the implication that I've somehow imposed unreasonable expectations on Oscar in the five minutes I've known him.

I resent that you think I'd reject him. I'm not an asshole, even though you seem determined to treat me like one."

"I'm looking out for Oscar. I'm his mother, and that's my job."

"I understand your motivations, Beata. But I'd like you to recognize the reality here. Oscar came looking for me, and now I'm here. I don't specialize in family law, but there is an excellent lawyer at my firm who does, and I'm sure she would tell you that kids at Oscar's age get a say in decisions about parental access."

"Are you threatening me?"

"Not at all. I'm telling you that Oscar's views matter, and he's made it clear that he wants me in his life. I'm asking you to respect his wishes, as well as mine, and propose an arrangement that would be acceptable to you."

At the moment, all Beata can think is that she'd like to go back in time and use the sperm bank of her imagination, and create a whole new life in which Oscar is her child and hers alone. In that life, she'd do everything right, and she'd be enough, and Will Shannon wouldn't be sitting in her kitchen, with his suit and his law degree, asking her oh-so-reasonably for permission to break her son's heart. That's an arrangement that would be acceptable to her.

The doorbell rings. "Excuse me," says Beata. She goes to the front door. Eloise is standing on the porch. "This is a terrible time, Eloise. It couldn't be worse."

"Why don't I come in and help?"

"You can't," Beata says. "Help, I mean. You can't help. Or come in. There's a situation with Oscar."

"Eloise?" Will has come into the front hallway. "I thought I heard your voice."

"Will? What are you doing here? Beata, why didn't you tell me that you knew Will? I've mentioned him to you a bunch of times. My work friend? The one I play tennis with?"

"What are *you* doing here?" asks Will. "It's strange, I was just thinking about you." To Beata he says, "Eloise practises family law at my office."

"I know," says Beata.

They focus their sharp eyes on her. "What's going on here?" says Eloise. "Beata?"

Another fatal error, Beata thinks. She knew, right from the beginning of her relationship with Eloise, that this outcome was a possibility. She even tried to end the relationship a few times early on, before it got too serious, but Eloise was stubborn. And she was in love, and prone to magical thinking as a result. She could find endless reasons to avoid office parties, couldn't she? She could train herself not to react whenever Eloise mentioned Will's name in conversation. And who knew what the future held? She and Eloise might not work out. She could postpone a collision, perhaps indefinitely.

She sees now how foolish she's been. She says, "Will is Oscar's biological father."

"You have got to be kidding me," says Eloise.

"Who's she?" says Oscar, coming down the stairs.

"Go back upstairs," says Beata.

"Oscar's the boy who came to see you at the office?" says Eloise to Will. "I can't believe it."

"Tell me about it," says Will.

"He was Beata's son, and I didn't recognize him. This is so fucked up." Eloise turns to Beata. "Why don't I know what your son looks like, Beata?"

"I showed you a picture," says Beata.

"He was wearing sunglasses!" Beata has never heard Eloise raise her voice before.

"Oscar, please go back upstairs," says Beata. "Right now."

"No," says Oscar. "I can hear everything anyway."

Eloise extends a hand to Oscar. "We haven't met, Oscar," she says. "I'm Eloise, your mother's girlfriend."

"Her girlfriend," says Will. "Okay. Because this wasn't weird enough."

"Eloise!" says Beata.

"You told me you weren't interested in dating," says Oscar. "You told me you didn't have time."

"My personal life is personal, Oscar," says Beata. "I wasn't ready to tell you yet, as Eloise knows."

"Just out of curiosity," says Will, "how long have you been seeing each other?"

"Two years," says Eloise.

"And, Beata, how much of that time were you aware that I worked in the same office with your girlfriend?"

"Most of it."

"And did it occur to you that it might be appropriate to contact me at that point?"

"This is not a cross-examination," says Beata.

"It is, actually," says Will.

"What were you thinking, Beata?" says Eloise.

"I was protecting my son."

"I resent that," says Will. "Deeply."

"So do I," says Oscar.

"This is a grown-up conversation, Oscar. You shouldn't be here," says Beata.

"I shouldn't be here?" says Oscar. "You're talking about my life. You were protecting *me*? That's fucked up, Mom. You don't care about me. You only care about protecting yourself from your own stupid decisions and lies." And before she can react, Oscar's gone, the front door slamming behind him.

"Well," says Will, "he's not wrong."

"No," says Eloise, "he's not."

MARCH

CHAPTER 10

Zoe

Zack is fussing. "Are you sure you're ready?"

"You're the one who's been pushing me to do this!"

"I know. But I want you to have a good experience out there."

So does Zoe. Up to this point, she'd rate the experience as mildly negative overall. She's weathered the complete pre-dating cycle, from winks and pokes, to light-hearted messages peppered with emojis, to gentle inquiries about relationship status, to frank expressions (some far too frank, with regrettably personal photos attached) of interest. She's had her hopes raised and dashed. She's bowed out graciously and been ghosted mysteriously. It's all normal, she's been assured by seasoned veterans, and terribly time-consuming, and vaguely enervating.

Tonight, though, she's breaking the online seal and leaving her house to meet an apparently single, male human, IRL. (Although she can never remember what the acronyms mean. She has a dictionary of online jargon bookmarked.) The human in question is Dave, a divorced entrepreneur who loves to travel. "It will be what it will be," she says.

"Very philosophical," Zack says. "That's a smart mindset. And you look fantastic. But take it slow. Manage your expectations."

"It's a drink, Zack. I know how to have a drink without ending up married or dead in a ditch."

"I worry about you."

"That's extremely sweet, but completely unnecessary."

"I feel like I'm sending my baby off to college for the first time."

"I'm older than you are."

"I'm proud of you."

"God, Zack, you're making me a thousand times more nervous. Shut up, will you?"

Zack follows her to the front door. "Break a leg. I've got my phone. Text me if you need a rescue, understood?"

"Remember that Will and Oscar are coming at seven thirty. You guys can decide what to order, okay? I'll text you if I'm going to be later."

She blows Zack a kiss and closes the door gently in his face. She's arranged to meet Dave at a bar around the corner, so she doesn't have far to travel in heels. She talks a good game, but she's rattled, honestly, by how off balance she feels. She hasn't been on a date with anyone except Richard since her early thirties, which means, she realizes, that she's never been on a date with a grown-up before. What do they talk about?

She snags a table by the window, with a view of the street and the entire room. Control the environment, remove the element of surprise: this is an experiment, and she's going to manage the variables. She orders a glass of wine.

"Zoe?" Unfortunately, you can't control for random dudes appearing out of nowhere. She has to get rid of this one quickly; Dave will be here any moment.

"I'm so sorry," Zoe says. "I'm terrible with faces." This isn't true, but it's convenient. "Remind me how we know each other?"

"We don't," says the man. "At least not yet. I'm Dave. You look exactly like your picture!"

"Oh," says Zoe. Dave looks nothing whatsoever like his picture. "Of course. What was I thinking! Nice to meet you." She stands, and they shake hands. Dave removes his coat and settles into the seat opposite.

"So," he says.

"So," she says. "Here we are." It takes three seconds, she's read, to decide whether or not someone is attractive; this date is a mistake. But she needs to fill at least a half-hour for the sake of civility.

The server brings her drink. "What will you have?" she asks Dave.

"Water's good for me," he says.

Panic sets in. Why isn't he drinking? Is drinking frowned upon at a first meeting? Is she sending the wrong signals? Why did he suggest meeting for a drink? Or was she the one who suggested it? She can't remember. What if he can't drink for medical reasons? Does he think she's insensitive? Or that she drinks inappropriately? Does she? Her brain is a hamster on speed. Is she having a full-scale anxiety attack right here in the bar? Why is she freaking out when there's zero chemistry anyway?

"How long have you been dating?" Dave is speaking and she forces herself to pay attention.

"Not long," she says, pleased at how normal she sounds. "I separated a few months ago."

"Ah," he says. "How are you finding it?"

"Kind of disconcerting, so far."

"It can be. I've been at it for a couple of years. It definitely gets easier." He smiles, and she recognizes the smile from his online pictures. "The worst part is that you get tired of listening to yourself give the same introductory speech over and over again. You start to think, am I as boring to my date as I am to myself?"

There is no need for alarm. A grown-up first date, Zoe sees, is a cocktail party for two, and she can chit-chat with the best of them for thirty minutes. She leans in. "You said you were an entrepreneur?"

"That's right."

"What a coincidence! So am I. What kind of business are you in?"

"I'm in tech."

"Fascinating!" Zoe wonders if she can shorten this down to twenty minutes. "What do you do?"

"I execute and lead."

"You execute and lead what?"

"Projects."

"Better than executing people, I guess." Neither of them laugh. "What kind of projects?" She wishes that Dave would pick up some of the conversational slack. She feels herself starting to sweat.

"I know you're new at this," says Dave, "but this feels like a job interview, not a date."

"My apologies," says Zoe. In fact, she thinks it would be a great leap forward in online dating if she could review CVs instead of profiles. Dave and his mysterious employment would never have made the cut.

"Don't worry about it," says Dave. "I can be oversensitive about my career."

"Totally normal," says Zoe, her inner alarm system ringing at full strength.

"So, this place is cool," says Dave. "Have you been here before?"

"I have. I live close by."

"Nice! I wish I could afford to live downtown."

"I thought you did," says Zoe.

Dave looks sheepish. "I put that on my profile, didn't I? Sorry about that. Some women are really shallow about that kind of thing. I didn't want to get ruled out just because I live in the suburbs."

Zoe, whose profile includes the restriction "must live downtown," swallows the last of her drink and signals for another. "Do you like to travel?"

"I love it!"

"Great!" says Zoe. "Any recommendations? Where's your favourite place to go?"

"Las Vegas," he says. "I do a road trip down there every couple of years."

"I've never been there."

"What? Are you ever missing out! We should go!" Dave laughs, high-pitched and reedy. "A road trip is a great way to get to know someone."

"I'm sure it is." Zoe hates road trips.

"I hate to fly. You have a completely different experience on the road."

"No argument here. It kind of limits you, though, don't you think?" She realizes that she sounds judgmental, but she can't possibly date someone who hates to fly, for god's sake. How would they go to Paris? Or Cambodia? Or Machu Picchu?

"Only if you want to leave the country. And why would I? There's so much to see right here, and you don't need a passport." He picks up the bar menu. "Did you want some food?" Does he mean that he doesn't have a passport? He couldn't mean that. Or could he? She has no idea who this man is, and she doesn't want to. She wants to go home.

"No," she says. "I'm heading out to dinner soon. Don't want to spoil my appetite."

Dave sighs and closes the menu. "I'll pass too. I have to be careful with the bar snacks these days. Digestive issues. Hereditary. My father's had most of his colon removed.

So, how did a gorgeous woman like you end up single?"

"My husband left me," said Zoe. She is utterly disoriented in this conversation. Is there some way to leave immediately without hurting his feelings? She wishes she could close her eyes and teleport somewhere, anywhere, else.

"Cheater?" he asks. Zoe nods. "Sucks, doesn't it? My wife took off with her trainer at the gym."

"Was it a surprise?"

"Not exactly," says Dave. "She hadn't had sex with me in five years."

"Oh," says Zoe, willing him to stop speaking.

"She always had some reason, you know, for our problems in the bedroom—she was stressed about our tax problems, my sleep apnea machine kept her up at night, things like that—but in the end I had to accept that the spark was gone."

"I'm sorry," says Zoe. She is. She is nothing but sorry.

"That's okay," says Dave. "It all happens for a reason. We wouldn't be here together if our spouses hadn't cheated on us, right?"

"That's true," says Zoe. She loathes Richard for placing her here, in this bar, with Dave.

It can't continue. She looks at her phone. It's been twenty-five minutes, and she's pulling the rip cord. "How did it get so late? I apologize for running off, but I'm due at dinner." She signals for the bill, hands over her credit card.

"So soon? That's too bad. I get it, though. It's always a smart idea to keep a first date short, just in case."

"Exactly."

"When do you want to get together again?"

"Let me check my schedule."

"Can I walk you home?"

"No!" says Zoe. "I mean, thank you very much for the offer, but I'm not going home right now." They're now standing outside the bar, and she sees no alternative but to hail a cab.

"I'll text you!" says Dave, as she climbs into the car.

She closes the door and waves. "I'm not going far," she says to the driver, and directs him around the corner. "I'm sorry."

The driver shrugs. "It's your money," he says.

Zack is waiting as she walks in the door. "How did it go?"

"I'm not ready to talk about it." Zoe hangs her coat in the closet and walks towards the kitchen.

"Don't be discouraged. It was a useful experiment."

"Zack. I said I'm not ready to talk about it."

"Talk about what?" says Oscar.

"Surprise," says Will. "We're early. I'm sorry. Would you like to take a rain check? We haven't ordered the food yet."

"No, no," says Zoe, giving Oscar a hug and Will a kiss on the cheek. "I'm grumpy because I had a horrible first date. Ignore me. I'm glad you're here. I'm going to change my clothes and I'll be right back."

"You look fantastic," says Will. "Whoever he was, he was lucky."

"Not as lucky as he wanted to be," says Zoe. She closes

the door to her room and sits down on her bed to take off her shoes. Her door opens and Zack comes in.

"If we're going to live together, there need to be some ground rules," says Zoe. "I said I didn't want to talk about it."

Zack sits down next to her. "Or you could talk about it," he says.

Zoe bursts into tears. "How did I get here, Zack? This isn't the life I was supposed to have." He puts his arm around her shoulder and kisses the top of her head. She wipes her eyes.

"Do any of us have the life we think we're supposed to have?" Zack asks. "I certainly don't."

"Richard ruined my life."

"Richard is unworthy of that sentiment."

"But I wasted so much time, Zack."

"And there's so much of it left. You are going to have a beautiful life, I promise."

"But not with Dave."

"Obviously, not with Dave."

"I'm going to wait a few months before trying this again."

"Okay."

"Remind me!"

"I will. I'm going to go and order the food, okay?"

"Yeah." Her phone is lighting up with text messages. "I'll be there in a minute."

All of the messages are from Dave, at five-minute intervals:

Thanks for a great time!

Did you check your schedule?

I really want to see you again.

Did I misread things? I hope not.

Did I do something wrong?

What can she say? She and Dave are living in a world she barely recognizes. She herself has done almost everything wrong: so many of her decisions have been misguided that most of her adult life looks like a mistake. Why does no one online admit to loneliness, to misadventure, to regret? Failure is the one experience most of them share, all of these disappointed, broken people trying to crawl out of the wreckage—her people now, all of them part of an accidental community, a club nobody wanted to join in the first place. She feels a tenderness towards them all, even Dave, with his cheerful, oblivious incompatibility.

She texts, *This isn't the right fit for me. I'm sorry. I hope you find everything you are looking for.* And then she stuffs her phone under her pillow, so she can't see it any longer.

Maybe she should forget dating altogether. She could get a dog instead, an adorable little dog who could come to work with her, and go on vacations with her, and Zoe could become one of those middle-aged ladies in the park who wears nothing but fleece and leaves the house without showering and talks to strangers ad nauseam about her dog's ailments. Or perhaps not. Zoe shakes off the chilling image of herself in fleece, changes into skinny jeans, and puts her hair up in a ponytail.

She walks into the kitchen. "What are we eating?"

"Holy shit, Zoe," says Will. "You look exactly the same as you did in college. It's freaky."

"Swear jar," says Oscar.

"We don't have one of those here," says Zack. "You're old enough to know that your aunt and uncle have filthy mouths. What happens at Uncle Zack's house stays at Uncle Zack's house."

"This is not Uncle Zack's house," says Zoe. "But make yourself comfortable, all the same."

"We're having Thai food," says Zack. "I'm going to go and pick it up in fifteen minutes. Take a load off."

Zoe sits and feels the day begin to slide off her shoulders. "What's new with you, Oscar?"

"Mom's being weird," says Oscar.

"That's not entirely fair," says Will. "Having me in the picture is a huge change for your mom, and she's doing her best to adjust. Let's cut her some slack, okay?" Will turns to Zoe. "Oscar has expressed a desire to stay over at my house more often, and we're trying to negotiate a schedule that makes sense for everyone."

"I don't know why it's such a big deal," says Oscar. "It's not like she's alone. Eloise is there all the time now."

"Don't you like Eloise?" says Zoe. "I do, a lot. She's my divorce lawyer."

"I like Eloise," says Oscar. "She's funny. And she's nice to me and my mom." He pauses. "I want my mom to have someone in her life besides me. It's too intense when it's only the two of us."

"Do you worry about her?"

"Sometimes. I want her to be okay when I'm not around."

Zoe gives him a hug. "Your mom is totally okay, buddy. She's been upset lately, but she's going to be fine. She wouldn't want you to worry about her."

"Does it bother you that your mom is dating a woman?" Zoe is glad it's Zack who asks the question.

Oscar gives him a withering look. "No one my age cares about that stuff."

"Ouch," says Zack.

"Anyway, she's always said that I should feel comfortable dating either boys or girls, and that she's dated both." He blushes. "I like girls, though."

Zoe reminds herself to call Beata to check in. Zoe likes Beata, and Nina for that matter, although she feels that she doesn't have a lot in common with either of them; Beata's been preoccupied with Oscar since her twenties, and Nina's hard to read, on the rare occasions when she's home. Mariana, on the other hand, is the sister she never had. Up until now, Zoe never felt that she needed to cultivate multiple ties within Mariana's family, but she senses that family relationships are reshaping themselves in the wake of Zack's show and Oscar's revelation. She wants to be sure that she's on the right side of family history. She should organize a cousins' dinner before Nina goes back overseas.

"Time to get the food," says Zack. "Oscar, why don't you come with me?"

The door closes behind them, and Zoe turns to Will. "So, I take it there's been some drama," she says.

"Yeah," he says, heavily. "I'm trying to get my bearings."

"As we all are."

"I'm not diminishing the pain of online dating," says Will. "I've been there, repeatedly, and it sucks. But that's a game with rules I understand. This one? I have no idea what I'm doing."

"Parenting, you mean?"

"Parenting a teenager without any recognized parental rights, and with a mother who resents my involvement."

"Isn't Eloise helping smooth the waters?"

"She's trying, but she's in a tough spot. If Beata sees me as the enemy, Eloise can't take my side."

"I get that."

"So do I." Will sighs. "I'd love to bring the temperature down on this whole situation. I'm not used to emotional outbursts. I come from a long line of people who repress their feelings."

"That's how the Hennessey family rolls," says Zoe. "Lydia is only the most famous of our collection of large personalities."

"That's my point," says Will. "I'm not a Hennessey."

"But your son is, which makes you a Hennessey by proxy."

"I'm not sure how I feel about that," says Will.

"Just know that once you figure it out, you'll have licence to express it as loudly and inappropriately as you like."

Will laughs. "Thanks."

Zoe pats his hand. "That's what family's for," she says.

CHAPTER 11

Beata

B eata has been wearing her bathrobe all day. She put it on when she rolled out of bed this morning, and it's still on now that the sun has set. She feels better than she has in weeks.

"Bathrobe Day should be a national holiday," she says. She imagines people dropping their kids at daycare in bathrobes, sitting around in meetings in bathrobes, negotiating treaties in bathrobes. Living in peace and harmony, in bathrobes.

"Oh?" Eloise isn't listening. She reorders her Scrabble tiles.

"Are you stuck?" Beata is no Scrabble champion, but she tries to hold up her end and finish her turns in a timely way. It can be boring playing with Eloise, who spends endless minutes searching for the most advantageous and impressive combination of letters and points.

But she's in a bathrobe, so Eloise can take her time. They're at a spa-hotel for the weekend. It's their anniversary: two years since the night they met. Eloise is the sort of person who keeps track of things (like anniversary dates) and who keeps things on track. Lately, she's been keeping Beata on track. Or perhaps more accurately, she's been keeping Beata on the rails. Beata is aware that she isn't at her best. She hasn't been sleeping well.

"Not at all," says Eloise, continuing to shuffle the tiles.

Beata leans back on the sofa and looks into the fire, glass of wine in hand. There is nothing to worry about in the here and now, not even her Scrabble perform-ance. Her first word, *prayer*, was a respectable twenty-two points. She closes her eyes, savouring the quiet. By some miracle, they have the common room to themselves.

Two years. Oscar has changed so much in that time, from a skinny, sweet kid to a volcanic teenager. Many would say—her mother among them—that her atten-tion has been fixed too rigidly on Oscar, and that the nat-ural process of separation is unnecessarily traumatic as a result. But none of those people have been single parents. It is a terrifying responsibility to make all of the decisions, knowing full well that many of them will look misguided in hindsight. When she decided to create her blog, it was with her earlier self in mind as an audience. If she can alleviate even one other single parent's fear and loneliness, *Mindful Mothering* will have been worth the effort.

She's changed too, over the past two years. Eloise has no idea what a huge step Beata has already taken in mak-ing space for a romantic relationship. There were years that she barely remembers, when Oscar was young and she was in school and then building a career that could support them both, years where she hardly slept and rarely socialized. She would no more have considered dating in those days than she would have thought of robbing a bank; and actually, the extra money would have been more useful than the sex. In the intervening years, she dated casually, but never made the emotional investment in a sustained relationship until she met Eloise.

And now Will Shannon is a fourth person in their once-tidy universe of two. She wishes she could press pause and give herself time to find her feet. She accepts that change is the only constant, but surely it could happen at a slower pace?

She says, her eyes still closed, "You can throw them back and forfeit your turn."

"Don't be ridiculous," says Eloise, laying down the word *yearn*, with the *a* on a double-letter score. "Nine points," she says.

Beata expects Eloise to curse, but she seems strangely satisfied with her meagre score. Beata gives herself permission not to care, if Eloise doesn't. She puts down the tiles for *girl*, five points. Eloise counters with *nuptial*, for twenty-two points.

"Doesn't it have two *u*'s?" asks Beata.

"No," says Eloise.

"Are you sure?" Beata sounds it out.

"Do you know how many prenuptial agreements I draft every year?"

Beata refuses to argue about spelling. She places *jug*

on a double-word score. Eloise carefully places letters on either side of it to spell *conjugal*, scoring a pedestrian eighteen points, while eschewing at least three double-word score opportunities that Beata can see. Beata spells *loose*. Eloise slams down *vow* for nine points.

"Okay," says Beata. "I'm getting the sense that this isn't really about the game." ·

"Why would you say that?"

"Well, for one thing, you put an *l* on a triple-letter square. And you threw away a *v* and a *w* just now. Is there something you want to talk about?"

"I don't know, Beata. What do you think?"

"I think you seem upset," says Beata. This is true. Eloise has been out of sorts all day. Beata has been ignoring Eloise's brooding silence, grounding herself, working to remember that Eloise is responsible for her own emotional states. But ignoring the value of a Scrabble move? Eloise is more deeply troubled than Beata knew.

"Let's cast our minds back to last night," says Eloise.

Beata does. She dropped Oscar off at her parents' house and picked up Eloise at the office. The traffic wasn't as bad as she had expected and they arrived at the hotel in plenty of time for dinner, which was delicious. The restaurant catered to vegetarian guests, and Beata was pleased with the availability of vegan dishes. They returned to the room and unpacked. She had a bath and phoned her mother to check on Oscar. She and Eloise made love, and they went to sleep. All in all, it had been an exceptionally pleasant evening, from Beata's point of view.

"You don't remember, do you?" says Eloise.

"Remember what, Eloise? Could you tell me what's bothering you instead of sulking because I can't figure it out?"

Eloise glares. "I proposed to you," she says.

"What?"

"I asked you to marry me." Another couple in bathrobes, having just entered the common room, make horrified eye contact with Beata and with each other, then turn and practically run out the door.

"You did not!"

"I definitely did."

"Was I awake?"

"I'm having some doubts on that score."

"That's awful!"

"I'm sorry you feel that way."

"No, I mean, it's awful that you proposed, and I missed the whole thing!" Beata takes Eloise's hand. "I'm truly sorry that I hurt your feelings. Please forgive me."

"What if you had heard me?" Eloise is watchful. "What would you have said?"

Beata wishes she had a different answer, but she doesn't. "I don't know."

"You don't know? How am I supposed to take that?"

"I would hope you'd take it as the truth. I love you. But I don't understand why we're talking about marriage all of a sudden. We only just told people that we're seeing each other."

"It was your choice not to tell people about us, not mine. We've been together for two years, long enough to know how we feel."

"Let me catch up." Beata feels her heart racing. "I need a minute. And I think we should have this conversation in a more private place." Eloise seems oblivious to the fact that three more bathrobe-clad guests have advanced into and retreated from the room in the past few minutes. "Can we go back to our room?"

They head upstairs. "Why don't I order us some tea and cookies from room service?" Beata asks. Eloise has a weakness for cookies, and the baked goods are excellent here. Beata places the call to the front desk, and they sit on the bed, facing each other. Beata takes Eloise's hand. She can tell that Eloise is starting to soften.

"What about moving in together?" says Eloise. "That's a smaller step."

"Than getting married, sure," says Beata. "But it's still an enormous deal. And what about Oscar? Hasn't he got enough going on without us adding to it?"

"Beata," says Eloise, "Oscar is not the person resisting change here. Oscar went out and found his father on his own initiative."

Beata doesn't like the way this conversation is going. Why is Eloise being so combative today? And where is this desire to get married coming from? Eloise is the last person on earth Beata would have expected to harbour a secret longing for matrimony. "But why marriage?" she says.

Eloise crosses her arms over her chest. "Are you opposed to marriage in general, or are you opposed to marriage with me?"

Beata thinks about the people she loves most, who also happen to be some of the people she understands least. Her parents were madly in love once, passionate about social change and each other, her mother a Ph.D. student in political theory, her father a young dentist running a free clinic on donations and grants. They married, vowing to make their union a utopian partnership of equals. But then her mother became famous, and when it turned out that "revolutionary leader" was a job that was poorly and infrequently paid, her father left the free clinic for private practice. Resentment ensued, on both sides, and now their marriage drifts ever further from help on dark currents of disappointment. Beata suspects this is why she and her sisters have been slow to embrace the married state. And Mariana, the only one of them to try it, regrets the attempt, according to their last conversation.

"My family," says Beata, "is untalented at marriage."

"That sounds like a self-limiting belief," says Eloise. "In addition to which, it doesn't answer my question." Beata grits her teeth. It irritates her when Eloise co-opts ideas that she's learned from Beata and uses them against her in an argument.

There is a knock at the door. Eloise opens it and returns with a tray. There is a brief and silent ceasefire, in which they drink tea, and eat cookies, and regain their composure.

Beata says, "Leaving aside all of the political arguments I could make against marriage, I haven't seen much evidence that it strengthens relationships. I haven't thought specifically about marriage to you, because today is the first time I've ever considered it, and also the first time I ever considered marriage to any specific person. So please don't turn this into a referendum on whether or not I'm serious about you. It's not fair."

"What's not fair is to waste my time in a relationship that isn't moving forward," says Eloise.

"I don't understand how we got here," says Beata. "I thought we were having a nice, romantic weekend."

"I don't understand a lot of things lately."

"Such as?"

"I still don't understand why you lied to everyone about Oscar's father, for starters," says Eloise. "Why invent a whole story about a sperm bank? It doesn't make sense. You must have known that he would ask about his father someday."

"I told you, I wasn't looking that far ahead. I was young. I found out I was pregnant. I barely knew Will. I didn't tell anyone because I assumed that if I did, I would be under pressure to terminate the pregnancy— not only from Will, but from my friends and family. It was easier to invent a story that would deflect people's questions."

"And when we started dating, and you knew that Will was my friend? You didn't think you should come clean at that point?"

"What can I say, Eloise? I did what I thought was in Oscar's best interests at the time."

"Did you? I think you have a habit of conflating Oscar's best interests with your own."

"Now you're being mean."

"Oh?" Eloise brushes cookie crumbs from her robe. "That's not how I see it. I'm beginning to wonder how much energy you really put into figuring out what matters to other people."

Beata catches her breath. "That's a horrible thing to say."

"It's an honest thing. It's an authentic thing. You implied that Oscar would be shocked to learn that you were in a relationship with a woman, so I didn't push it. But it turns out the only problem he has with our relationship is that you didn't trust him enough to tell him about it. So now I wonder, were you honestly concerned about his reaction, or were you misleading me to buy time?"

"I had no way of knowing how Oscar would feel about it. I overreacted."

"And what about Will Shannon? You dropped him in this situation with no warning, and he's coping with incredible maturity and generosity. Don't you think it's time to admit that if you'd told him about Oscar at the outset, he would have helped, and all of you would have been better off? I've been trying to stay neutral, but you made a mistake, Beata, and you should own it."

"I never said I wanted you to be neutral."

Eloise stands up. "Good. Because I'm in the middle of your mess too, and I'm entitled to have opinions about it."

"No one's stopping you," says Beata, stiffly.

"I've been stopping me! I've been second-guessing myself, and walking on eggshells, and trying to be a good girlfriend. But I'm done now. I want a clear commitment from you, Beata, and soon. It's past time someone around here cared about *my* best interests."

APRIL

CHAPTER 12

Mariana

"Thanks for the lift," says Mariana, jumping into the passenger seat.

"Thanks for doing the gig," says Zoe. "Who knows? Maybe it'll be fun."

"As long as it's paid, I don't care."

"That I can promise," says Zoe. "What's happening with Harmony? Did you meet with her yesterday?"

"I did. She made me an offer."

"That's great!"

"It is."

"But?"

Mariana looks out the window. "Don't get me wrong. It's an excellent job, and I'm grateful to you. But it's the first time since I had a career that I've taken work for the sole purpose of paying the bills."

"A lot of people would call that lucky," says Zoe. "But I get it. I do. It's not forever, Mariana."

"Maybe it is." Mariana feels tears pricking the corners

of her eyes. "I'm a single woman with two young children. I can't rely on Dev to cover anything unexpected that may come up in the future. What if one of the kids has a health issue, or needs special education of some kind? It's all on me. Meaningful work is a luxury I can't afford any longer."

"Mariana." Zoe pulls into a parking spot and turns off the car. "What's this about? Did something else happen?"

Mariana wipes her eyes. "I got my buyout offer from the paper."

"Wasn't it what you were expecting?"

"It was. I can pay my lawyer and buy Devlin out of the house. It's exactly what I needed it to be."

"And?"

"And it feels like a second divorce. I loved journalism for a lot longer than I loved Devlin Kelley. I don't know who I am if I'm not a journalist."

Zoe squeezes her hand. "You're still a journalist. It will always be part of your identity. But you're entitled to a bigger self than one narrow job description, right?"

Mariana blows her nose. "I guess."

"You are. Mariana, I know you feel like last week's garbage. I've been there, and recently. Christmas was hell. It takes time to feel normal again, but you will. In the meantime, you may have to fake it until you make it."

Zoe's client, Chloe, is at the door when they arrive. "Can I borrow Zoe for a second?" she says. "Feel free to mingle."

"Do not mingle," says Zoe. "Chloe, we've talked about this. This is not a mixer, and no one is mingling. Wipe those words from your vocabulary. We are providing opportunities for fabulous individuals who happen to find themselves unattached—in this case, the opportunity to attend an upscale literary event with like-minded people. That's your brand. It's fun and cool and not at all desperate. Understood?" Chloe nods, eyes wide. "Now, what's the problem?"

Chloe huddles with Zoe while Mariana snags a glass of wine from a passing server. She has to pull herself together. If she is to preserve some vestige of her former status, it will be through public events like this one. She needs to hit it out of the park.

"Mariana," says Zoe. "There are a few logistical issues that I need to deal with. Can you prep the speaker for the Q&A while I do that?"

"Absolutely," says Mariana. She is determined to act as if she has her psychological house in order for the rest of the evening, and not only for Zoe's sake. "How much time do we have before we're on?"

"Half an hour. Just the broad strokes, okay? Leave a little mystery. I don't want it to feel too scripted."

"Zoe," says Mariana. "I know how to interview people. It may be my one natural skill. Go and do whatever it is you have to do."

"That's my girl," says Zoe. "Tim is the tall guy in the purple shirt over there. Silver hair, glasses." She points.

"Target located," says Mariana. "Moving in." In fact, she recognizes Tim Carver from the author photo on his book. "Tim?" she says, extending her hand. "I'm Mariana

Goldstein-Hennessey. I'm the one interviewing you tonight."

"It's great to meet you," says Tim. "Thanks so much for doing this. These presentations are way more engaging when I can bounce off someone else."

Mariana feels a blush rising at the idea of bouncing off Tim, who has a dimple and warm eyes with thick lashes, and who is undoubtedly married. God, she's sex-deprived. "A lot depends on chemistry," says Mariana.

"How's ours?"

"Workable," says Mariana.

"Did you read my book?"

"You're very direct."

"I'm a therapist," says Tim. "It's an occupational hazard."

"I read it and I liked it. Anything you want me to ask about specifically?"

"Not really," he says. "I was curious. You can ask whatever you want."

"Does that mean you like surprises?" asks Mariana.

"I do. Don't you?"

"No. I hate them."

"Interesting," says Tim.

"Interesting in a therapeutic sense or in a small-talk sense?"

Tim laughs. "So suspicious."

"All good journalists are suspicious."

"All good therapists are curious."

"We're both nosy, in other words," says Mariana.

"My secret is out. And since you're wondering, I have

read you for years and I'm a fan. Your city hall exposé was genius."

"I wasn't wondering about that."

"Really?"

"Okay, I was."

Tim grins. "I do have a question, though, from one nosy person to another."

"Fire away."

"What's it like having Lydia Hennessey for a mother?"

"Did you watch the TV show?"

"I did."

"I will never admit this publicly and will deny having said it if asked," says Mariana.

"Accurate, was it?"

"Scarily so."

"I had a feeling. Your cousin wrote it?"

"Zack, yes. He's been in the doghouse ever since."

"With you?"

"With my mother. And the other sister he included in the show. And possibly the sister he didn't include. And probably my dad, on my mother's behalf."

"I assumed your dad was out of the picture," says Tim.

"That was a dramatic device so that my mother's character could go on dates. They may not be happy, but my parents are definitely married."

Zoe strides over. "Are you guys ready?"

"This is my cousin Zoe," says Mariana. "Zoe, meet Tim."

"Zack's sister?" says Tim.

"Do you know Zack?" asks Zoe.

"Not at all," says Tim.

"Okay, then," says Zoe. "That was confusing. I'm going to introduce you, and when I do, come up on the stage and have a seat. There are microphones on the chairs. Don't forget to switch them on." She takes the stage, smiling widely. "Welcome, everyone. How many of you never expected to be single?"

Lots of hands go up. "Neither did I," says Zoe. "And it can be overwhelming. But that's where Perfect Pair Matchmaking comes in. It's a bespoke dating service that takes the stress out of single life. Your perfect pair is out there—maybe even in this room. But are you ready to meet that person? Tonight's event is about making sure that you are." The audience applauds. "We're fortunate to have two fantastic guests here tonight. Tim Carver is the bestselling author of *Second Time Lucky: Finding Love after Divorce* and a sought-after couples' therapist. Mariana Goldstein-Hennessey is an award-winning journalist and my favourite cousin. Let's give them a warm welcome."

Mariana takes the microphone as the applause dies down. "Thanks, Zoe. Tim, I want to start with a question that might seem provocative. You're incredibly positive about women's chances at finding love in their forties and beyond. That doesn't square with the anecdotal experiences of women I've spoken to. What accounts for that disparity?"

"Excellent," says Tim. "I love this question. You're hitting on one of the most self-destructive dating myths that I talk about in the book, namely the belief that love is increasingly difficult to find as you age."

"Since when is that a myth?"

"Since always. Statistically, both men and women at mid-life are wiser, more experienced, and more compassionate than their younger counterparts. And they have a clearer idea of what they want out of life generally and relationships more specifically."

"Come on, Tim. Isn't it true that the pool of available men shrinks as women age, because many men want to date younger women?"

A woman in the audience calls out, "You tell him, sister!"

Tim holds up his hands. "I don't deny that some men want to date younger women for a variety of reasons. But it's by no means true of all men, or even most men. Again, I think this is a pervasive myth that all the good men are taken and the ones that are left are shallow players. My research, and my observations in my own practice, don't support that view."

"The frustration is real, Tim." Tim's soothing tone is getting on Mariana's nerves. Is he patronizing her? "There are a lot of perimenopausal women out there watching their former husbands take up with yoga instructors." She pauses for a groundswell of cheering from the women in the audience. "What do you say to women who are discouraged?"

"I say that you'll never attract the relationship you want if you don't even believe it exists."

Mariana raises her eyebrows. "Are you a proponent

of manifestation, Tim? Are you saying that I can imagine my ideal relationship into being?" Out of the corner of her eye, she sees Zoe signalling to her to stop talking, but Mariana ignores her. She hasn't had a good fight since Devlin moved out.

"I'm saying that no one wants to go on a date with someone who's expecting him to fail."

"Exactly!" yells a man from the audience.

"Dating requires a mindset of openness and curiosity," says Tim. "You can't rule people out based on irrelevant criteria before you even get to know them."

Mariana sees where he's going with this, and she isn't surprised. "Women should lower their standards, then?"

"If their standards are that they'll only date CEOs who play professional sports, are over six feet tall, and spend their weekends curing cancer for fun, yes." The men in the room holler their support. "There is no one perfect match. Any given person has many potential successful matches, if she is willing to let go of status-based fantasies. And, let me finish, that pool of matches will look quite different as we move through life. We change, and the qualities we need in a partner will change also."

"I hear you saying that any relationship will evolve inevitably towards incompatibility and divorce," says Mariana.

"How could you possibly have heard that?" says Tim.

Zoe hops up on stage. "Okay, we've got a battle of the sexes up here! Thanks for keeping it real, you two. Now let's give our audience a chance to get in on the debate."

Zoe casts a warning glance over her shoulder at Mariana. "But first, let me ask a question. Tim, if you could offer one piece of advice to everyone here, what would it be?"

"A relationship at this stage should be an enhancement to an already rich, full life. Don't make the mistake of thinking that a relationship is a shortcut to the life you want. Build the life you want, and the relationship will be much easier to find."

"Great advice!" says Zoe. "Questions from the audience?" She points. "Go ahead."

A woman in a suit asks, "I have a public profile in my industry, and it makes me self-conscious about dating. I know that anyone I date can search up all kinds of information about me. How do you navigate that?"

"I get it," says Tim. "Old notions of privacy, and of parcelling out personal information over time, have really gone by the wayside. And, of course, there are safety implications as a result of that."

"Perfect Pair provides specific counselling on dating safety," says Zoe. "Talk to Chloe after the presentation."

"But, as you say," Tim continues, "the issues are more acute for those of us who have an online presence. As a first step, I want to encourage you to be open about the fact that you're single and looking for a partner. Often the discomfort we feel stems from embarrassment that we're single. We worry that we'll be judged." Tim takes a sip of water. "Imagine being a therapist and self-proclaimed dating expert. No pressure there, right?" The audience laughs. "If I'm so smart about relationships, why am I single? But if I'm going to get hung up on what other people might think, I'm going to stay single."

"Any more questions for Tim?" asks Zoe.

"Did you just say you're single?" asks Mariana.

CHAPTER 13

Zoe

Zoe has been here, in this tiny conference room, all day.
It is a kind of sensory deprivation cell, decorated in
shades of beige with innocuous landscape prints on each
wall. There is no view to the outside, no sense of time
passing. Richard is with his lawyer in another room down
the hall, and the mediator shuttles between them as they
move towards an agreement. Eloise is with her, mostly, but
sometimes she leaves to take a call, and Zoe is left staring
at the landscapes. One is an English country scene with a
windmill. One is a rustic hillside with a ruined castle and
cows. Neither is a place she wants to visit.

She begins to understand that the divorce process
is designed to wear everyone down, that only the most
intransigent, the most rage-fuelled, the most aggrieved
ex-spouses can sustain that heat in the face of such relentless boredom. After a full day of sitting here contemplat-
ing the wreckage of her life, she is ready to do almost
anything to not have to sit here again. The mediator has

assured her that Richard is coming around to an understanding of his own responsibility for self-sufficiency. This may be true, or it may be a ploy to engage her sympathy. She is beyond caring. Whatever she wanted before today is irrelevant. She wants only one thing, and that is for her marriage to be well and truly over.

She texts Will Shannon. *Are you in the office? I'm dying of boredom in conference room 26.*

Three dots appear immediately. *I'm out at a meeting. I should be back around 5. Will you still be there?*

I hope not!

Are you close to a deal?

I have no idea. Remind me to never get divorced again.

Absolutely. Easily preventable. I'll check in when I get back.

Eloise returns to the room. "The mediator is about to come back with their final offer for the day," she says. "He'll present it, and then we'll have some time to go over it and consider what we want to do, okay?"

Zoe nods, and Eloise invites the mediator in. He lays out Richard's offer. Zoe only half listens. She examines the cows in the landscape painting. There's something wrong with the perspective. The cows are too large in relation to the castle. "There's something weird about the cows," she says.

"The cows?" says the mediator.

"I think we need a short break," says Eloise. She escorts the mediator out into the hallway and returns a few minutes later. "I think we should pack it in for today, Zoe."

"No," says Zoe. "Let's finish this."

"You're tired, and that's completely understandable," says Eloise. "It's been a long day. We're close to a deal, but I'm not going to let you sign it unless I'm confident that you've thought it through."

Zoe stands and stretches. "I'm going to go for a walk for ten minutes," she says. "Can I do that?"

"Your ex-husband has a yoga mat in his room, so I can't see why not," says Eloise. "Take fifteen. Why don't I go and get some coffee that isn't revolting? What do you want?"

"A vanilla latte. Super hot, super sweet."

"That's the spirit," says Eloise. "See you soon."

Zoe walks out to the elevators and rides thirty floors down to street level. She steps out into a courtyard surrounded on all sides by skyscrapers, and she sits on a bench. It's damp and chilly, and she's the only one out here among the empty planters and dirty puddles. She pulls her sweater around her shoulders, shivering. When she feels alert again, she heads inside and up to the thirtieth floor, where she chugs her injection of fast-acting refined sugar.

"I'm ready," she says. "Take me through the deal."

Eloise does, point by point, and Zoe listens. "So the upshot here is that I sell the house, and give him all the proceeds plus a quarter of my retirement savings in a lump sum, and then I'm done with him forever?"

"Yes."

"And he has no claim on my business whatsoever?"

"None."

"And he can't come after me for anything else, even if he continues to be a feckless loser?"

"That's on him."

"And what do you think about the deal?"

"I think it's in the ballpark. I think to get closer to what you want will take a lot of time and money, and probably involve going to court, and it won't be worth it."

"So you'd sign it?"

"I'd sign it. But I'm not you, and this decision is yours. It comes down to whether or not you want to spend more money at this point for an uncertain result, which, even in the best-case scenario, won't be a whole lot better than the deal in front of you."

"When does the house have to be sold?"

"He wants to put it on the market as soon as possible. There's wiggle room if you want more time to get it ready for sale."

"No," says Zoe. "I want to wash my hands of the whole mess."

"You're ready to sign?"

"I'm ready," she says.

An hour later, she walks into the house that no longer feels like her home. There's been a death, and now there's work to be done, lots of it. Every closet, every drawer, every shelf, must now be emptied, sorted. Every item must be categorized, boxed, donated, or moved. And then there's the small matter of finding a new place to call home, and of serving Zack his eviction notice.

In their separation agreement, Richard has specified

five items of household furniture that he wishes to keep. He has invited Zoe to set them aside and notify him when they are ready to be collected. How efficient! How considerate!

She goes down to the basement and surveys the skis and bikes and camping equipment—all purchased in pursuit of a marriage improved on the foundation of shared interests, none of which were ever sincerely shared. She sees a baseball bat that belongs (belonged) to Richard, and considers using it to smash his five items to smithereens. *Smithereens*. It's a word that isn't used often enough. *In her forties, Zoe Hennessey's life was blown to smithereens.*

A mountain of stuff, she thinks. What a waste of money. She is disgusted with her past consumerism. In the future, she will buy only what she needs. She will relocate to a tiny home and embrace minimalism and restraint. In a surge of reforming zeal, she wraps her arms around two pairs of skis, hauls them to the staircase, and launches herself upward at a run, which morphs into a spinning jump as the curved end of one of the skis catches on the handrail. Zoe twists in the air, watching the skis fly over the banister and clatter across the basement floor as she falls backwards, tucking her head forward into her arms and connecting hard with her hip and shoulder.

"Ow!" she whimpers, as she slides down three stairs and lands. She uncurls her body and rests beside the skis. "Fuck you, universe," she says, giving the finger to her ceiling. It's stained, she realizes. She'll probably have to get it painted before she sells the house. It's all so unfair, she thinks, and bursts into tears.

Is this how her life is going to be now? One pathetic misadventure after another, until she becomes a sad old lady who never bounced back from her divorce? She's seen what's available out there on the dating scene, and it's grim. She's been on ten first dates this month, after a self-imposed post-Dave hiatus that lasted five days. From her preliminary data, it appears that of the men who are within five years of her age, moderately sane, and employed, there are none who a) have healthy relationships with the people closest to them, b) share at least some of her interests, and c) are comfortable with a woman who is professionally ambitious. She could, of course, lower her standards. Perhaps the universe is trying to teach her humility. Well played, she thinks, and wipes her eyes.

Her phone is ringing. She pulls it out of her pocket. The cover is smashed but it's functioning.

"Hello?"

"Hey, Zoe. It's Will. I heard you settled with Richard, and I wanted to check in. How are you?"

"I've fallen and I can't get up," she says.

He laughs.

"No, really," she says. She starts to giggle. "I can't move."

"What are you talking about?"

"I fell down the stairs."

"Are you hurt?"

"I'm not sure. I think maybe."

"I'm leaving the office right now, and I'll come right there. Will you be able to let me in?"

"No, but the back door is open. I'm in the basement."

She disconnects the phone and closes her eyes. Her mind drifts. She could have a good life as a terminally single person, she thinks. She has friends who can pick her up off the floor. That's all you need, really. And a dog. But not a cat. A cat will eat you if you fall down the stairs and die, but a dog will sit beside you until help comes. It's a well-known fact. She looks up and sees Will at the top of the stairs.

"Oh my god," he says. "Don't move."

"I'm on it," she says, as he comes down and kneels beside her.

"Wiggle your fingers." She does. "Now your toes." She does. "Do you think you can stand up? I'll help you." He lifts her to her feet. "Let's see you walk."

She takes a few tentative steps and lifts her arms above her head. She's moving like Frankenstein's monster, but there's no sharp pain. "Nothing's broken," she says, relieved.

"Did you get a medical degree when I wasn't looking? I'm taking you to the hospital for an X-ray."

"So that we can sit in uncomfortable chairs for hours to be told that I pulled a bunch of muscles in my upper back and bruised my ass?"

"Hmm," says Will. "That's a persuasive argument. Here's a compromise. We'll put a hot pack on your shoulder, I'll give you a massage, you'll take a hot bath, and we'll see if we can get you feeling better. If not, I'm taking you to the hospital. Deal?"

"Deal."

Zoe climbs the stairs without assistance, wincing when Will isn't looking. She lies down on the living room sofa, while Will heats a hot compress bag in the microwave.

"Here," he says, placing it on her shoulder. "How's that?"

"Hot," she says.

"That's a good thing. Does it hurt if I touch you here?" He puts a hand on either side of her spine.

"It feels tight."

"That's because it is." Will's hands are gentle. It's been so long since anyone has touched her. That it should be Will Shannon is a comfort; she knows she is safe with him. She feels the tension begin to ease.

He lifts the heating pad. "I'm going to try to work on your shoulder, but I'll only touch it lightly, okay? Try to relax."

Zoe tries. How many times in her life, she wonders, has she been asked to relax? Normally it feels passive-aggressive to her, a way of protecting the other person's comfort rather than her own, a way of suggesting that she's too intense, high-energy, demanding, and ambitious. So what? Why should she be otherwise? Why is "relaxed" considered desirable in all cases? She thinks of all of the men she's gone on dates with over the past month, most of whom she would have described as "relaxed." And did she want to sleep with any of them? She did not.

It doesn't bother her when Will asks, though. He doesn't have an agenda. He is trying not to hurt her. She relaxes. She lets go of any responsibility other than breathing in and out. She feels the pain recede. And then—how extraordinary!—she feels a flicker of desire. How surprising, she thinks, and how welcome: if her body can remember arousal now, covered in bruises, with her shoulder in knots, she can't be entirely dead inside. What a gift. She sighs with relief.

"Where did you learn how to do this?" she asks.

He laughs. "I'm a natural." His hands still briefly, lifting away from her neck, and then they land again, spreading like wings across her shoulder blades. "There," he says. "It's loosening up. Should we keep going?"

"You should. I'm going to keep lying here. Do you think I should get a dog?"

"Why?"

"Because cats will eat you if you die alone and dogs will wait until help arrives."

"What if help never comes?"

"I don't know. I mean, dogs are still animals, I guess."

"So it's more a question of how long it takes them to eat you." He adds some pressure. "You aren't going to die alone, Zoe. Don't be ridiculous."

"You don't know that."

"I have a fair idea."

"Why?"

"Because you're a delight, even lying on the floor in a heap."

"I am?"

"You absolutely are."

She wants to see his face. "I'm going to sit up."

"Ambitious," he says. "I'm here if you need help."

She pushes herself back onto her knees and slides her legs out from underneath, one by one. It's slow, and not especially graceful, but Will never moves from her side. "Success," she says. Their eyes meet and hold. God, he's beautiful.

"How do you feel?" he asks.

"Much better," she says. "Thanks to you."

He smiles. "No ambulance ride?"

"Sorry to disappoint."

"I've known you for over twenty years, Zoe," he says, smoothing a strand of her hair behind her ear, "and you've never once disappointed."

"That's an impressive record," she says, struggling to keep her voice light. The air is shifting between them, and something is coming into being that has never been there before. "I'd hate to risk it."

"Little fear of that," says Will. And then he leans in and kisses her, gently, and she kisses him back, less gently, and it's a long time before they come up for air.

When they do, she says, "How's my record holding?"

He laughs. "Holding strong," he says, and pulls her in for more.

CHAPTER 14

Beata

"The hands-on side of the clinic is growing," says Beata. "There's more demand for appointments in the evenings and on Sundays. We definitely have room to add a part-time person and keep them busy."

She's in the breakout room on the second floor of the Holistic Healing Partnership offices for her monthly partners' meeting. There are five of them: Clarice, a craniosacral therapist and acupuncturist; Jessica, a naturopath; Mike, a Gestalt psychotherapist; Sasha, a child psychologist specializing in play therapy; and Beata herself. Downstairs, where Beata works, they operate four treatment rooms and employ a full-time receptionist. In addition to Beata and Clarice, there are six healing arts specialists. Upstairs, there are four offices designed for individual counselling, along with the large breakout room for group therapy and training.

"Do you have someone in mind?" asks Mike.

"I do," says Clarice. "I know a fabulous woman who

does reflexology in addition to traditional massage. If you agree, I'd like to invite her in to meet everyone."

They agree. They usually do. It's one of things Beata loves most about her business partners. Each and every one of them is invested—personally and professionally—in harmony.

"What's the report from the second floor?" asks Beata.

"We have bad news and good news," says Sasha. "The bad news is that Marsha has decided to retire. It's not unexpected, but we'll miss her. She's given us three months' notice, though, so we have some time to find a new occupant."

"And the good news?"

"It's related," says Mike. "Ben Jackson called me last week asking about office space."

"I thought he was travelling the world and loving it," says Beata. Ben is a therapist whose TED Talks and bestselling books on nurturing intimacy in marriage have made him a sought-after lecturer. He's a friend, and he uses their building for his weekend couples' retreats when he's in town.

"His daughter is expecting in the summer. It's his first grandchild," says Mike. "He and his wife are planning to be here a lot more once the baby's born."

"That's amazing news," says Clarice. "Does everyone agree that Mike should reach out to Ben about Marsha's office space?"

They do. "Are there any other issues on the agenda?" asks Beata.

"Could we talk to the landlord about replacing the fridge in the kitchen?" asks Sasha.

"Absolutely," says Beata. "I'm seeing him later this week. It shouldn't be a problem." The Holistic Healing Partnership is located in the building that once housed Marvin's dental practice. Marvin stills owns it, as he has for thirty years, during which time it's increased exponentially in value. Five years ago, Marvin was ready to retire, but he wasn't ready to sell an asset that was continuing to appreciate in a booming real estate market. So when Beata and a group of her friends approached him about refurbishing the building and becoming an investor in their wellness clinic, as well as their landlord, he didn't need much persuading. It's been a happy arrangement for all concerned. "Is that everything for today? Then we're adjourned. Thanks, everyone."

The meeting's over, but the group lingers. The only downside of their business success is that they have less time to socialize with each other. "How's Oscar doing?" asks Sasha. Beata has asked for Sasha's advice about Oscar on countless occasions over the past few years, and she's always been generous with her time.

"Full of rage," says Beata. "Much the same, in other words."

"He'll come through it," says Sasha. "Hang in there. Just keep showing up and loving him. His anger will wear itself out eventually."

"This is fascinating," says Mike. "It's like you're living with your disowned part."

"My what?" says Beata.

"We all have parts of our personalities that make us uncomfortable, and that we disown or disavow," Mike explains. "You, for example, disown your anger, but here you are, living with a literal embodiment of it. I know it's miserable, but it's a huge growth opportunity for you."

"I don't disown my anger," says Beata. "I don't have any anger."

"Everyone has anger," says Mike. "It's a basic human emotion. You can deny your anger all you want, but it will find an outlet somewhere. You know that as well as I do, Beata."

Her mind wanders to Bethany, her alter ego on *After the Revolution*, dripping with crystals and self-help aphorisms, and prone to incongruous outbursts of hostility. Do other people see a side of her that she doesn't? Honestly, there are days when she could strangle Zack with her bare hands. "Maybe," she says. "Or maybe I don't give in to anger because I'm empathetic and grateful for my many blessings."

"That's a possibility, I guess," says Mike. He looks unconvinced.

She picks up some groceries on the way home, allowing for a few of Oscar's favourite non-organic items. "I'm home," she calls. Silence greets her. She goes up to Oscar's room and knocks on the door. "Are you in there? Come have some lunch, honey. I went to the store."

"I'm not hungry," he says, through the door.

"Come on, Oscar. You're growing. Your body needs the fuel. I'll make you something."

"I don't want anything right now."

Beata opens the door. Oscar is still in bed. "It's almost noon. You should get up. It's a gorgeous day outside." She opens the curtains.

"Jesus, Mom!" Oscar shields his eyes from the light.

"What do you have on today?"

"I'm hanging out with my dad later. Now could you please go away?"

"Oscar," she says, "we've talked about this. I support you spending time with your father, but I need to be involved in the decision-making about the schedule. You need to keep me informed."

"I'm telling you now."

"Do you have any specific plans together?"

"It's none of your business."

She's had enough of being treated like the enemy. "I am your mother. Everything about you is my business."

Oscar springs out of bed. "I told you to get out!" he shouts. "If it were up to you, I wouldn't have a dad at all."

Beata retreats into the hallway, and Oscar slams the door. She hears him moving around inside the room. "That is not true," she says, loudly. "I only want what is best for you."

The door opens. Oscar is dressed and carrying a backpack. "As if you have any idea what that is," he says. He brushes past her and heads downstairs.

"I'm talking to you, Oscar. Where are you going?" She follows and arrives in the foyer in time to see the front door close behind him.

How did she get here? she wonders. She's done everything she can think of to be a good parent. She's been patient, and loving, and attentive to her son's emotional well-being, right from the start.

It might have been otherwise. She was very young, only twenty, when she got pregnant. She'd been the baby in a busy family with a famous parent and had struggled to carve out her own identity. She was smart, but never academically driven like Mariana or Nina. After high school, she did a year at art college before deciding she lacked the talent for it, and then she headed west. She was dabbling in organic farming when she came home for a visit, dropped in at Zoe's party, and met Will Shannon.

Motherhood was the making of her. As soon as she discovered that she was pregnant, she knew she'd have the baby. It was a relief in a way, to be sure of something for once, even while her family and friends were wringing their hands. Oscar's arrival was her rebirth. And now Oscar hates her.

The phone rings and she answers it, glad of the distraction.

"Beata? It's Will Shannon."

"Is Oscar with you?"

"He is."

"That's good," she says. "He stormed out of here earlier."

"I know. I'm sorry. I'm sure his behaviour is distressing for you."

"It is," she says.

"I'm afraid this call won't help."

Beata sits down. "I'm listening," she says.

"Oscar has asked if he can stay with me for a while."

"How long is a while?"

"He's talking about staying for the rest of the school year. At this point, I think we should be talking about this in the short term, like the next week or so."

"I see." Beata does see. She sees everything she has done wrong from the first moment of Oscar's life—from before that, even. She sees herself going to Zoe's party. She sees herself talking to Will, enjoying his unabashed good looks and charm. She sees herself going home with him, no strings attached. She sees herself taking a pregnancy test, in the bathroom of the organic farm. She sees the test result, an invitation from the universe to grow in unexpected ways.

"Beata? Are you still there?"

"Yes." Her voice is thick.

"I'd like the three of us to talk about this. Could I bring Oscar over so that we can hash this out?"

"No. Not today. Maybe tomorrow." She's crying.

"I know this is very upsetting, and I'm sorry. Are you all right? Can I do anything for you?"

"No," says Beata, and she hangs up. She lies down on the floor, feeling its solidity under her. She scans her body, noting the twisting of her guts and the pounding of her heart. She breathes to remind herself that she is alive, even though this is the worst moment of her life. She fishes her phone out of her pocket and dials. "Eloise," she says, "something terrible has happened."

She feels rather than hears Eloise sigh. "What has Oscar done now?"

"He wants to move in with Will."

"Beata, try to see this as temporary. He's acting out. He's angry."

"You shouldn't have come over that day!"

"You're upset. But even still, I'm not going to wear this for you. Oscar is angry because he is a young man who just discovered that he has a perfectly nice father that he never knew about, and that the person he most trusts kept that information from him for his entire life."

"It was for his own good!"

"It was principally for your own good, and when you are ready to admit that, you'll be in a better position to understand why Oscar is so angry."

"What am I going to do?"

"You're going to love him and let him figure this stuff out. You say that's your parenting philosophy, right?"

"Yes." Beata blows her nose.

"Well, this is your chance to prove it."

Beata bursts into tears. "Why are you being so cold?"

"Beata, do you know what I do all day? I dismantle bad relationships. And what I see here is the potential for a great one. We love each other. We have fun together. We want the same things, long term. It's rare to find that, and we should invest in it. But all you want to do is focus on your son. I'm not even in the picture. So I have to ask myself what I'm doing. It doesn't make sense to keep trying so hard if it isn't what you want."

"It is what I want!"

Eloise's voice softens. "Then tell me how I can help."

"Will wants to come over with Oscar tomorrow and make a plan."

"Sounds sensible to me."

"Can you be here too?"

"Yes," says Eloise. "If that's what you want, I'll be there."

MAY

CHAPTER 15

Mariana

"Where's Daddy?" whines Iona. "I want pancakes."

"Pancakes!" shouts Siobhan, "pancakes, pancakes, pancakes, pancakes!" She bangs on the table, upending her bowl of cereal in a cascade of Cheerios and milk.

"Time out!" Mariana yells, hustling two sobbing, hungry children into their room and closing the door behind them. She, too, feels like sobbing. After three months of separation, she is beginning to understand that while she has become immune to Devlin's charm, his daughters have not. Without him in the house, they are demanding, angry, and downright unpleasant, and she lacks the capacity to coax them into good cheer.

It is enraging that Devlin has emerged as the preferred parent. At the end of his custodial weeks, the girls return home to her with cotton candy matted in their hair, expecting to stay up until midnight watching movies in her bed, wanting breakfast for dinner and candy for breakfast. Her week is spent re-establishing routines, enforcing screen time and bedtime, shovelling vegetables and fibre into them, and compensating for Devlin's shortcomings. They hate her for it.

And really, can she blame them? She isn't the fun one. Even if she were effervescent by nature, structural impediments preclude her from taking that role with them. Isn't this the complaint of mothers the world over? That they do all of the ugly, unsung work to hold a family together and are reviled as nags, while men show up for school concerts twice a year and are worshipped as exemplars of modern fatherhood? She's been writing about these issues for years, forewarned and forearmed, but still, inevitably, defeated.

Her self-esteem is at a historical low. Divorce at her age is a parade of indignity and sleep-stealing, energy-sapping worry: body dysmorphia, financial fear, sexual insecurity, reluctance to trust, and anxiety about her children's futures—in particular, what they'll say about her in therapy (which should, in her opinion, be a recognized phobia). There are, she will admit, moments of unexpected connection. Zoe, a few months ahead of Mariana in the cycle of recovery, has been a tireless cheerleader, available for emergency pep talks whenever Mariana becomes convinced that she's going to be living under a bridge. Like now, for instance.

She dials. Zack answers. "Why are you answering Zoe's phone?" she says.

"She's in the shower and I saw that it was you. Everything okay?"

"No," says Mariana.

"What's going on?"

"I'm the mean parent, and I hate it."

"Then be the fun one."

"It's not that easy."

"It really is," says Zack.

"Someone has to be the mean one! Do you want the girls to die of scurvy? Do you want their teeth to rot out of their heads? Do you want them to be entitled assholes like their father?"

"Assuming that's a rhetorical question, I think you should focus on the here and now."

"You aren't as good at pep talks as Zoe is."

"Are you having a good experience of parenting right now?"

"No."

"Are your kids having a good experience of your parenting?"

"No."

"That sounds like a more pressing problem than scurvy. That's all I'm saying." Mariana hears Zoe's voice in the background. "It's Mariana," says Zack. "She's having a bad day."

Zoe comes on the line. "How can I help?"

"Do you want to go out for pancakes?" Mariana realizes that she sounds completely pathetic. "You know what? Never mind. Carry on with your day."

"Sure," says Zoe. "We love pancakes." Mariana hears Zack in the background. "Yes, you do, Zack."

"He doesn't have to come," says Mariana.

"Oh, but he does. He's making amends. We'll get a reservation and text you with it in the next fifteen minutes. Hang in there."

By the time Zoe's text arrives, the desire to leave the house has passed and Mariana regrets her cry for help. Kicking herself, she washes the girls' faces and blows their noses, gets them dressed, loads them into the car, and drives across town. By the time they arrive, she's exhausted.

Zoe and Zack are already seated. "How did you get a table for five on a weekend?" asks Mariana. "How do you even know about this place?" It's usually packed here. The coffee is hot, the food isn't horrible by moderately discerning adult standards, and most importantly, there's a ball pit in the basement—an unbeatable combination for a rainy Saturday with kids.

"Magic," says Zack. "And connections." He addresses himself to the girls. "So what's it going to be, ladies? Chocolate chip pancakes with whipped cream? And some hot chocolate to go with it?"

"Yes!" they shout.

"Girls," says Mariana. "Don't go crazy."

"Mariana," Zoe says. "It's okay. Take some pressure off yourself. You don't have to be perfect today."

They place their orders, and Zack stands up. "Come on, girls. Let's hit the ball pit." The girls leap up. "Text me when the food gets here," he says to Zoe.

"He doesn't have to do that," says Mariana, watching them go. "It's not like I was ever mad at him. Not like my mother and Beata, anyway."

"You may as well have the benefit of his atonement," says Zoe. "By the way, did you get my email about dates for a cousins' dinner?"

"I did," says Mariana. "They're all custodial dates for me. Can you send another batch?"

"At this rate, it'll be summer before we manage it," says Zoe.

The coffee arrives. "Oh, thank god," says Mariana.

Zoe laughs and takes a slug of coffee. "Let's use our time wisely. What's going on with you?"

"Aren't you angry?" Mariana asks.

"At you? No. I told you I wasn't. You wouldn't believe the feedback we got from that Perfect Pair event. The battle of the sexes was a huge hit. Just give me a heads-up next time you want to start a fight at one of my events, okay?"

"That's not what I mean. I want to know why you aren't walking around in a cloud of divorce-fuelled rage. Your husband cheated on you. I don't see you snapping at people for no reason or provoking strangers into arguments. What's wrong with me? I feel like a crazy person."

"Who says I'm not?"

"You don't look it."

Zoe sighs. "You know what I do when I get mad? Like incredibly livid?"

"I don't know. Punch pillows?"

"I cry. I burst into tears and turn into a blob of self-pity. I actually think your way of dealing with it is healthier."

"Your way is more attractive, though."

"Attractive to whom?"

"I don't know. People would rather be around someone sad than someone angry. I feel contagious."

"Who are these people you keep talking about?"

Mariana thinks. "The women in the schoolyard. The neighbourhood moms. I have this sense that they're avoiding me."

"Do you like them? Are they your friends?"

"That's not the point. The point is that I feel like everyone I know is choosing Devlin and it isn't fair."

"Injustice is good. Be angry about injustice. But maybe try to take it up a level from playground politics."

"Any suggestions? Because I am seriously one bad day away from blowing it all up."

"Saved by the food!" says Zoe, as the server arrives, laden with plates. "Let me text Zack."

The girls reappear, and they all eat their way through mountains of pancakes. Mariana has to admit that life is less daunting with a full stomach. The brief window of well-being closes, though, as the girls renew their whining: "Mommy, we want to go back to the ball pit."

"I'm out," says Zack. He kisses Mariana on the cheek. "I have to run a few errands."

"You've done more than your duty," says Mariana.

"I'll stay, if you want the company," says Zoe.

"Please," says Mariana.

The ball pit is surrounded by benches for parents, and Mariana and Zoe take seats as the girls dive in. "Oh, fuck," says Mariana under her breath.

"What?"

"Hide me."

"How am I going to do that?"

"Never mind," says Mariana, planting a bright smile on her face and waving. "It's Alison and Paisley. They were friends before the split. I saw them at the school the other day and they pretended they didn't see me."

"Bitches," hisses Zoe. "Why are we smiling?"

"Because we don't want them to know that we know that they chose Devlin," Mariana hisses back. "Hi, Alison! Hi, Paisley! How are you?"

Alison and Paisley exchange a charged glance, stand, and come to sit next to Mariana. "Mariana!" says Paisley. "What a surprise! I usually run into Devlin here!"

"We can't let him have all the fun," says Mariana. "This is my cousin, Zoe." They all shake hands.

Alison leans in. "I was so sorry to hear about your split. Devlin was telling us all about it at Katie's birthday party last week. He says you've been having a really rough time and not getting out much. It's great to see you spending time with family. Family is so important." Alison puts her hand on Mariana's arm. Mariana resists the urge to shake it off.

"Well," says Mariana. "I'm sure it's hard for him also.

It's a big transition. But, you know, it was my decision. So."

"Devlin said it was mutual," says Paisley. "But of course there are two sides. I think you're being very brave."

Mariana sees what Devlin has been doing. He's been on a charm offensive to recruit the entire neighbourhood onto his team, leaving her socially isolated, and, more humiliatingly, branded as a depressive, jilted loner.

"And it must be fantastic to have Devlin so involved in the kids' lives," says Alison. "I mean, if I got divorced, Ed wouldn't have the faintest idea what to do with my boys. He literally wouldn't know where to start. But Devlin is at pickup every day. He even offered to volunteer for the Family Fun Fair committee!"

"He doesn't have a regular job, so that makes him more available for stuff like that," says Mariana.

"Why don't you check on the girls?" says Zoe.

"I can see them from here. They're fine."

"Are you still a member at the Fitness Room?" asks Alison. "I haven't seen you there in ages. Dev's there all the time."

"I'm still a member. It's hard to find time these days." It's hard to find a time when she can be sure she won't run into Devlin flexing his muscles. His flexible employment schedule makes him predictably unpredictable, and irritatingly fit. Whereas she grows wider with every passing month. She really needs to do something about exercising. She adds it to her mental list, along with "get a hobby," "meditate," "be more social," and "volunteer."

"Why don't you come out for drinks after parent night next week?" asks Paisley. "You should! You can catch up with everyone." Alison jabs Paisley in the ribs. "Ouch."

"Is something wrong?" asks Mariana.

"Not at all," says Alison. "We'd love for you to come. But I asked Dev earlier this week, and he's coming, so you might not want to."

"No," says Mariana. "I might not."

"And also"—Alison lowers her voice—"Devlin told me that he might bring someone with him."

Paisley blanches. "I didn't know that! I mean, I knew he was dating, but I didn't know he was bringing her next week. God, I'm so insensitive! I'm sorry, Mariana. Can you forgive me?"

"Sure," says Mariana. "I doubt that you could help yourself."

"Mariana," says Zoe, "I think Iona needs you."

"She's fine," says Mariana.

"You knew that he was dating, right?" says Paisley. "I will feel so horrible if you didn't know before now!"

"Far be it from me to deprive you of the opportunity to feel horrible," says Mariana.

"Sorry?" says Paisley.

"Mariana!"

"Zoe, for god's sake. I've got this," says Mariana, as a voice comes over the loudspeaker.

"Attention parents, the ball pit has been soiled. I repeat, the ball pit has been soiled. Children are required to evacuate the ball pit. Please collect your child immediately."

Mariana's head swivels to her children, who are sobbing in the ball pit, covered in vomit.

"I tried to tell you," says Zoe.

"I want Daddy!" howls Iona.

"Oh, those poor, sweet girls," says Alison. "Divorce is so hard on the children."

CHAPTER 16

Zoe

I'll have a double espresso," says Zoe. "Extra hot, please."
She doesn't usually drink coffee this late in the afternoon, but it's been a long day and she has a date tonight.
She smiles. It's early in the game, but she's feeling more
optimistic than she has in a very long time.

"For here or to go?" asks the barista. It's the one she
used to lust after, before he mistook her for a stepmom.
She hasn't interacted with him since. For several months
after the Christmas debacle, Zoe avoided MainLine altogether, and when that became untenable, she positioned
herself in the queue so that she could order from the girl
with green hair instead. Today, seeing no flash of recognition whatsoever on the barista's face, she realizes that she's
stopped caring. And what if she *were* a stepmom? It's a live
possibility, and not a horrifying one, now that she's dating
someone fantastic who has a kid.

She goes home with her coffee, rotating her shoulder as she walks. It's still stiff from the fall a few weeks

ago, but making progress, thanks to regular massages from Will's magic hands. She's looking forward to another session with those hands tonight. Will is every bit as good in bed as she guessed he might be, and then some. Playful, intense, athletic, even surprisingly tender. Who knew that romance could sit so effortlessly on the foundations of a two-decades-long friendship? They're keeping things under wraps for now, until they figure out where the relationship is headed. They're being responsible, adult. At least outwardly. Underneath, she's as giddy and distracted as a teenager with a first crush. She wants to pass notes in class with cartoon hearts, and stay out past curfew, and wait for him at his locker to steal a kiss. It's absurd and completely intoxicating.

She opens the door to the house. "Hey," says Zack. "You're still going out tonight, right?"

"I am," she says. "If all goes well, it might even be a sleepover."

"Look at you," says Zack. "Back in the saddle. Who's the mystery man?"

"I don't want to jinx it," she says. "He has the potential to be a keeper, and I need all the luck I can get."

"I don't think luck has much to do with it," says Zack.

"You might, if you'd been married to Richard."

"Richard was a jackass from day one," says Zack. "That was poor judgment, or love blindness, or the inexperience of youth, but it wasn't bad luck. And he got worse over time because you babied him."

"He was moody," says Zoe. "I'll give you that." She can

admit, at least to herself, that she devoted considerable emotional energy during their marriage to circumventing Richard's snits and sulks.

"Is that why you guys never had kids? Because Richard needed too much attention?"

"You know what?" says Zoe. "There's such a thing as too much honesty." But Zack's not wrong. It took her far too long to figure out that Richard changed the subject whenever she talked about their future children, and over time, she mentioned them less frequently, as her eggs got older and he became more dyspeptic. It makes her sad to think about all the ways she sold herself out in order to keep the peace. "I'm going to have a shower," she says.

In the bathroom, she examines her body. She looks younger than her age, she knows. She's taken care of herself. Her belly is still flat and toned, where other women her age have become marsupial. She's strong. She could have a child in her forties, if she wanted to. But does she? She'd never choose single motherhood, after watching Beata struggle through it. And her romantic life, however promising, is embryonic.

No, she thinks, as she dries her hair. This isn't the time for maternal considerations. And what if that time never comes for her? Would it be a tragedy? She could be like the fierce maiden aunts of her grandmother's generation, the ones who were left without marriage prospects after all the young men were killed overseas, the ones who made themselves indispensable to fatherless families after the war: the Ednas, Ethels, and Ediths, the Marjories, and

Mildreds, and Mavises. Those women didn't wallow in self-pity. They took their lumps. They got on with the business of living.

She gets dressed and calls out to Zack that she's leaving.

He comes to the door to see her off. "Have fun," he says. "Let me know if you're staying out."

"I will," she says. It's a warm evening, and she walks the few blocks to her favourite local restaurant. Will is already seated with an open bottle of wine on the table. He stands and kisses her cheek, formally.

"Everything okay?" she asks.

"Absolutely," he says. He doesn't make eye contact. "Can I pour you a glass of wine?"

"Please. Long day?"

"Not especially." He lifts his wine glass and taps it against hers. "It's good to see you. You look lovely."

"Thank you. How was your weekend?" Will and Oscar had been planning, with Beata's blessing, to spend the day together on Saturday.

"It was eventful."

"Did you see Oscar?"

Will nods.

"How's he doing?"

"He's going through some stuff. He isn't getting along with his mother right now. He's decided that he wants to move in with me for a while."

"That's big news." Zoe puts her wine glass down. "How's Beata taking it?"

"Not well. She's upset. Very upset. It seems that she

and Oscar had a fight about the time he's been spending with me, and it escalated."

"Poor Beata. What does Eloise say?"

"She's a pragmatist. She's encouraging Beata to do family therapy with Oscar to try to cool things down. But Eloise and I both expect that he'll be at my place a lot more often from now on."

Zoe reaches across the table and squeezes Will's hand. "Quite the plot twist."

Will pulls his hand away. "You could say. Four months ago, I didn't know he existed, and now I'm a custodial parent, for all intents and purposes. I have to say, I did not see this coming."

"You can handle it," she says, encouragingly.

"Maybe," he says. "I hope so. Did you ever meet my parents?"

"I don't think so," says Zoe.

"They were not great role models for parenting. They were absent a lot, and when they were around, they loathed each other. I was mostly raised by nannies, and my great-aunt. This is a massive learning curve for me."

"Will?" His eyes meet hers. "What are you trying to tell me?"

Will's expression is pained. "Oscar is furious with his mother, mostly because she lied about me, but also because she lied about Eloise. I just arrived in his life and I need to build trust with him. He's volatile. What if he reacts negatively to my relationship with you? I can't run the risk that he'll feel displaced or deceived."

"We could test it out with him, see how he feels."

"He hasn't even called me Dad yet. What if he pushes me away? I love this kid, Zoe. I don't want to be a phase that he outgrows."

"Where does that leave us?"

Will's expression is resigned. "I like you hugely, but we're barely out of the gate as a couple. It could go south. Statistically, based on my averages, it's likely. And you're an important adult in Oscar's life. I can't afford for you to become another girlfriend I've let down and pissed off."

"Do I get a say in this?" Tears prickle in her throat.

"Please try to understand." He takes her hand. "I've never been a parent before, and it's way harder than I thought it would be. And there's not a lot of time left before he's grown up, so I don't have the luxury of making stupid mistakes and hoping he'll forgive me for them. I have to put what he needs ahead of what I want."

"It's not me, it's you?"

"I understand if you're angry. I deserve that."

"This sucks," says Zoe. She wipes her eyes with a napkin.

"Yes," says Will. "It sucks."

"I need some time to process this," she says. "I should go."

"What can I do to make this okay between us, Zoe? I really want to have you in my life, and in Oscar's life."

Zoe gathers herself and meets Will's eyes. "I understand the reasons for your decision," she says. "I don't necessarily agree with them, but I respect that you're trying to do your best for your son. I'm Oscar's family. I'm not going anywhere."

"Thank you," he says. "Can I walk you home?"

"I'd prefer not," says Zoe.

At home, she shuts the front door behind her and leans against it.

"Zoe, is that you?" Zack sounds panicky.

"Yes."

"I wasn't expecting you until later." Zack's head appears in the doorway to the living room. "Please don't kill me."

"What have you done?" Zoe hears jingling in the next room. "What's that noise?"

"It's temporary."

"What's temporary?"

"The dog."

"The *dog*?" Zoe steps around Zack and goes into the living room, where there is, indeed, a dog. It's small, though not delicate. Its chest puffs out in a defensive stance, and its eyes are watchful. "Explain."

"A set designer I used to work with heard about this gang of Chihuahuas that were scooped up by animal protection services in Texas. Terry got involved in the campaign to bring them here, and he signed up to adopt one himself. The whole process took a couple of months, and then last week, the dog finally arrived and, bam, his kid got watery eyes, a runny nose, hives, the whole works. Yesterday, his wife told him the dog has to go, but he doesn't want to put it back in a shelter after all it's been through."

"Admirable sentiment. Why is it here?"

"He needs to find a permanent home for the dog, but that might take some time. So I said I could provide emergency housing."

"You remember that this is *my* house, right?"

"You're moving. The house is sold. You're getting rid of most of the furniture. Can we agree that it's not a disaster if the dog makes a mess? I mean, look at her. How big a mess could she make?"

"It's female?"

Zack nods.

"Does she have a name?" Zoe holds out her hand and takes a step towards the dog. The dog's ears twitch and she cocks her head to the side, but otherwise, she doesn't move. She watches Zoe as if there is nothing a human could do to surprise or disappoint her. She has no expectations either way. She can take care of herself.

"Terry's kid called it Muffin."

"Her name is not Muffin." Zoe addresses the dog. "No wonder you gave that kid allergies." The dog barks.

"Last month you said something about quitting dating and getting a dog. This is like a trial run."

"Hush," says Zoe. "I'm talking to the dog." She moves to the far end of the sofa, sits, and pats the seat. The dog jumps up, maintaining a distance between them. Zoe holds out her hand. The dog cranes its neck and sniffs the gap between them. Zoe wiggles her fingers, and the dog stretches out to tap its wet nose against them. Zoe reaches behind the dog's ear, finds the sweet spot, and scratches. "Who's going to help look after you?"

"I can help," says Zack.

"If you're going to help, you'll have to live with us when we move."

"Are you serious?"

"I'm serious. A dog is a big responsibility."

"You want me to keep living with you?"

"If that's what you want."

Zack tackles Zoe in a hug, and the dog leaps to the far end of the sofa.

"You're scaring the dog."

"Sorry." Zack beams. "This is amazing."

"Shh."

The dog inches back across the sofa until she is an easy patting distance from Zoe. She rests her head on her paws, a homely miniature sphinx. Zoe reaches out and kneads her fur. The dog curves its muzzle around to lick Zoe's hand and then flips over so that Zoe can rub her belly.

"What are we going to call her?"

"I don't know about you," says Zoe, "but *I* am going to call her Mavis."

CHAPTER 17

Mariana

Mariana arrives for her first day at FairMarket Beauty, open to the possibility of not hating it. It took weeks to agree on terms with her old employer and with her new one, and most of her initial excitement has dissipated. At this point, she doesn't expect to like it, but she's confident that she can more than tolerate it, and that's enough. She's armed herself with a mantra: *Remember how much they are paying you.* It's an amount worth a fair bit of nonsense, in her estimation.

She's flattered to be met by Harmony Delacroix herself, who is not wearing shoes. "Mariana!" says Harmony. "I can't tell you how delighted I am that we were able to make this work!"

"I feel the same way," says Mariana.

"Please come in," says Harmony. "I've assembled the Mother Board in our main ideation room."

"I'm sorry?"

"The Mother Board is what we decided to call our

executive team. FairMarket is run by women, and our main customers are women, so we want the language we use to reflect women's distinct values and approaches. Also"—Harmony winks—"we think it's cute."

"It's totally cute," says Mariana. Almost unbearably so, in her view.

"Here we are," says Harmony, opening a door.

Mariana looks around the room, taking in the executive team/Mother Board, which consists of five women in athletic wear who are all sitting or lying on yoga mats.

"I feel overdressed," says Mariana.

Harmony laughs. "We don't always dress like this. But most of us keep a change of clothes here. I like to incorporate movement into our discussions around new concepts or opportunities for growth. And we have an in-house yoga instructor at lunch twice a week."

"How refreshing," says Mariana.

"Thank you for saying so," says Harmony, folding her hands in prayer position and inclining her head. "Also, many of us prefer not to wear shoes in the office, so that we can be more attuned to the energy of the earth. You should do as you wish, but know that we have radiant heat in the floors so that our feet don't get cold."

"Thanks," says Mariana.

"You've arrived at a perfect time," says one of the women. "We're starting the summer cleanse tomorrow if you want to get in on it."

"We encourage everyone at FairMarket to practise radical self-care," says Harmony. "We support all kinds of strategies—you'll find a napping room here, as well as a juice bar and a meditation sanctuary. We do company-wide cleanse challenges every season as well. What's the theme this time, Daria?"

"Ayurvedic," says Daria. "There's a three-day option, a seven-day option, or a twenty-one-day option. We don't recommend that last one if you're pregnant, by the way."

"I'm not," says Mariana. "But I think I'll pass on the cleanse this time around. Maybe in the fall?"

"You have to do what's right for you," says Daria. "I'm the director of community relations, by the way. It's wonderful to have you here."

"I know some of you have busy mornings," says Harmony, "so let's form a circle and get right to it."

Mariana pushes a yoga ball into the circle formation, and sits. She is embarrassed for herself, and not because she's wearing a business suit. She unbuttons her jacket.

"Mariana, what we want to do as a group is get a read on who you are, so that we can learn how best to integrate you into our community," says Harmony.

"I appreciate that. Would you like me to tell you a few things about myself?"

"Not in words," says Harmony. "We're going to close our eyes and try to read your energy signature for fifteen minutes or so. You can close your eyes as well, or keep them open, but try to keep your breath even and smooth." She meets Mariana's eyes. "I know you've been in work environments up until now that were all about the head. Our company emphasizes the knowledge of the body as well as the mind. It's very powerful. You'll see. Ready?"

Harmony and the other women close their eyes and begin breathing rhythmically. Mariana's mortification is complete. She needs to dissociate from this experience, immediately. She closes her eyes, so that she can no longer see her new colleagues attempting to read her aura, and wills herself to think of something, anything, else.

She's glad that the twins have gone to Devlin's as of this morning. Now that they are all in family therapy, and Devlin has committed to maintaining some consistent routines, the transitions are easier, and she hates him less. Her therapist has been trying to persuade her that hating Devlin is a crutch that prevents Mariana from addressing her underlying sadness at the end of her marriage. Mariana isn't sure about the underlying sadness, but she's prepared to agree that decreasing rage levels are desirable. Rage is exhausting.

She wonders if it's too soon to start dating. She's starting to feel acutely deprived of sex. It's not that she and Devlin were all that active after the twins arrived, but a quick no-muss no-fuss screw was generally available when she wanted it. Now she's not sure how to go about obtaining what she wants. She's taken stock of her assets. She's definitely attractive enough in low light to take someone home from a bar, but she doesn't go to bars except when she's boozing with fellow journalists. And fundamentally, she's a practical, safety-first sort of person. She might not need a lot of frills, but anonymity isn't her style. "You can exhale," her (female, divorced) doctor had said at her last appointment, when the test results came back clean in the wake of Devlin's extracurricular antics. "But you need to be careful out there. You'd be shocked at how many STIs I'm treating these days. Modern dating is all commitment issues and gonorrhea."

"Hmm," says Harmony. "I just picked up a shift in your field."

"I can't imagine why," says Mariana, and she forces herself to think about meadows of lavender and eucalyptus groves for the next few minutes.

"Interesting!" says Harmony. "I'm sure I speak for all of us when I say how delighted we are to be working with a writer of your calibre." She stands. "Why don't we go to my office and we can talk for a few minutes about how I want to use your talents here."

Mariana shimmies off the yoga ball and waves to the other women as she follows Harmony out of the room.

"As you'll see, we don't use a traditional office model," says Harmony, as she strides through an open space that looks more like an open-concept living room/dining room. "Most of our contributors work out here or in the garden or kitchen spaces, so that they can cross-pollinate more easily. And we have the ideation rooms when we need to meet at a particular time for a particular purpose. But there are a few dedicated work spaces. I have one of them." She opens a door and waves Mariana into a spectacular room with a large desk and a floor-to-ceiling window overlooking a garden. "Please have a seat."

"Thank you." Mariana sniffs. "Is something burning?"

"Oh, that's palo santo."

"Sorry?"

Harmony reaches under her desk and pulls out a dish with a smoking wood fragment. "It's a mystical tree from South America. The wood has incredible healing properties. It prevents autoimmune disorders, depression, anxiety, even the common cold."

"You don't say." What has she done? This is so much worse than she dreamed it could be.

Harmony leans forward. "Mariana, it's a gift to have such an effective communicator on board. And you already understand our mission so clearly! When I read the profile you wrote, I knew we had to recruit you. It's such a relief to give an interview and feel understood at the end of it. You'd be amazed at how often I give an interview and then find myself completely misrepresented. It's infuriating."

"I hear that a lot."

Harmony sighs. "What can we do? You need a media profile to get your message out. But so many journalists take refuge in cynicism. They'd rather tear someone down than take a risk of their own. It's sad." She opens a mini-fridge beside her desk. "Would you like some kombucha?"

"I'm fine."

Harmony pours a glass of tea. "Anyway, enough about that. Let's talk about what you're doing here. As you know, our pure essence beauty line is revolutionizing the industry." Mariana keeps her expression neutral, and nods. "Lately, we've been moving into the broader wellness space with a new website that has extensive content relating to self-care, exercise, and relationships."

Mariana nods again. "I saw that, yes."

"So the next frontier for us, as I see it, is to create, or more often curate, products that support our wellness agenda."

"You want to monetize the content?"

"I want to offer products, and maybe even services, that support our customers in achieving their wellness objectives." Harmony looks past Mariana. "Perfect timing! Here's Daria. Come in."

Daria takes a seat next to Mariana. She's changed out of her yoga clothes into skinny jeans, a kimono, and prayer beads. "Okay, so let's talk like sisters here," says Daria. "We decided to test the market on our wellness initiatives with a couple of events earlier this year. We were very careful about the invitation list, but even still, there was a breach."

"What kind of breach?"

"A group of activists," says Harmony. "They call themselves Doctors Against Quackery." Mariana smothers a giggle. "They're on a mission to debunk all of the spiritual aspects of wellness. They are at war with what they call 'pseudoscience.'"

"They're very aggressive," says Daria. "They sued one of our competitors for misleading advertising. It was a complete overreaction."

"In any event," says Harmony, "as we develop our products for market, we need to be mindful of these skeptics."

"Haters," says Daria.

Harmony inclines her head. "Enlightenment is an individual journey. It's important to remember that we don't all get there at the same time. I can tell from Mariana's energy field, for example, that she can be skeptical." She waves away Mariana's protest. "It's an asset. You'll help us anticipate criticisms and neutralize them. Some healthy skepticism in-house will keep us from getting ahead of our audience."

"Quite so," says Mariana. "It would be helpful to me to have some specific direction from you about how you'd like me to spend my time over the next few weeks."

"To start with, I'd like you to review the copy for our new products. We have several in stock and ready to offer to our customers, but we want to make sure we don't attract any unpleasantness when we go public. You can work with the marketing group to approve the wording for the website and to flag any concerns. If necessary, you can consult with our outside counsel."

"No problem. I can't imagine that will take too long."

"Wonderful! And then we have some larger initiatives that I want you to drive. There's the overall communications plan for FairMarket's wellness mandate, obviously. Right now, when people think of FairMarket, they think of organic beauty products—creams, massage oils, cosmetics. I want them to think of a holistic approach to living—what they wear, what they eat, what kind of exercise they do, where they travel, everything. I want FairMarket to be a lifestyle for our customers, the way it is for the people who work here. Which reminds me, Daria, could you get Mariana some product samples? I want you to have intimate knowledge of the products you're writing about."

"Absolutely," says Daria.

"Sounds good," says Mariana. "I'll look forward to trying them out."

"You'll never look back," says Harmony. "Trust me. Wellness is addictive." She takes a sip of kombucha. "The other major project is a launch of the wellness initiative before the end of the year. I want to have a summit meeting of the best thinkers and writers who support our mission. I have a few ideas, obviously, but I'm hoping that you'll generate a list of speakers, along with a thematic mandate. We'll want maximum media exposure, but we'll want to control the message."

"It's called the free press for a reason," says Mariana. "There's a limit to what we can do on that front. We don't control what people say about us."

"Well," says Harmony, "in my experience, there's some wiggle room there. Let's find it. Only some of the best things in life are free." She laughs. "What isn't is on our website. Ha! I'm writing your copy for you."

Remember how much they are paying you, thinks Mariana.

"I have an appointment now, but I'll be checking in with you tomorrow to see how you're settling in," says Harmony. "Daria, can you take it from here?"

"Sure," says Daria. "Let's find you a place to write."

"Oh, and Mariana?" says Harmony. "Take some palo santo wood with you and try it out. You'll be amazed at the physical and psychological benefits. We're going to sell it on our website."

JUNE

CHAPTER 18

Beata

A re you sure you're ready for this?" Beata asks.
"I've been ready for months," says Eloise.

"They mean well, but they can be a lot to take in. My mother has no filter whatsoever. Don't take anything she says personally, okay?"

"Your mother is Lydia Hennessey. She can basically say whatever she wants." Eloise, it turns out, is a Lydia Hennessey super-fan. Beata is not sure what to think about this.

"Don't say that. You have no idea what you might unleash."

"I deal with high-maintenance people all day, and none of them have inspired me as much as your mother has. I'm prepared to cut her some slack," says Eloise. "Let's focus on what you need to stay calm."

"I'm completely calm," says Beata. "I'm known for being calm. Don't tell me to be calm." The doorbell rings. "Oh my god. Why are we doing this again?"

Eloise sighs. "Because we're in a committed relationship and it's past time I met the rest of your family."

Beata goes to the door. "Remember that you were warned," she says. "Hi everyone!"

The Goldstein-Hennesseys flood into the house.

"Eloise!" Lydia Hennessey pulls Eloise into an embrace. "I'm Lydia Hennessey. We are so pleased to meet you. And this is Marvin, and Mariana, and Nina."

"Hi," says Eloise.

"Give her some room to breathe," says Beata.

"She's fine," says Lydia. "For heaven's sake, Beata. We aren't going to break her. Why on earth my daughter decided to keep you a secret, I have no idea."

"I'm glad we're getting the opportunity to meet now," says Eloise.

"Likewise," says Lydia. "Beata, ask Nina about her news."

"You have news?" asks Beata. "Also, we don't have to stand in the hallway. I have a living room."

"I signed a one-year contract at Western General Hospital," says Nina, as they file out of the hallway.

"I thought you were picking up shifts at your friend's walk-in clinic until your next overseas assignment came through," says Beata.

Beata's family has a tendency to talk over one another, and it can be a challenge to break into the conversation. Eloise makes an attempt. "I understand you're with Physicians for Peace," she says to Nina. "They do such incredible work. I attended their fundraiser last year."

"Thanks for your support," says Nina. "And yes, I've been with them for the last five years, but I've decided to take a break."

"Only for the year?" asks Beata.

"Indefinitely," says Nina.

"How's my building?" asks Marvin, before Beata can follow up on Nina's remark. "Is everyone enjoying the gold-plated fridge? I can't believe how much appliances cost these days."

"Your building is worth even more than it was when you installed the fridge two months ago," says Beata, "and you know it. Don't be a curmudgeon."

Marvin smiles, a rare occurrence these days. "It's one of the few privileges of old age, my girl." He pats her knee. "I'm proud of you."

"Did you know that I spoke at one of the first rallies for sexual diversity?" says Lydia to Eloise.

"I did know that," says Eloise. "Actually, I've heard you speak a few times, starting when I was a university student."

Lydia smiles. "Well, then, we're not strangers at all." She leans in. "I want you to know, for the record, that we're absolutely comfortable with Beata dating a woman."

"No one's keeping a record, Mom," says Mariana. "Also, consider the possibility that Beata didn't tell you about Eloise because she thought you'd make a production of it."

"What do you mean? When do I ever make a production of anything?"

"I have to say, I've never understood how some-one can be equally attracted to men and women," says Marvin.

"I'm completely with you on that," says Eloise.

"Okay," says Beata, standing. "Let me get Oscar down here to say hello. And Eloise, do you want to help me with the drinks?"

"Sure," says Eloise, rising from the sofa and following Beata out.

"Are you okay?" Beata asks as soon as they're out of earshot. "They're a lot, I know."

"I'm fine," says Eloise. "More than fine. I think your mother really likes me. Why don't you go and get Oscar while I pour the wine?"

"If you say so." Beata calls up to Oscar, and he appears without argument or delay, thumping down the stairs and into the living room.

Lydia sniffs. "Oscar, are you wearing cologne?"

"It's body spray," says Mariana. "All the teenage boys wear it. It's marginally better than the B.O."

"Did you know there's a genetic reason for the way teenage boys smell?" says Lydia. "It's nature's way of pre-venting incest."

"Is that true?" asks Mariana. Oscar looks horrified.

"Eloise, Beata tells us that you're a divorce lawyer," says Nina.

"Not only divorces," says Eloise, filling wineglasses. "I deal with marriages as well, and adoptions. Family issues of all kinds."

"Do you have any interest in getting married your-self?" asks Lydia.

"Mom!" says Beata.

"As a matter of fact," says Eloise, "I would love to get married someday."

"Isn't that wonderful," says Lydia.

"I'm going to put the finishing touches on dinner," says Beata. "Eloise, do you want to help me?"

"Mariana, why don't you help her?" says Lydia. "I want to visit with Eloise."

Mariana rises and follows Beata into the kitchen. "There's no point in trying to separate them," she says. "Eloise can handle herself."

Mariana smells like sandalwood and has prayer beads looped around her wrist. "How's the job at FairMarket going?" Beata asks.

"It's tolerable," says Mariana.

"You should touch base with Nina," says Beata. "She's involved with Doctors Against Quackery. They did some kind of protest against FairMarket right before you started there."

"Nina's part of Doctors Against Quackery? Aren't they a bunch of cranks?"

"Who told you that? They're small, but they're legit. FairMarket skates awfully close to the line with some of the claims it makes about its products."

"I'm surprised to hear you say that." Mariana's brow crinkles. "You love natural remedies."

"Only when they work," says Beata. "Can you take the

salad out to the table?" She follows her sister with another platter of food. "Okay, everyone," she calls. "Come and sit down."

"Oscar," says Lydia, taking her place at the table. "Sit here with me and tell me all about your father. No one has told me the first thing about him."

"There are reasons for that, Mom, as you well know," says Beata.

"His name's Will," says Oscar. "He's a lawyer. He works at the same law firm as Eloise."

"But what's he like?" asks Lydia.

"He's nice," says Oscar.

"Do you know him well, Eloise?" asks Mariana.

"I do. Will's a close friend. He's a terrific person."

"Well, we would like to meet the gentleman responsible for our grandson," says Lydia.

"I can ask him, if you want," says Oscar.

"Oscar and Will are still getting to know each other," says Beata.

"We don't bite," says Lydia. "Do we, Eloise?"

"Not that I've noticed," says Eloise.

"Cheers, everyone," says Beata, raising a glass. She needs to distract her mother. Oscar bangs his glass against hers. His hands are enormous, she notices. When did that happen? "Not quite so hard," she tells him. He rolls his eyes.

Her plan works, and the table breaks into smaller conversations that aren't about Will Shannon. By the time the main course is finished, Beata is actually enjoying herself.

Lydia rises from her chair. "If I could take the floor for a moment," she says, "I have something to tell all of you." There's a serious note in her mother's voice, and Beata realizes she's holding her breath. Please let it be good news, she thinks. Please let her and Dad be healthy. Across the table, she sees the same trepidation in her sisters' faces. "This October," she continues, "one of the largest feminist demonstrations in history—and certainly in your lifetimes—will happen right here, in our city."

"Mom!" says Mariana. "You scared me."

"Me too," says Beata.

"Me three," says Nina.

"Your mother has a flair for the dramatic," says Marvin.

Lydia is annoyed. "It's huge news, girls. Organizations across the country are coordinating sister marches, each one led by a giant of the feminist movement. But the one here is projected to be the largest. And I've been chosen to lead it."

"Bravo!" says Eloise.

"That's amazing, Mom," says Mariana.

"Congratulations!" says Beata.

"I expect all of you to be there. Especially you, Oscar. The men of your generation need to stand arm in arm with your sisters in the struggle for equality."

"We'll all be there," says Nina.

"Tell us more about it," says Eloise.

"I met with the organizing committee this week," says Lydia. "They're an inspiring group of women, with very ambitious plans. They've expressed an interest in having me attend their meetings so that they can take advantage of my experience."

"They'd be crazy to pass up the opportunity to learn from you," says Eloise. "I mean, you've been at every major feminist rally for decades."

"Not *every* one," says Lydia, modestly.

"I'm going to get the dessert organized," says Beata. She walks into the kitchen and opens the freezer to get the ice cream. When she turns, she's startled to see Nina.

"I don't want to be alarmist," Nina says, "but you might want to hurry."

"Take the cake," says Beata. "I'm right behind you."

"You're perfect for her," Lydia is saying to Eloise. "You have our full support. Go for it."

"What's going on?" asks Beata.

"Nothing at all," says Lydia. "Oh, yum! That cake looks sinful."

Beata slices into the cake. "Dad? Cake and ice cream?"

"Beata," says Eloise, standing up and walking over to her. "I have an announcement too. I love you, and if you're willing, I'd like to join your incredible family."

"Yes!" says Lydia.

No, no, no, thinks Beata.

Eloise gets down on one knee. "Marry me," she says.

CHAPTER 19

Zoe

W hat are we doing today?" asks Zack. "Unpacking
more boxes?"

They've been in their apartment for several weeks now,
but there are still a few boxes stacked in the kitchen.

"Later," says Zoe. "I'm taking Mavis out for a walk
now. I want to unplug for a couple of hours."

"Unplug how?"

"Turn off my phone. Disengage from social media.
Become unavailable."

"Why?"

"Mariana and I are doing an online course together
and it's one of the assignments."

"What kind of course?"

"Do you promise not to laugh at me?"

"Yes."

"It's a happiness course."

"As in, the philosophy of happiness?" asks Zack.

"More the psychology. Specifically, how to be happier."

"That sounds like a scam, Zoe."

"There are many psychologically proven strategies to boost your own internal happiness levels without relying on external factors, like relationships," says Zoe primly. "Every week, the course covers a different strategy and your homework is to experiment with it."

"Who's offering this course, exactly?"

Zoe colours slightly. "FairMarket is branching out into wellness programming."

"So, not Harvard, then?"

"Piss off, Zack. You said you wouldn't laugh."

"Sorry. What's your experiment this week?"

"Mavis and I are exercising, enjoying nature, and disconnecting from our devices."

"Is Mavis trying to boost her happiness levels?"

"Are you in or out?"

"In."

"All right then." Zoe holds up her phone. "Three, two, one," she says, and they power off in unison. She feels an unfamiliar thrill. How rare it is for her to be unreachable these days. "Let's go."

"Go where?"

"Mavis will figure it out for us. She's extremely intelligent."

"So you keep telling me," says Zack.

At the entrance to their building, Mavis pauses and sniffs the air. "Lead on, Mavis," says Zoe. Mavis heads north at a trot. She turns left at the first corner to lunge at a flock of pigeons, and continues west.

"How long is Mavis going to be in charge of the day's agenda?" asks Zack.

"Until we have a better one. Anyway, it's a gorgeous day."

"So tell me what's happening on the dating front," says Zack.

"Nothing remotely promising," says Zoe. Since she and Will have gone back to being friends and sort of relations, she's taken a deep dive into online dating again. She's on four sites, where she's presenting four alternative versions of herself (all accurate; she contains multitudes): the fun-loving extrovert who likes a night on the town, the ambitious entrepreneur, the devoted friend- and family-oriented woman who loves nothing more than a night at home with loved ones, and the arts and culture maven. Each of her profiles is generating equally abysmal prospects, and often the same ones. Available men in the online dating pool bear a depressing resemblance to a holiday fruitcake: unloved, rejected, and re-gifted year after year, website after website. She's spent evenings with Eric the usability engineer, possessed of four kids from two wives and nasal allergies; Sumul the radiologist, obsessed with an obscure form of music called "mathcore" that sounds to Zoe like a bar fight at the end of a bad night; Brian the pilot, who doesn't live in the city, or even the country, but likes to have sparkling companionship wherever the friendly skies take him; Fernando the highly anxious director of a small and (reading between the lines) failing theatre company; and Tyler the life coach and motivational speaker, whose claim to fame is having jumped into the shark tank at the local aquarium, naked, before being fished out by security. It's draining and nowhere near as fun as it should be, which is why she's agreed to do the happiness course with Mariana.

They continue west for a half hour, and Mavis shows no signs of slowing down until they pass a large farmers' market, and she pulls them into the park, nose twitching.

"Do you think it would be fun to have a food truck?" asks Zoe.

"I've never thought about it until now," says Zack, "but since you ask, no. I don't."

"I don't know," says Zoe. "It's kind of an open-road fantasy. Like it's just you and your truck, and you have everything you need to make a living right there. No office, no aggravation."

"Except the aggravation of working out of a hot, stinky truck all day long. And figuring out where to park your truck. And dealing with the public. I hate the public."

"So it's not your fantasy," says Zoe. "I get it."

"It's not your fantasy either. What kind of food do you like enough to make day in and day out?"

Zoe thinks, and comes up empty. "You make a good point."

"Thank you."

"Did Mom tell you that she's throwing a wedding shower for Beata and Eloise?" says Zoe. "She says it's because Lydia is so busy with the Women's March coming up, and she wanted to make sure that Beata's wedding didn't fall through the cracks."

"Passive-aggressive, no?"

"I think Mom was hoping to make a point, but I'm not sure Lydia even noticed. She said she thought it was a nice idea and she was sure Beata would appreciate it."

"I don't have to go, do I?" asks Zack.

"Probably not. I think it's an old-school, women-only thing."

"I'm strongly in support of that," says Zack.

Zoe laughs. "How do you think Oscar's doing? Has he said anything to you? He seems okay, but I haven't had a conversation with him about it."

"You mean how's he doing with the whole 'my mom's been dating a woman for two years and didn't tell me and now they're getting married and I also have a new dad that I didn't know about'?"

"Yes. That."

"We haven't had a deep, meaningful chat, but guys don't do that, as a rule."

"I'm asking for your read on the situation."

"My take is that he's fine. He's entitled to some teenage angst, like the rest of us were."

"Beata's worried about him."

"When is she not? She's been all over that kid since he was born. He's entitled to withdraw and fester and speak in monosyllables for a few years. It's a time-honoured tradition. Most of the men you know did exactly that at his age."

"Most of the men I know are complete disasters."

"Let's keep it friendly," says Zack. "Moving on, Beata forgets that her mother drove her nuts when she was Oscar's age. She used to imitate Lydia, do you remember?"

Zoe smiles. "I do, now that you mention it. She used to be hilarious." Her smile fades. "Before she had Oscar."

"Yeah." Zack sighs. "Who knew she'd be such a helicopter parent?"

"I didn't understand then what it must have been like for her, having the baby, living with her parents, going back to school." Zoe remembers feeling horrified at the turn Beata's life had taken. She realizes now that Beata must have noticed her discomfort, and her failure to offer support. "We were assholes."

"Speak for yourself. I didn't shun Beata like the rest of you. I was her favourite babysitter, did you know that?" Zack puts his feet up on the coffee table. "I wish she'd get over being mad about the show."

"It didn't help that you and Courtney were tabloid fodder for a couple of years." Zack's tempestuous relationship with Courtney Marcus, the actress who played Beata/Bethany on Zack's show, added an incestuous flavour to the already-unpalatable airing of family laundry.

"The show was *fiction*," says Zack. "Bethany was not based on Beata. Why is it so hard for people to understand that?"

"Because it was a show about a famous feminist with an eerie resemblance to Lydia, and her children."

"I could spend the afternoon itemizing all of the ways

in which the fictional family differs from Lydia's family."

"And yet," says Zoe, "there's a line and you got too close to it. Whether or not you stepped over it is a matter of interpretation. Mariana thinks not, Beata and Lydia think so. That's their prerogative. You had to know you were running a risk."

"What does Nina think?"

"I don't know," says Zoe. "She doesn't have an alter ego on the show, and if I had to guess, I'd say she wouldn't care that much if she did. But who knows? She's a tough one to pin down. When she's not living on the other side of the planet, she's crazy busy. You know that dinner I've been trying to schedule for the five of us? I've circulated four sets of dates, and she can't do any of them."

"Maybe she's avoiding me."

"I doubt she gives you that much thought."

"Maybe not," says Zack. "That would be a refreshing change. What's she doing these days? I thought she'd have gone back overseas by now."

"Mariana says she's taken a contract in the ER at Western General. I guess she wants a break."

"Makes sense to me," says Zack. "But then, I wouldn't have put my hand up in the first place. Nina must have nerves of steel." He points to a truck. "Want some tacos?"

"More than anything," says Zoe. They get in line.

It's been ages since Zoe visited a farmers' market. She and Richard had been the sort of people who went every weekend, three seasons a year. They had also been the sort of people who hosted elaborate dinner parties, and appreciated good coffee, and supported the arts. It seems to her now that these had been rather slight foundations for a marriage. She assumed that these activities were shorthand for deeper shared values: *We are the kind of people who support community projects. We are the kind of people who prioritize relationships with friends. We are the kind of people who value risk-taking and artistic expression.* But actually, it strikes her, with prickling clarity, that they shared a love of good cheese, coffee, and conversation, and not much else.

"What kind do you want?" asks Zack. "I'm buying."

"One chicken, one shrimp. I'll grab a spot on the bench over there."

Zoe sits and remembers the dinner parties she used to throw when she was married. Richard, ever predictable, would insist that the guests sample the espresso from his machine. And she'd say: "He'd rescue that machine first if we had a fire. He loves it more than he loves me." And he'd say, "I do!" And everyone would laugh, right on cue. But once the cracks opened up in her marriage, she stopped using the line for a laugh. It wasn't funny. It was true: Richard didn't love her.

Zack arrives with the tacos. "What would you save in a fire?" she asks.

"A fire where?"

"At our place, I guess."

"You," he says. "Mavis." He reaches down to scratch her ears. "Even though she's very gassy."

"What else?"

"My camera, maybe?" he says. "The notebook beside my bed where I scribble down ideas in the middle of the night?" He shrugs. "But I probably wouldn't have the presence of mind to rescue anything. I'd be that guy standing outside naked when the firefighters arrived. I'm not much of a planner. What about you?"

"I had a box under the bed when I was married that had the stuff I'd save. Wedding pictures, memorabilia, tickets from concerts, that kind of thing. Like a little time capsule of my life."

"Where is it now?"

"I went through it when we moved and threw everything out. It was more likely to start a fire than be the thing I wanted to rescue in a fire." Zoe feeds Mavis a piece of chicken from her taco. "Who loves chicken?"

"This is giving me some insight into the gassiness," says Zack. Mavis wags her tail. "Do you miss him?"

"Richard?"

"No," says Zack. "Will."

"No one is supposed to know about that."

"We both know that I do. I'm not telling anyone, I'm asking how you are."

"I'm sad," she says. "The timing was awful, but still. It had potential."

"I thought you guys were good together."

"Yeah." Zoe turns her face up to the sun and closes her eyes. "You lose so much more than a marriage when you get divorced. You lose your confidence, and all kinds of people—not necessarily your closest friends, but so many acquaintances that the whole landscape of your life shifts—and your world view. It's disorienting." She opens her eyes and scratches Mavis under her chin. "With Will, I started to think it had all happened for a reason, you know? That all the horrible stuff had been a precursor to the main event. And now I feel every bit as awful as I did when Richard left, but with way less optimism about the future. It's like I've make no progress at all. It's humiliating."

"Try having your love life spread across tabloids in every supermarket in the country. I'm a gold medallist in the humiliation Olympics." Zack leans back on the bench, raises his face to the sun. "You aren't stuck, Zoe. You're in the middle of your story. It can get messy, but as long as you're moving forward, you'll be okay."

"What if I end up somewhere I don't want to be?"

"Then you do what I'm doing," says Zack. "You figure out how you screwed up, and you start writing a new chapter."

CHAPTER 20

Mariana

M ariana," says Harmony. "Would you mind stepping
into my office?"

"Sure," says Mariana, glancing at her watch. It's the
end of the day, and Mariana has a date. She hasn't been on
that many dates at all since she kicked Devlin to the curb,
and most of them have terminated at the screening stage
(a low-commitment coffee or drink). This one is higher
stakes, though, and she doesn't want to be late.

"Can you believe it?" asks Harmony, settling behind
her desk. "You've been with us a whole month."

Actually, Mariana can believe it. There's an Alice in
Wonderland quality to FairMarket Beauty. Since joining the company, she's changed her wardrobe, her diet,
and her exercise routines, not to mention her life goals.
The sound of keyboards clicking in the newsroom, the
smell of stale coffee and recycled air, the adrenaline rush
of a perfect quote—these are all fading in her memory

like antique newsprint. "It's gone by very quickly," says Mariana, and this much is true.

"I've been reviewing the product descriptions on the website today. I understand they went live last week?"

"That's right. It took longer than we projected to get the wording approved by our lawyers."

"I'm sorry we had to get the lawyers involved."

"Oh?" says Mariana. She wonders if Harmony is unhappy that she's incurred legal costs. She could have sworn that she'd been instructed to consult with the legal team.

"They have a tendency to make the products sound unappealing."

"Yes, I noticed that. We had to go back and forth with them a few times."

"I guess what I'm saying, Mariana, is that I was hoping you'd be able to inject a bit more flair into the descriptions of our new wellness products. Take the essential oils, for example." Harmony taps on her keyboard, turns the screen towards Mariana, and reads aloud: "'Celebrate your inner Earth Mother with this essential oil, combining red raspberry, clover, and lady's mantle, herbs long associated with fertility. Not to be consumed orally, this specially formulated oil is best enjoyed using our Essential Diffuser.'" Harmony purses her lips. "What happened to the wording we discussed? 'Formulated by FairMarket's dedicated naturopathic practitioners, our Earth Mother Oil regulates fertility naturally, drawing on the ancient healing powers of red raspberry, clover, and lady's mantle, fertility herbs cultivated by midwives throughout history.'"

"The lawyers didn't like it," said Mariana. "They felt it came too close to promising unsubstantiated medical results. Also, they thought we might get sued by the professional organization representing midwives."

"And what about our fair-trade copper bracelets, 'a perfect accessory for any season and nature's cure for inflammation'?"

"They're fine with the perfect accessory part, but not the cure part."

"Oh, come on!" says Harmony. "What about our Warrior Tea? I thought we were going to say that it harnesses the power of nature's own cancer warriors with a scientifically proven blend of antioxidant herbs and fruit extracts."

"It isn't scientifically proven, and if we claim that it is, we might inadvertently discourage someone from seeking appropriate medical care for her symptoms."

"Mariana," says Harmony, "the future of the wellness industry is health care adjacent. That's what our customers want—natural, beautiful products that bolster their health and which they can access in the privacy of their own homes."

"I understand it's not what you wanted to hear, Harmony, but the company is growing and it's under more scrutiny. Isn't that part of the reason you hired me? To make sure that the public claims we make about our products can be defended?"

Harmony closes her eyes and takes several deep, cleansing breaths. "I'd like to take some time to reflect on this," she says.

"Take all the time you need," says Mariana. "I should get going, but I'll be in the office all day tomorrow."

"There is one other item. We've been approached about providing a major sponsorship for an event this fall. Perhaps you've heard that there's going to be a Women's March?"

"I had heard that, yes."

"The organizing committee has sent us a proposal for funding, and I'm considering it seriously."

"I'd love to see us get involved," says Mariana. "It should be an inspiring day. You should talk to Daria about the community relations impact. If we do fund it, I'll make sure we get a lot of traction from a communications standpoint."

"The speakers haven't been announced yet, but a little bird tells me that your mother will play a prominent role." Harmony looks expectant.

"I've heard the same."

"So I'm wondering out loud, Mariana, could we persuade your mother to partner with us? She's a woman of amazing power and substance. And a real beauty as well."

Mariana sighs inwardly. It's never straightforward, being Lydia Hennessey's daughter. "I very much doubt that my mother is involved in the fundraising aspects of the march," she says. "So I'm not sure what kind of partnership you have in mind."

"Nothing specific," says Harmony, "only that providing funding would make more sense from a business perspective if we could get some cross-pollination. Maybe your mother could be the face of our 'Beauty at Any Age' line? Or at least donate her image for a special campaign around the march itself?"

"Harmony," says Mariana, "these are all interesting ideas, and I'm not rejecting them out of hand. Right now, I have another meeting to get to. Why don't we regroup tomorrow?"

"As you wish," says Harmony, folding her hands together. "Be well."

Mariana races out of the office and jumps into her car. She's rattled by her conversation with Harmony. And now she's running late. She takes a deep breath, Harmony-style, and reminds herself of her current dating philosophy: every date is merely practice for some future date that will validate her present attitude of unearned optimism. The romantic landscape may be unpromising (and it is), but she's in training: all she needs to do is show up groomed, outfitted, accessorized, and armed with a few conversational gambits, and she's made some measurable progress towards her goal (having a date at some point in the future that doesn't suck). It's strange how she and Zoe have switched positions: Zoe's confidence in dating has dropped lately, while Mariana's has increased.

Tonight, though, Mariana's nervous, because she's going on a date with Tim Carver. First of all, she's not completely sure it's a date: the first and last time they met, they got into a public argument. Still, they've kept in touch since then, striking up a friendly, slightly flirty (or is it her imagination?), occasionally combative banter by text. Secondly, she may have miscalculated her outfit; this one (flattering jeans that Zoe helped her choose and a low-cut bohemian top from the FairMarket Beauty clothing line) is designed to telegraph that she's on a date, but what if she isn't? She doesn't think these are problems people used to have as often in the pre-digital age. And lastly, she isn't sure her neuroses are adequately contained to escape the notice of a therapist.

Her phone rings. "Hi, Zoe," she says. "I was just thinking of you. I'm on my way to a date."

"A date! Who's the lucky guy?"

"Would you believe Tim Carver?"

"Tim from the singles night? The couples therapist? Oh my god, are you dating him?"

"Yes, that Tim. No, I'm not dating him. I'm having one date with him. I think. I'm not entirely sure."

"Do you want to be having a date with him? I wasn't sure you liked him that much at the singles event."

"We got past that. We've been texting."

"No kidding," says Zoe. "Well, never mind, then. I was going to see if you wanted to come over and watch girl movies with me."

"Maybe on the weekend, if you don't have plans?"

"I have no plans," says Zoe. "I'm on hiatus from dating."

"Why?" Mariana wonders if there's something Zoe hasn't told her.

"I need a break every now and then. I got too invested in the last guy I went out with," says Zoe.

"Who was that? I don't remember you telling me about him." What kind of guy managed to knock Zoe off balance?

"I'll tell you about him another time," says Zoe. "Good luck on your date. We'll talk before the weekend."

Mariana parks and walks to the restaurant. Tim arrives at the door at the same time.

"Have you been here before?" he asks. "They have a nice patio in the back."

"I haven't," she says. "But sitting outside sounds wonderful. It's a gorgeous night." They find a table in the garden, and Mariana orders a large glass of something with high alcohol content. "This place is a find."

"Isn't it great? I've been coming here for years." Their drinks arrive, and they clink glasses. "I was really sorry to hear that you'd left the newspaper. It's a sad commentary on the print journalism industry that they couldn't keep someone as talented as you are."

"I'm flattered."

"It's true," says Tim. "So many of my favourite writers have left for the private sector. How are you finding the transition, by the way?"

"I like the salary," she says. "I like the hours. But I feel homesick, if that's the right word? There's nothing like a newsroom, even in its diminished state." She sips her drink. "What made you decide to be a couples therapist?"

"Have you heard of the Love Lab?"

"At the University of Washington? We did a story on it a few years ago. They've figured out how to predict which marriages will survive, right?"

"That's the one. I spent some time there while I was doing research for my doctorate. It was fascinating. Initially, I planned to pursue an academic track, but I ended up preferring the couple interviews to the data crunching."

"I didn't realize you had actual scientific research to back up your theories about healthy relationships," says Mariana. "I feel like I owe you an apology, again, for arguing with you on the panel."

"Yeah, well, I still ended up divorced," says Tim drily. "Did you want to ask me why?"

"I usually wait until later in the date to ask the divorce questions," she says. Tim tilts his head, and her stomach falls. "If this is a date. Which I'm not sure it is. Is it?" She considers running for the door.

"No," says Tim. "But only because I don't date people who've been separated less than two years."

"Ever?"

"Ever since I learned the hard way that it was a necessary sanity saver."

"But what if you meet a perfect person and she's only been single for eighteen months?" Mariana's curiosity overwhelms her desire to flee.

"That's never happened, but if it did, I'd explain my rule and tell her that I hoped she'd still be available in six months."

"I think you're completely nuts," says Mariana.

"Very likely," says Tim. "I am a therapist, after all."

"I'm totally over my husband, and it hasn't been two years yet."

"It's amazing how all the divorced people I meet are convinced that the usual milestones don't apply to them. You've been separated, what, six months?"

"Four."

"Why would you want to rush the process?" asks Tim.

"Because the process is excruciating," says Mariana.

Tim laughs. "Do you want to talk about something else? Books, plays, sports?"

"All right. Who's your favourite author?"

"Chekhov."

"Chekhov? Seriously? That's your answer?"

"What's wrong with Chekhov? He's brilliant."

"His characters all sit around drinking vodka and talking about how futile their lives are. Which is fine, if that's your jam and you aren't trying to be, say, relatable."

"Who's yours, then?" asks Tim, slightly defensive.

"Jane Austen," says Mariana.

"Her characters all sit around drinking tea and talking about how futile their lives are."

Mariana laughs. "What about movies? What kinds of movies do you like?"

"I like superhero movies. All of them, no matter how ridiculous. Is that a more acceptable answer?"

"Yes," says Mariana. "As long as you like the girl superheroes as much as the boy superheroes."

"Obviously," says Tim. "I might even like the girls more."

Mariana leans back in her chair. "Do you have rules about being friends with people who've been divorced for less than two years? Because I could use a friend who likes superhero movies."

Tim smiles. "I'm far more flexible when it comes to friends," he says. "Especially if they're the sort of people I'd like to date when the time comes."

JULY

CHAPTER 21

Beata

W e need to start making some decisions," says Eloise. "Okay," says Beata. There are a lot of conversations like this these days, and they are riddled with pitfalls. Predictably, most Saturday mornings now begin in this way, before she is alert enough either to avoid them or to navigate safely through them.

"Do you have strong preferences for the music?"

"I don't think so."

"Not even for the ceremony? We could have recorded music, which is less expensive, or we could have a musician or even a trio?"

"Classical, you mean?"

"Not necessarily," says Eloise. "Although I was leaning in that direction."

"Okay."

"Of course, a lot depends on the venue. Are we hoping for outdoor or indoor?"

"I hadn't thought about it."

"I'd appreciate it if you'd put away your phone, Beata. Availability is limited for September. People plan weddings a year in advance."

Beata puts her phone down. "We could do that, too, you know."

Eloise exhales. "We agreed on September. I'm going to look at a few restaurants today. Do you want to come with me?"

"If you want me to," says Beata.

"What I want is for you to venture the occasional opinion. It's important that it be a meaningful day for both of us."

"It will be meaningful no matter where we have it," says Beata. "And no matter when. I don't understand why we're rushing and creating all this stress."

"I'm stressed because you aren't interested in a single one of the details." Eloise pauses and collects herself, as if dealing with a particularly unreasonable client. "How about I narrow the list down to several options, and then you promise to help with the final selection."

"Sure."

"Oscar is more engaged in this process than you are," says Eloise.

Beata is aware, and it's why she hasn't managed to halt the wedding train. She'd rationalized, when she accepted Eloise's proposal, that they would be able to create a tradition of their own, something low-key and meaningful. But Eloise, who was a bridesmaid at all four of her brothers' weddings, has been waiting patiently for her turn. And she's arranged for Oscar and Will to be their best men. Which means that Beata can't put her foot down without risking another round of blended-family strife.

"I hear that you're feeling disappointed in my participation," says Beata.

"You could say," says Eloise.

The phone rings. "Don't answer that," says Eloise. "This is an important conversation."

"It's my mother," says Beata. "I'm answering. Hi, Mom." Eloise scowls and bangs her coffee mug on the table.

"Do we have a date yet?" asks Lydia. Beata regrets having answered the phone. She wonders if the universe is punishing her. But why? For keeping Oscar's father from him? Surely good intentions count in the karmic calculation.

"Not yet."

"Are we leaning towards early September or late September?"

"I don't know."

"Beata! The colour scheme will be completely different! Early September is still summer, late September is fall. I need to give the florist some direction!"

"Eloise is working on it, Mom," says Beata. "We were just talking about it, in fact."

"Do you have a dress yet? You're not going to wear a pantsuit, or something awful like that, are you? I see that a lot with celebrity lesbians. One wears a wedding dress for the ceremony and one wears a suit."

"Have you been to a lot of celebrity lesbian weddings?"

"I've seen the pictures in *People* magazine, Beata. Don't be snarky, it doesn't suit you. I don't think you appreciate how much work goes into planning a wedding. Particularly when it's happening right before the Women's March. It's essential that we plan ahead."

"Okay, Mom." There's a lot about this wedding that Beata doesn't appreciate, starting with her mother's collusion. What could she do but say yes, with Eloise beaming and her whole family, including Oscar, clapping and cheering? She hadn't anticipated how much momentum could be created by two exceedingly high-energy personalities—Eloise and her mother—with a shared vision of tulle and chrysanthemums.

"Let me speak to Eloise." Beata hands the phone over and goes upstairs. She can hear Eloise speaking in an animated voice. She closes her bedroom door.

The phone rings, which must mean that Eloise and her mother's conversation has ended. Or that her mother hung up by accident, a frequent occurrence, and is now calling again.

"Mom!" calls Oscar. "The phone's for you!"

Beata doesn't answer. Maybe they will assume that she's asleep. The door opens, and Oscar walks in. Beata waves him off and mouths, *I'm not here.*

"It's Aunt Mariana, and she knows you're here," he says, handing her the receiver and walking away before she can hand it back. It's time to cancel her landline, Beata thinks.

"Hello," she says.

"Mom says I need to take you shopping for a wedding dress."

"Why is everyone trying to torture me?" asks Beata.

"Do you love Eloise?"

"Yes."

"Do you love Mom?"

"Yes. Mostly."

"Do you have strong views of your own about what your wedding should look like?"

"No."

"Is it weird that a cynical divorce lawyer is a secret romantic who wants a white wedding with all the trimmings? Is it surprising that your feminist mother is going Bridezilla all over it? Maybe, but so what? Stop spoiling their fun."

"Isn't it enough that I'm telling them to do whatever they want and I'll show up?"

"If it were enough, they'd stop bugging you. You need to show a little enthusiasm."

"Why are you calling me?"

"Because I'm coming over with Nina in a half-hour to take you shopping for a wedding dress."

Half an hour later, Beata climbs into Mariana's car. "Don't you need an appointment to go wedding dress shopping?" she asks.

"You do if your friend isn't the editor of the wedding supplement at the local paper of record," says Mariana.

"This was worth pulling strings for? Seriously?"

"You know what Mom's like when she gets an idea in her head," says Nina, from the back seat. "And anyway, I haven't had a day off in weeks. Mariana promised me lunch in addition to shopping."

"It'll be fun," says Mariana. "It's Mom's first wedding, to be fair. Devlin and I ran off to city hall, which she mentioned several times today. She's invested in this one."

"At least she isn't coming on this excursion," says Beata. "Wait a minute, she isn't coming, is she?"

"No," says Mariana.

"Not for lack of trying," says Nina.

Mariana pulls up in front of a boutique with an enormous white dress in the window. "You guys," says Beata.

"They have all kinds of different styles," says Mariana. "Trust me. If you don't find anything, at least you can tell Mom and Eloise that you spent a few hours trying, right?"

"A few *hours*?"

"Come on," says Nina. "The sooner we get you into a few dresses, the sooner we can have lunch."

The boutique is swarming with customers, and Beata considers making a break for it. "Let me find our consultant," says Mariana. She looks at Nina. "Don't let her escape."

"You probably haven't been to many weddings in the past few years," says Beata.

"You might be surprised," says Nina. "Extreme situations can be clarifying in lots of ways. People go with their guts, seize the moment. They let go of the details—what their family might think, or whether they can afford it, or what they should wear." Nina gestures around the shop with a smile. "Our chaplain was pretty busy, and not only for funerals."

Mariana returns with a young woman in tow. "Greta's going to help us."

"Who's the bride?" asks Greta.

"I am," says Beata.

"Is there a particular style you had in mind? Maybe some pictures from magazines that appealed to you?"

"Nope," says Beata.

"Let's get her into a fitting room," says Mariana. "Beata has more of a bohemian style, wouldn't you say, Beata?"

"Wedding dresses can surprise you," says Greta. "It's fine not to have any preconceived notions of what you want. Why don't I bring you some different options and you can see how they suit you? In the meantime, would you like some champagne?"

"Definitely," says Beata.

Greta moves them to the fitting area, finds them chairs, and fills their champagne flutes. "I'll be back with a few options," she says.

"Just out of curiosity," says Mariana, "why does Eloise want a traditional wedding?"

"It's how she was raised," says Beata. "She's the oldest of five. She helped raise her four younger brothers, who all adore her to pieces. They're all married with kids, and she's been a bridesmaid at every single wedding."

"Have you met them?"

"They all live on the other side of the country," says Beata. "I didn't really have the complete picture of how close they all are until we got engaged."

"Are they comfortable with you being . . ."

"A woman? Apparently so. One of the wives called to say hello the other night and told me that the whole family is thrilled to be celebrating their first gay wedding."

"That's sweet," says Nina.

"It is," says Beata.

"What about Oscar?" says Mariana. "He seems to be on board."

"He is," says Beata. "I didn't give him enough credit, I guess. I wouldn't say he's excited about the wedding—having to dress up and be on display for a day isn't his idea of a good time—but he's keen on Eloise moving in and joining the family. They like each other."

Greta arrives with two long bags draped over her arm. "Are we ready? I thought we'd start with two of our most popular styles and go from there." She pulls a curtain across the room and divides it. "Beata, you come to this side for some privacy, and I'll help you with the gowns."

Beata follows Greta and strips down at her instruction. Greta opens the first bag, revealing a flash of satin and tulle. "Close your eyes, and put your hands in the air," says Greta, throwing the dress over Beata's head and fastening it. "And . . . open! What do we think?" She pulls the curtain aside so that Mariana and Nina can see.

"No," says Beata.

"The high-necked Victorian look is really big this

year," says Greta. "Very royal wedding. Not every bride has the height to pull it off, but you do. Imagine it with a floor-length veil!"

"I don't think so."

"Beata," says Mariana. "Can you try to be open-minded? This is supposed to be fun. What does your dream dress look like?"

"I don't have a dream dress."

"Never mind," says Greta. "You'll know it when you see it." She releases Beata from the first dress.

"Maybe a softer line," suggests Mariana. "Something more fluid and romantic?"

"I was thinking the same thing," says Greta. She slides the curtain closed and unzips a second bag. "This one has been a huge hit this year. It's perfect for a garden wedding. And if you want a more bohemian look, I have some floral crowns that you could try." She slides the dress over Beata's head.

"I look like the elf princess from *The Lord of the Rings*," says Beata.

"Is that good?" asks Nina. "Can we see it?"

"No," says Beata. "To both of those."

"Certainly, it's a distinctive look that won't be to everyone's taste," says Greta, stiffly. She unfastens the dress and helps Beata out of it. "Perhaps you might like a more contemporary style?"

"Yes," says Nina, from the other side of the curtain. "Let's try that. And maybe give us a few minutes?"

"I'll be back," says Greta. "There's a robe over there."

She points to a flimsy piece of rayon hanging from a hook and exits, yanking the curtain aside and exposing Beata in her underwear.

Mariana hands Beata the robe. "I get the sense," she says, with some delicacy, "that there's more going on here than a rejection of this season's wedding dress trends."

Beata finds that she can't meet Mariana's eye. "I don't need help choosing a wedding dress," she says. "I never asked for that. I never asked anyone to plan a wedding for me. Everyone acts as though they're doing me this huge favour, stepping in and putting their lives on hold to celebrate me. *I don't need that.*"

Into the silence, Nina says, "What *do* you need?"

"I don't know," says Beata. "I never get to ask myself what I need. I've been responsible for a child since I was practically a child myself. I've never had the kind of freedom that most people have in their twenties and even thirties before they decide to settle down. Do you want to know what I dream about? Being free of responsibility."

"How do you feel about feathers?" asks Greta, appearing with another bag.

"Whatever," says Beata.

Greta unzips another bag and pulls out what appears to be a giant feather boa. "Take off the robe, please." She pulls the dress over Beata's head without fanfare. "You'll need to invest in some shapewear, of course, but you'll be doing that anyway. The dress could not be more on trend."

"I look like a lumpy chicken," says Beata. "This dress

is ridiculous." She looks at the price tag. "Five thousand dollars? Are you crazy?"

"Okay," says Nina. "I'm calling a time-out."

"Thank god," says Beata. "Get me out of this thing."

"Let me help you," says Mariana.

"For the last time, Mariana, I don't need your help." Beata has rarely felt so angry. She reaches behind her for the zipper and yanks it down. "Where were you when I had a tiny baby? Where were you, Nina?"

"Stop!" Greta flutters her hands. "The feathers are extremely delicate! Please be careful."

Beata peels her arms out of the sleeves. "This. Is. Not. My. Dream." She pushes the fabric down over her hips and lets it pool at her feet.

Greta rushes forward and sweeps the dress into her arms, releasing several feathers into the air. "No," she says, as the feathers drift back down to the floor. "Oh, no."

"I'm very sorry," says Beata, but Greta holds up a hand. "We charge for repairs," she says.

CHAPTER 22

Zoe

Zoe is in a goal-setting phase. She's experimented with every happiness strategy known to psychology, and the only one that seems to make a dent is focusing on positive action in support of concrete goals. Gratitude is too much effort, meditation is an invitation to wallow, and she can't operate her business without a phone in her hand, so unplugging is out of the question. Goals, though, she can do. Like learning to kickbox. And building her business. And not thinking lustful thoughts about Will. Shannon.

Every morning, she rises early and spends a few minutes reflecting on her goals. She imagines not being consumed by lustful thoughts about Will. She imagines how liberating that would feel. She visualizes obstacles (his arms, his smile), and she makes resolutions about how to overcome them (in place of his smile, she forms a mental picture of her entire extended family screaming at her and each other). Then she goes to the gym and works off any residual sexual energy. On the upside, her business is growing faster than even her most optimistic projections. She's brought in a raft of new clients, and she's hiring. And she's looking seriously fit.

This afternoon, she's kickboxing with her trainer, Clyde, a former MMA fighter. He, too, is a great believer in goals, and also in aphorisms.

"Zoe!" says Clyde, as she walks into the kickboxing studio. "Did you come here to kick ass and take names?"

"As usual."

"Sweet," says Clyde. "Let's do it."

Zoe puts on her gloves, which are pink.

"Ready? Jab and cross, right side and then left. Go."

Zoe makes a fist and swings. Clyde dances out of the way. "Damn," she says. "Stupid."

"Hey, hey. That's no way to talk to yourself. You're here and you're fighting. Showing up is half the battle."

"You still have to win the other half, Clyde," says Zoe, panting, as she tries to land a punch.

"You need to visualize, Zoe. Don't hit me where I am. Hit me where I'm going to be."

"If I knew where you were going to be," puffs Zoe, "I'd be hitting you. Shit." She puts her hands on her hips and bends over, winded.

"Get back in here! You miss a hundred percent of the shots you don't take."

"What about missing a hundred percent of the ones I do take, Clyde?"

"Go again. Like I said."

Her shot glances off his shoulder.

"Contact. Harder!" he says.

"You're letting me hit you." She swings again.

"I said harder."

"That was harder!" She punches.

"You can do better than that."

She punches again.

"Now I'm starting to feel it. Keep going."

"Aren't we supposed to do the other side? Or, you know, some kicking?"

"Not until I get a real punch out of you. Again." Clyde takes a swing at her and connects with her upper arm.

"Ow!"

"Like that. Come on, Zoe. I know you have it in you. Pretend I'm your ex-husband. Let me have it."

Zoe swings again.

"Better," says Clyde. "Now the left. Really come at me."

She launches herself at Clyde and he dances away, landing a roundhouse kick on her thigh. "Stop that," she says.

"Stop? Does a zebra stop when it's being chased by a lion?"

"Eventually, I guess," says Zoe.

"And then what happens?"

"It gets eaten?"

"Exactly. You see my point."

Zoe doesn't, but she's concentrating on breathing and standing upright. She swings, misses, absorbs another blow to the arm.

"Okay, seriously. Ow." Zoe takes off her gloves.

"What's up today, champ? You're usually tougher than this."

"I don't know," she says. "I'm not feeling it today."

"Your problem isn't feeling, it's thinking. You think too much. Overthink a fight and you get knocked out, simple as that. Start swinging or get out of the ring."

"I'm out," she says. "I'm beat, Clyde. See you next time."

Zoe picks up groceries on her way home from the gym. She's cooking dinner for Will and Oscar tonight. She isn't sure why she invited them over; in hindsight, it seems like a mistake. She's trying to prove to herself that she's bigger than her misery, but she isn't, in fact. With Zack away for a couple of days in LA, she's been indulging in weepy family dramas on television, and they aren't having the cathartic effect that she'd hoped they would.

She's running late by the time she's showered and dressed, and she's barely started the meal prep when she hears Mavis going crazy at the door. Oh well, she thinks, she'll put her guests to work in the kitchen. Oscar could use a few life skills. But when she opens the door, Will is alone. He leans down and scratches Mavis behind the ears, while she squeals adoringly.

"Who's a beautiful dog?" he says. "Yes, you are. The *most* beautiful dog." He straightens up. "Oscar got a better offer," he says to Zoe. "I suspect it involved a girl, but I wasn't provided with complete information. I'm supposed to pick him up in a few hours."

"Do you want to cancel with me? I won't be offended if you want a night on your own."

"Not at all. That is, not unless you want to."

"No!" She realizes she has spoken too quickly and too loudly, but there's no help for it now. "Please come in. I haven't made much progress with dinner."

Will hands her a bottle of wine. "What did you have planned?"

"Nothing fancy. Steak and salad. Chocolate mousse cake."

"Nature's perfect meal, aside from the salad."

"I'll even let you drive the barbecue."

Will grins. "I'll let you—what's the word?—*compose* the salad."

"Gallant to the last," says Zoe.

"I hope so," says Will. Their eyes meet, and they both break contact quickly.

Zoe hands him an apron. "The steaks are in the fridge."

"Got it. Can I pour you some wine?"

"Thanks. How's Oscar doing?" Will hands her a glass.

"I'm no expert, obviously, but I think he's doing really well. He's enjoying the summer. He did well on his report card. He seems to have friends, not that I've met them. They interact solely by text from what I can tell. He's doing filmmaking camp next month and he's looking forward to it."

"He and Beata are doing okay?"

"They're in a better place, which is a relief. The family therapy has been helping a lot with their communication.

And he really likes Eloise, now that he's had a chance to get to know her. I get the sense that Eloise is a calming influence over there."

"How often is he staying with you?"

"It varies. I don't want to get too used to it, in case it's a phase he's going through. He tends to spend two or three nights a week at my place."

"You like it?"

"I love it. It feels like he's always been around. He decorated the spare bedroom so he has a space that's his own."

"You're a dad."

"Yeah. How crazy is that? Six months ago, I didn't know he existed. Now I want to slow down time so I have a few more years with him."

"You're doing a fantastic job with him, Will. We all think so. Even Beata."

"Oh. Well." Will clears his throat. "Thank you. That means a lot to me." He looks at his watch. "I should go and see about the barbecue." He steps outside and slides the balcony door shut.

Zoe smiles. Will has never been one for extravagant displays of emotion. But she knows few people, male or female, who would have committed as unconditionally as Will has to an angry teenage boy appearing in their life out of nowhere. He was thrown into the deep end of emotional experience and chose to swim, and in her book, he deserves a huge amount of credit. And he looks ridiculously cute in an apron. Damn, she thinks. Another resolution shot.

"These steaks look gorgeous," says Will, stepping back inside.

"So do you," she says, and covers her mouth with both hands. "Oh, shit. I said that out loud."

Will puts the plate down on the counter. "You did."

"I'm sorry."

"Why? I liked hearing it. So do you, by the way."

Zoe catches her breath as Will crosses the room to stand in front of her. "But we aren't supposed to . . ."

"We aren't supposed to what?"

"Do this. We aren't supposed to . . . we're supposed to be platonic. For Oscar."

"Oscar isn't here. And I'd like to kiss you."

"Okay," says Zoe, all out of arguments, and she closes her eyes and pulls him in. And then they are all hands and mouths and need, and clothes are flying everywhere, and she says, with all of her willpower, "Wait." He stops. "Aren't you hungry?"

He laughs. "Not in the way you mean."

She's surprised at how natural it feels to kiss him again. Underneath the layers of sadness and frustration, her desire to be with him is as fierce as ever. Sex with Will is so much fun. She's forgotten how affectionate he is in bed, and how frankly appreciative of her body, middle-aged though it may be. As hard as she's tried to convince herself to give him up, she can see that her arguments barely made a dent in her consciousness. She wants him, and not even she can persuade herself otherwise.

Later, she composes exquisite steak salads, and they

sit at the kitchen counter and devour them, along with enormous slices of chocolate mousse cake. "Why can't more dates be like this?" says Zoe.

"Hard conditions to replicate," says Will. "But I've been thinking. Maybe I was too rigid before."

"Not in the least."

"I mean," says Will, "about our seeing each other with Oscar in the picture. Ahem."

"Are you blushing? Did I make you blush?"

"Certainly not," says Will, who is visibly pink.

"Aren't we still worried about Oscar freaking out? Not to mention Beata?"

"Let's say this were a new relationship," says Will. "What if today were day one? Wouldn't we give it a little time to make sure it's real before telling everyone about it? Wouldn't we be entitled to some privacy to figure it out?"

"I'm listening."

"What if we didn't plan any family events over the next few weeks? I'd spend time with Oscar, and I'd spend time with you separately, and there wouldn't be any need to pretend around him."

"And we'd be a couple on our own time?" asks Zoe.

"Right."

"And we wouldn't be telling Beata, or anyone else. Except Zack, because I don't see any way to keep it a secret from him." Will nods. "And how long would this experiment last?"

"We'll have to play it by ear," says Will. "We might decide that it isn't a fit, and then we'd go back to normal with no one the wiser. Or we might decide to go public, in which case, we'd have to navigate that." Will's phone rings. "It's Oscar," he says. "Hi. You ready? A half-hour? Okay. Where? Sure. I'll see you then. Text me the address."

"You have to go?"

"I do. I'm sorry. I wish I could stay longer. I hate to cut this conversation short. Do you want to think about it, and we can talk again tomorrow?"

"I'd love to talk tomorrow, but I don't need to think about it," says Zoe. "I'm in."

AUGUST

CHAPTER 23

Zoe

Zoe loves wedding showers. She loves the corny speeches, and the old-timey games, and the way the older ladies get bawdy when the bride opens boxes of naughty lingerie. She loves the esprit de corps, the recognition that women are all in this business together, this business of being women in a world run by men. She loves that they use these ostensibly innocent gatherings, meant to celebrate traditional milestones of mating and procreation, to pass along the knowledge of how to manage it, how to manage living with and loving men, from one generation to another.

Obviously, this particular shower is a variation on the theme, but much of the conversation remains that same: the reality of love, its possibility and promise, its evolution and endurance. She's grateful to have a boyfriend in this company, even a secret one. Wedding showers (and baby showers too, now that she thinks of it) are excruciating when you're single.

"I hope this won't be too difficult for you, darling," says her mother, who is in full hostess mode. Zoe's affection for wedding showers is genetic; her mother leapt at the opportunity to have one for Beata.

"How so?"

"Because of the divorce," Judy whispers.

"You don't have to whisper, Mom. Everyone here knows that Richard and I broke up."

"It's bad luck to talk about divorce at a wedding shower."

"Says who? Did you make that up? You did, didn't you?"

"Well, it surely isn't *good* luck, is it?"

"You have your party face on." Zoe furrows her brow and offers her best imitation of her mother's wild-eyed expression.

"Throwing a surprise party is stressful, Zoe. What if Beata isn't surprised?"

"Maybe that wouldn't be so bad. Not everyone likes surprises, you know."

"Well," says Judy, "Beata can certainly dish them out, so maybe she should learn to take them."

"I wouldn't put that in your speech," says Zoe.

"I'm not making a speech," says Judy. "Your cousin Mariana is doing it. That reminds me, sweetie, could you circulate around and get all the ladies to sign the card for Beata and Eloise? We'll present them with their gift after Mariana's speech." Judy sighs. "I wish Eloise had agreed to a theme, and individual gifts. It gives some structure to the party when you spend an hour going around in a circle, opening them. Also, the women tend not to drink or squabble as much."

"Spoken like a true veteran of the shower circuit."

"But Eloise was adamant that one pooled gift was better. Apparently, Beata doesn't like being the centre of attention." She shakes her head. "It's bad luck to break with tradition."

"I think you'd feel better if you stopped inventing superstitions."

Judy looks at her watch. "Beata and Eloise will be here in ten minutes. I need to finish up in the kitchen."

Zoe pours herself a glass of wine and scans the room, which has filled up while she's been chatting with her mother. Zoe waves at Nina, who comes over and gives her a hug.

"I'm sorry, I'm sorry," she says. "I know I owe you dates for the cousins' dinner. I like the idea, honestly."

"That's okay," says Zoe. "Beata's given us another reason to get together. Well, except for Zack. He's worried you're mad at him, by the way."

Nina laughs. "I haven't even seen the show," she says. "And I change the subject whenever anyone tries to talk to me about it. Tell him he can take me out for lunch if he's so worried. I'm sure I can manage to schedule lunch with one other person."

Zoe's mother's voice breaks through the party chatter. "They're here, everyone! Everyone quiet! Hide!"

"Oh, for god's sake," says Zoe to Nina. She raises her

voice so that it echoes in the room. "Don't hide. Remain calm. There is no need to hide."

"Surprise!" yell the guests closest to the door. Zoe moves to stand next to Mariana.

"Why are we torturing Beata?" says Mariana. "Hasn't she made it clear that she doesn't want this sort of fuss?"

"I think it's sweet," says Zoe. She wishes that Mariana would turn on the charm, if only to make Judy happy. "I mean, think about how it would look if we didn't have a shower for Beata. People would think it was because she was marrying a woman."

"Beata looks like she's being roasted over hot coals," says Mariana. "She's never been into traditional stuff. Like marriage, for example."

"I wouldn't include that in your speech," says Zoe. She hopes that Mariana isn't too edgy today. Aren't journalists supposed to be able to read the room? If Mariana can, it isn't always obvious.

Beata comes up. "I need to talk to you," she says to Zoe.

"Sure," says Zoe. "Do you want to go into the backyard?"

"That would be fine."

"Congratulations, by the way." Zoe opens the screen door off the kitchen, and they step out.

"Oh," says Beata. "Thanks."

"Are you having fun?"

"Would you be?"

"Yes. I mean, I *am* having fun. Aren't you?"

"Of course! Who wouldn't be having fun at their own wedding shower?"

"Are you feeling okay, Beata?"

"Since you ask, I'm overwhelmed. With emotions. So many big emotions."

"That sounds sort of normal," says Zoe. "Getting married is a huge transition."

"I guess," says Beata. "But I don't see that as the issue. I need to ask you a question. Are you dating Will Shannon?"

Zoe freezes. No one knows about them. She has plausible deniability. She decides to exercise it. "No?"

"Is that a question? It sounded like a question."

"It's not a question."

"So, I should interpret that to mean you are not dating him. Or in any way romantically involved with him."

"I'm not exactly saying that. I'm sort of saying that."

"I'm looking for a clearer answer about what is going on with you and Will," says Beata. "Let me ask again. What's your relationship with my son's father?"

"It's early," says Zoe. "We're figuring it out."

"Are you sleeping with him?"

"That is none of your damn business, Beata," says Zoe, her voice rising.

"It's absolutely my business," says Beata. "Hasn't Oscar had enough to deal with?"

Judy taps on the patio window and gestures for them to come inside.

"Whose fault is that?" says Zoe. "Not mine, and not Will's. You're the one who decided to keep secrets from Oscar. If there's fallout, that's your problem to deal with."

"What's going on, guys?" asks Eloise, stepping outside.

"Your guests want to spend time with you, Beata. Your aunt is getting agitated."

"Zoe is sleeping with Will."

"Oh," says Eloise. "That's unfortunate."

"So what if I am?" says Zoe. "Who are you to pass judgment?"

"If you cared about Oscar's well-being, you'd stop seeing Will," says Beata.

"You are so far out of line, Beata. Will and I are being responsible. We're taking the time to figure out how serious we are before we complicate matters by telling Oscar, which is a strategy that you of all people should understand."

"Come on, you two," says Eloise. "Let's take the temperature down."

"I was minding my own business when your fiancée showed up and started flinging accusations," says Zoe. "Here's the truth, Beata. You lied to your son about his father, and you lied to him about being in a serious relationship with Eloise, and you broke his trust. I don't intend to operate that way. I'm in the early days of a relationship with Oscar's dad, someone I've known and liked since college, and if it becomes more serious, he and I will sit down with Oscar and tell him what's going on. And none of that will have anything to do with you."

"Zoe! Beata!" Judy sprints out of the house, her voice bright and quavering. "Time for speeches! And lunch! Come on inside and join the party! Eloise, why don't you go in with Beata?"

Eloise takes Beata by the arm and they step inside the house. Eloise closes the door behind them.

"What on earth are you doing?" says Judy. "Is it too much to ask that you not think about yourself for five minutes? You're a grown woman, for heaven's sake. Smarten up."

"She started it." It comes out of her mouth before she has a chance to register that she sounds like a sulky teenager.

"I don't care who started it. You are ruining the party for all of the guests. I'm not even going to get into what you did to make Beata so upset. It's not my business. What *is* my business is the success of this event. So put a smile on your face and get inside. And if you dare make another scene, you can be sure that I'll have something to say about it!" Judy turns on her heel and storms back into the house.

Zoe follows, pausing at the bar to refill her wine glass. What a mess. She should have known that her relationship with Will wouldn't remain secret for long, but who could have predicted this kind of explosion? It's inevitable now that Oscar will find out and have his own reaction, whatever it is. But maybe that's for the best. Maybe it's time for both of them to confront whether or not they want to take this risk together.

She doesn't feel like putting a smile on her face. She doesn't feel like being a good girl. She's done enough of that for one lifetime. She is, as her mother says, a grown woman. She can choose. And if her choice causes a scene, so be it. She's done keeping the peace.

She walks into the living room and feels her mother glaring at her as she moves towards Beata. She leans in. "I can't speak for Will," she says, quietly. "But I care about him, and I'm entitled to some happiness of my own, even if it's inconvenient for you or anyone else. I understand that you want me to stop seeing him. But I'm not going to. I don't want to, and I won't."

CHAPTER 24

Mariana

Mariana hates wedding showers. She hates baby showers too, but wedding showers are the absolute worst: the stupid games, and the embarrassing sexual gifts, and the lies. Most of all, she hates the lies. The bride-to-be lying about how fantastic her relationship is, and the married women lying about how lucky the bride is to be getting married, and all of them trying to protect each other from the truth, which is that marriage has never been, and will never be, about the happiness of women. It is beyond the pale that they have to celebrate their subjugation by wearing hats made out of paper plates and bows. It isn't, in her view, made more palatable by the fact that two women are getting married. It's more evidence that the patriarchy has infected even the most subversively feminist of human relationships, the only ones where men are not required for any reason at all.

There wasn't any of this nonsense when she married Devlin, because she didn't tell anyone about their plans.

She didn't want a fuss. She wanted a neat, tidy, controlled, convenient wedding with no weird family rituals. There is a tiny part of her that wonders if she inadvertently attracted negative karma to her marriage by entering into it without a nod to the spirit world. It's all moot, though. That marriage is over, and now she's going to be single forever.

And she would have been fine with that fate. She would have vacationed with friends, immersed herself in challenging projects at work, raised her children, and volunteered in her community, all the while knowing that she was living her best life. But now, because of Tim Carver, she's destined for a fate worse than FOMO. She is mired, instead, in COMO, Certainty of Missing Out, because she knows that there is a thoroughly charming and decent single man out there, a man who is exactly the sort of person she'd fall for, and that he's unwilling to date her.

"How are you, dear?" asks Aunt Judy. "I hear that you have a fabulous new job!"

"Not really," says Mariana. "It's kind of gross, to be honest with you. I think I may have traded my soul and reputation to sell pseudoscience to suggestible women. And clothes. I also sell clothes."

"Well your blouse is just lovely," says Aunt Judy. "Would you like something to drink? Some punch? Or a mimosa?"

"I'll take a mimosa, thanks, without the orange juice."

"I'll get that for you." Aunt Judy pauses. "There was a

little kerfuffle between Zoe and Beata outside just now."

"A kerfuffle? What do you mean?"

"It's not important. It's in the past. We've moved on."

"Okay," says Mariana.

"But I was thinking that it would be nice if your speech could lighten the mood. I hate to ask you to make any changes to it at the last minute, but if you could make it funny—you know, add a few jokes—I'd be grateful."

"I'll do my best, Judy." Mariana has not yet written the speech, having planned for some casual remarks, delivered off-the-cuff.

"I knew I could count on you, Mariana. We'll do the toast before lunch, if that works for you?"

"Oh, sure. No problem."

Mariana takes a seat in a quiet corner. She needs to collect her thoughts. She's still unsettled by Beata's accusations of abandonment, not to mention her obvious reluctance to marry. And now Judy wants her to make a funny speech. With jokes.

"Mariana!" Lydia sits down next to her. "Is your speech ready?"

"Just about," Mariana lies.

"Good. I want everything to be perfect for Beata."

"I really don't get it," says Mariana.

"Get what?"

"Why this wedding means so much to you. It's not as though you cared when I got married." She sees her mother begin to protest and puts up a hand. "No, you didn't, Mom. Don't be revisionist."

Judy appears with a glass of prosecco, hands it to Mariana, and retreats immediately.

Lydia puts her hands on her hips and huffs. "Don't you think your sister deserves a nice wedding? Is this jealousy talking?"

"Far from it. Beata's wedding extravaganza is my idea of hell on earth. And, I might add, I see a lot of evidence that Beata feels the same way."

"I have no idea what you're talking about," says Lydia.

"Beata doesn't want a big wedding. She keeps saying so and no one seems to hear her. Instead, all of us are spending way too much time trying to persuade her that she should be more excited. Why?"

"Your sister has been on her own for her entire adult life. And now she's met someone wonderful, and I want to support her."

"You aren't supporting her. You're forcing a wedding down her throat. It's like you're overcompensating. Is it because you and Dad aren't getting along?"

Lydia's nostrils flare. "That is exceptionally rude, Mariana. My marriage is my own business and none of yours."

"Says you," says Mariana. "I might have another view on that if you were at all interested."

"This may come as a surprise to you, Mariana, but I don't consider you an expert on happiness. I see an exceptionally talented woman who is systematically destroying her life, and blaming everyone else for the results," says Lydia.

"I'm not destroying my life!" Although perhaps she is. A year ago, she was a respected journalist, married to a sexy Irish musician. Now she's a permanently single shill for a snake oil company. Even she has to admit that it's not an upgrade. "And even if I am, it's my choice to make."

"It's not your choice. You have daughters, just like I did. Do you think I did exactly what I wanted to do with my life? I did not. I had a responsibility to give you girls stability and security. And that's what I did."

"What is it you believe I should be doing, Mom? What would earn the Lydia Hennessey stamp of approval?"

"I'd like to see you make some effort to reconcile with your husband, for the sake of your girls."

"That is not going to happen, Mom. Anyway, I've been seeing someone else." This isn't precisely true, but it's close enough. She and Tim have been spending many platonic hours together, during which she routinely fantasizes about other, less wholesome pursuits.

"Your generation is so cavalier about marriage. You all want the shiny new relationship around the corner. Well, let me tell you, Mariana, no marriage failure is one person's fault. And whatever issues you brought to your marriage with Devlin, you'll take with you into your next relationship. If you haven't figured that out already, you will."

The gloves are off, and Lydia's too-pointed remark scores a direct hit. What if her mother is right? What if Mariana is hopelessly damaged and will never find love, with Tim or anyone else? What if that's what Tim means when he says she isn't ready? What if he knows she never will be? Mariana takes a swig of wine and says, "Devlin and I are finished, Mom. What kind of model do you think I'd be setting for Iona and Siobhan if I stayed? What would I be teaching them? That their self-respect is an after-thought? That lying and cheating is acceptable behaviour in a marriage?"

"Selfish people always resort to that argument," says Lydia. "As if children care about your unhappiness. They want their parents in the same house. I was miserable for most of your childhood, and did you notice? No!"

"Wrong again," says Mariana.

"Time for speeches!" says Aunt Judy, racing over with Nina a step behind her. "We need to start the speeches right away!"

"What's going on?" asks Lydia.

Aunt Judy looks as though she's about to burst into tears. "Zoe and Beata are arguing again."

"About what?" asks Mariana.

"It's something about Zoe sleeping with Oscar's dad," says Nina.

"Zoe's sleeping with Will?" says Mariana. "I can't believe she didn't tell me!"

"Stop talking about it!" says Aunt Judy. "We are not discussing it further! We are going to have speeches, and lunch, and give Beata and Eloise their present!"

"Beata seems quite upset," says Nina. "Maybe we should give her some time to cool down before we put her in the spotlight."

"Under other circumstances, I might agree with you, Nina," says Aunt Judy, "but half the guests overheard the fight, and the other half are gossiping about it. We need to shift the focus immediately. And I need to have a word with my daughter. Can you be ready to speak in five minutes?"

"Sure," says Mariana. "No problem."

"Good," says Aunt Judy, spinning on her heel and tearing out of the room.

"Everyone!" calls Lydia. "Everyone into the living room! We're going to have speeches now! Gather round!"

"This is a terrible party," says Mariana, mostly to herself.

"It could always be worse," says Nina. "Trust me."

"How long do you think we need to stay?"

"Is your speech appropriately joyful and tear-worthy? Aunt Judy is expecting you to save the day."

"It will be. And funny. No pressure at all," says Mariana, unfolding a cocktail napkin on a side table as the living room fills with guests. "Do you have a pen?"

"Seriously?" Nina hands her a pen, and Mariana bends over the coffee table and begins scribbling notes.

"Ready, Mariana?" says Aunt Judy, reappearing.

"Absolutely," says Mariana, continuing to write. She's spent a career skating right to the edge of deadlines, pulling all-nighters, blasting into her editor's office without a moment to spare. She likes the adrenaline rush, she realizes. How often has she made her life unnecessarily stressful just to feel alive? She is, she now understands, the polar opposite of mindful. She makes a mental note not to share this fact with Harmony Delacroix.

"Wonderful," says Aunt Judy. "I'll introduce you." She moves to stand in front of the fireplace and says, "What a pleasure to be able to gather today to celebrate my niece, Beata, and her partner, Eloise. I know I speak for the whole family when I say how much we are looking forward to the wedding next month." Everyone claps. "I've asked Mariana, Beata's sister, to make a toast to the happy couple. Mariana?"

Mariana stands, and as she does, she smacks her knee into the coffee table, causing several wineglasses to jump and slosh their contents onto the tabletop. She swears under her breath and reaches for her napkin/speech, only to realize that it's now soaked with wine and completely illegible. "I'm here," she says, and limps over to join Aunt Judy.

"First of all, I want to thank my aunt Judy for this lovely party. Judy is a wonderful hostess, and my sisters and I rely on her to provide us with at least one square meal a year." The crowd obliges with a laugh. Lydia does not join in. "As you know, Beata is the youngest of three sisters. She's always been the flower child of our family, a woman determined to chart her own path. Sometimes Beata's choices have seemed eccentric, and sometimes they've come as a big surprise to those of us who love her, but it's hard to argue with the results. She has a beautiful son, and a career she loves, and a terrific partner who will soon be her wife. Of course, Eloise isn't a stranger to us.

For those of you who don't know her, Eloise is a brilliant divorce lawyer, and several of us here today would be happy to provide a reference if you need one. See me after the speech." She pauses, and there is a strained silence. "Come to think of it, Eloise, now that you're joining officially, we should talk about a family discount." Still no laughter. So much for the jokes. She picks up the pace. "I never would have guessed that Beata, the free spirit, and Eloise, the hard-hitting, take-no-prisoners lawyer, would decide to embrace the institution of marriage. But that's the amazing thing about love. It's completely irrational. Eloise, we salute your courage. You can never say you didn't know what you were getting into. No one knows more of the dirty details of our family's inability to stay happily married than you do. So, let's raise a glass to Beata and Eloise. Congratulations and good luck!"

Mariana downs her drink amid scattered applause. Aunt Judy returns to centre stage. "Thank you for those unique remarks, Mariana," she says, with a dark look in her niece's direction. "Shall we open the gift?"

CHAPTER 25

Beata

Beata can't believe she's ended up spending a rare day off at wedding shower in her own honour. Had she been asked, she would have said, very politely and very definitively, that she'd rather pass, thank you very much. She has all of the stuff that anyone could ever need, plus the million fancy kitchen gadgets that Eloise has gradually brought over. Had she been consulted, she would have said that no good could come from putting all of the female members of her family, along with a sprinkling of family friends and neighbours, into Aunt Judy's living room for a weekend afternoon of female hazing in the form of get-to-know-you games and cringe-worthy marital advice. She would have said that this is not a club she has ever wanted to join. But she wasn't consulted, and now, after pretending to be surprised, she also has to pretend to enjoy being the centre of attention at a party she doesn't want.

She's been trying to stay mellow and retain a festive mien for the sake of family harmony. But since her confrontation with Zoe, it's all she can do to contain her fury, which has been building since last week, when Eloise came home from the office and said, "Is something going on between your cousin and Will Shannon?"

"With Zoe?" Beata said. "I sure hope not. Why?"

"Will and I were having lunch today, and I asked him how things were going with Oscar. He said it was great, but that he was working harder these days to plan their time together. I asked why, and he said that in the beginning, they'd spent a lot of time at Zoe and Zack's house while he and Oscar got to know each other, but that they aren't doing that anymore."

"So? That makes sense."

"Yes, but then he said it had been more efficient when he could see Zoe and Oscar at the same time. I asked if something had changed in their relationship, and he froze. It was weird. Initially, it made me wonder if Oscar and Zoe had argued. But I figured you'd know about it if they had. So then I wondered if Zoe and Will were seeing each other romantically."

"Did you ask him?"

"I did, but he changed the subject. I'm not ruling out the possibility of another explanation, I'm only saying that it made me curious. Would it upset you if they were dating?"

"Yes," said Beata. "It certainly would."

And now she's confirmed it. It's staggering, Zoe's self-absorption. There is an entire city of men, an entire internet of men even, and she's fallen into bed with the only prospect who should be off-limits. Beata wants to be generous, but it's hard not to draw the conclusion that Zoe is drawn to Will's very forbiddenness.

Beata forces herself to pay attention to Mariana's speech, although she's fuming inwardly at Zoe's final salvo. She should have known better than to hope that Zoe would do the right thing and break it off with Will. But she's learned that many if not most people aren't motivated by petty concerns such as moral duty. How often has she tried to convince herself that the universe is just and balanced, when in truth, the good she has done in the world has rarely, if ever, come back to her?

She poured all of herself into raising Oscar. She sacrificed financially, spiritually, emotionally, and physically. She gave up her youth, her flat and unscarred belly, her uninterrupted sleep, her disposable income, her savings, and her ability to travel to exotic places and take real risks. Whereas Zoe and Will had years of unfettered irresponsibility, only, it seems, to obtain the same status she holds as a parent without any of her investment. Beata knows there's nothing more toxic than resentment, yet she feels it coursing through her veins like poison.

Mariana is still talking, and saying something about the irrationality of love. Beata agrees. Love makes no sense at all. Take Oscar, for example. It seems there is nothing Oscar can do to make her not love him. He can stink and stomp and swear, and choose her sexy cousin and his GQ model–slash–brilliant and rich lawyer father over her, and she'll love him still.

Romantic love is, of course, more fragile than parental love, and this gathering is replete with supporting evidence for that proposition. She loves Eloise, but why can't it be on her own terms? Why should she have to conform to outdated social norms, at this late stage in life, to provide proof of love? Marriage, she thinks, is a whistle in the dark, a way of negating impermanence. It is a denial, not an acceptance. It is a fortification, not a journey beyond the walls. It is falsity, not authenticity. She feels invigorated by Mariana's speech. Love shouldn't require her to embrace illusions, and neither should Eloise.

"You need to smile," Eloise whispers.

"I don't need to do anything except be true to my authentic self," says Beata, loudly enough that several people look over at her.

"I'd argue otherwise, in this context," murmurs Eloise, "unless you want to make your aunt Judy cry."

Mariana finishes her speech, and there is a smattering of applause and a clinking of glasses. Beata turns to face Eloise. "I don't know how we got here," she says.

"This was a mistake," says Eloise. "You're overwrought. Let's take a breath and we'll go as soon as it's polite."

"I'm sick of being polite," says Beata. She feels reckless in a way that can't be explained by a couple of glasses of Chardonnay. "If being polite means setting aside your principles to make everyone else comfortable."

"Beata!" says Lydia, joining their huddle. "Your aunt Judy has worked her fingers to the bone to make this party for you, and a little gratitude wouldn't go amiss. By the way, have you asked Mariana, Nina, and Zoe about their being your bridesmaids yet?"

"In case it's slipped under your radar, Mom, I'm a grown woman who doesn't require your advice about how to behave in public. And no. I haven't asked them, because I don't want bridesmaids. That would be ridiculous at my age. This whole extravaganza"—Beata waves her arm to take in the entire room—"is absurd."

Eloise and Lydia exchange a glance that makes Beata want to jump on the sofa, scream, and break the teacups. "Pre-wedding jitters are very common," says Lydia. "I had them myself. You'll be much happier once the wedding is over."

"I was perfectly happy before," says Beata. "My life as an unmarried person suited me. I don't know why we're doing this. Explain to me how this makes our relationship better."

"It's what I want," says Eloise, her voice quiet. "So in that sense, it makes our relationship possible. Which makes it better, because it ensures that the relationship exists at all."

"Marriage has a lot to recommend it!" says Aunt Judy, widening the circle. "You don't know because you haven't experienced it yet. It's knowing that the person you love has committed to you for a lifetime."

"Exactly," says Lydia. "Thank you, Judy."

"Why are we so fixed on the notion of permanence?" asks Beata. "The nature of existence is impermanence. The only guarantee is that nothing will remain the same. Love dies, children grow up, bodies age."

"Judy, do you want to get the card for Eloise and

Beata?" says Lydia. "Maybe they should open it at home. It might be a good idea to send Beata home for a rest at this point."

"I'm not a toddler who missed her nap, Mom. Can you honestly say that marriage improved your life? You and Dad aren't happy together. If you'd had the choices then that I have now, would you really do it all over again?"

"Of course I would!" says Lydia. "I love your father!"

"But you don't like him," says Beata.

"We're committed to each other. We have children. We have grandchildren."

"Was Mariana happy when she was married? Was Zoe?"

"Don't bring me into this," says Mariana.

Beata points at Nina, who is standing at a slight remove. "Nina has a perfectly full life. No one bugs her about getting married."

"Why don't we have some cake?" says Aunt Judy.

"Does she get a pass because she's saving lives in war zones? Is that what it takes?"

"Nina is not in a committed relationship," says Lydia. "Nina doesn't have a son. Stop lashing out, or Eloise will wonder if you're mature enough for marriage."

"I was married," says Nina.

"What was that?" says Lydia.

"I said, I was married," Nina repeats, and they all turn towards her, a baroque tableau. A hush ripples outward from the group and falls over the remaining guests.

"When?" says Lydia.

"Last year, in Syria."

"You have a husband?" says Mariana. "Who is he?"

"Nils Larsen, another aid worker. A doctor from Norway."

"Why haven't we met him?" says Beata.

"Because he's dead," says Nina. "He was at the hospital when it was bombed. It was only three days after we were married. We were going to come home early in the new year and tell you, and then he died and you didn't know about him anyway, and it seemed easier not to tell you at all."

"Easier for whom?" says Lydia, whose grammar is perfect, even under duress.

"For me," says Nina. "Easier for me. Some things get to be about me. I thought this should be one of them."

"What the fuck, Nina," says Mariana, sitting down.

"And my thought about all of this is that you shouldn't get married unless you really, really want to," says Nina to Beata, as if Beata is the only person in the room. "Because when you lose that person, part of you dies. And it isn't worth it unless you're all in."

"Were you?" asks Beata.

"Oh, yes," says Nina. "I was. And so was he."

Beata's chest burns with all the words that she can't figure out how to say.

"I wish we'd had a chance to get to know him," says Aunt Judy in a gentle voice.

"Thank you," says Nina. "And thank you for all the work you put into this party. I'm sorry it didn't turn out the way you wanted."

"That's not important now," says Aunt Judy.

"Nevertheless," says Nina.

"Ladies," says Aunt Judy, raising her voice to fill the room. "We're going to bring the festivities to a close. Thank you all so much for coming. We'll see you at the wedding!"

"They won't, though," says Eloise. "They won't see us at the wedding."

"The party wasn't that bad," says Zoe. "I'm sure they'll all still come."

"I mean there won't be a wedding," says Eloise. She turns to Beata. "This has been a mistake. I started it, and I'm finishing it. The wedding's off."

SEPTEMBER

CHAPTER 26

Mariana

Mariana lies in bed and listens to the quiet in the house. It's Saturday, the girls are at Devlin's, and she's alone. She can stay in bed all day if she wants to, but it's complicated. Her desire to throw the covers over her head and burrow like an animal is strong. On the other hand, the sheets smell like Tim, and every time she catches his scent, she dies a little. This is because she seduced him last night, and then completely freaked out on him, exactly as he predicted she would, and she's quite sure he'll never want to see her again.

She replays the tape in her head over and over again, every excruciating detail of it. "You're lovely," he said, kissing her shoulder as he unhooked her bra. She understood that it was true for him, and she was glad beyond words to be with a man who believed her lovely.

"I don't remember having this much fun with kissing before," she said to him. Post-marriage dating made her feel young, in all the best ways: every kiss was to be savoured. It was all unexpected, all new.

Tim laughed, and kissed her again. "I've always been a fan," he said, and she tangled her fingers in his hair.

"I'm messing with your rules," she said.

"You are," he said.

"Do you regret it?"

"Not yet," he said.

She moved over to the bed and turned down the covers. Climbing in, she propped her head on the palm of her hand, striking what she hoped was an invitingly sexy pose. It had been so long since she'd made an effort to seduce someone. She felt self-conscious.

"Are you okay?" asked Tim. He was looking down at her with an expression of concern.

"Yes. Of course. Why do you ask?"

"You seemed to be somewhere else for a moment," he said.

"I'm right here," she said, reaching for him and pulling him down so that they lay facing each other. He stroked the line of her hip, kissed her gently. "Would you prefer it if I turned out the lights?" she asked.

"I'm fine either way. Would you prefer it?"

"I think so." She got up and flicked off the light switch. "How's that?" asked Tim.

"Better. Where were we?" she said. She manoeuvred herself underneath him and threw her arms around his neck. His mouth moved down the length of her body, and she closed her eyes. When was the last time she and

Devlin had been intimate like this? The memory eluded her. It couldn't have been that long ago, she thought. Their problems remained outside the bedroom until the very end. Even when she wanted to kill him, after the twins, he could still smile at her and she'd melt.

"Mariana?" said Tim. "Where are you?"

"I'm here," she said.

"I don't think so," said Tim.

She rolled to her side, away from Tim, so he couldn't see the tears in her eyes.

"Mariana," he said, in a calm voice, "tell me what you need right now. Do you want me to stay, or would you prefer to be alone?"

"I don't know," she said, and she began sobbing. "I'm sorry. I don't understand what's going on with me right now."

Tim rubbed her back. "You're grieving."

"What do you mean?"

Tim sighed. "Hypothetically," he said, "when a person is task-oriented, a marriage breakdown offers many distractions from painful emotions such as loss. Such a person might focus on the mechanics of separation—the legal issues, for example, or the logistics of shared custody—instead of the feelings she might have about the end of the relationship. And sometimes it isn't until that person contemplates a new attachment that those feelings surface."

Mariana felt ill with mortification. "Please forgive me."

"There's nothing to forgive. You're not ready, and that's okay. But I think we should get dressed and go into the other room and have some tea and relax. And when you're feeling like yourself, I'll go home."

"But I want to be with you. I do."

"Your head does. But your body has its own timeline. You don't recover from a trauma like a divorce overnight. You can't speed it up by being smarter and more determined than everyone else."

"How long?" Mariana felt the vise in her chest loosening.

"It's different for everyone," said Tim, "which is why two years is a safe bet."

"Are you mad at me?"

"Not at all," said Tim. "I'm mad at myself."

Mariana groans, shakes her head, and returns to the present. She needs a distraction that doesn't involve dating for the foreseeable future. Perhaps this is an opportunity to reconnect with her sisters, for example.

She picks up the phone and dials Nina. "Are you working today?" she asks.

"Not until tonight," says Nina. "What's up?"

"I need to get out of the house," says Mariana.

"I'm having lunch with Beata in an hour," says Nina. "Why don't you join us? She could use some cheering up."

"I'm on my way," says Mariana. She rolls out of bed, throws the sheets in the laundry, and showers the humiliation from her skin. She dresses fashionably, in samples from the FairMarket line, and puts on makeup. She may be romantically inept and professionally dissatisfied, but she can dress like a woman who has her shit together.

It's not until she arrives at the restaurant that she realizes how absorbed she's been with her own concerns lately. Are Beata and Eloise in contact with each other? How is Nina coping with her grief? She has no idea. She kisses first Nina, then Beata on the cheek and says, "How *are* you?"

"Much as you'd expect," says Beata. "It's nice to get out of the house."

"How's Oscar?"

"He's being exceedingly polite, which makes me nervous. I think he's afraid I'm going to break or explode or cry."

"Are you?" asks Mariana.

"I wouldn't rule it out," says Beata.

"What about you, Nina? What's going on?"

"I like being back in the ER. I've found an apartment near the hospital that I'm going to rent for the time being."

"I'm so glad that you'll be in town for a while. I've missed you. We all have. Which reminds me, have you talked to Mom lately?" Mariana asks.

"I talked to her this morning," says Nina.

"Did she say anything about the Women's March?"

"It was the main topic of conversation," says Nina, laughing. "Do you want to be more specific?"

"I was wondering if she was making any plans to celebrate with her out-of-town friends after the march," Mariana says.

"She hasn't mentioned anything to me," says Nina. "Has she said anything to you, Beata?"

Beata shakes her head. "She seems fairly distracted with the logistics of the march itself. Why do you ask?"

"Do you think we should throw a party for her?" asks

Mariana. "It struck me the other day that if thousands of people are showing up to listen to her speak, we should mark the occasion, do something to honour her legacy."

"The woman loves a party," says Beata. "And we all know I'm not giving her the one she really wants. Could we surprise her, do you think?"

"Normally, I'd say no," says Mariana, "but Dad says she's barely been home lately. She's at meetings for the Women's March every day."

"It would be great to get Dad involved," says Nina. "He needs a project."

"I'll talk to him," says Beata. "I bet he'll be willing to host it at their house, if we take care of all the details."

"I wondered about that," says Mariana. "I can run over there after the speeches end and get things set up."

"This is beginning to sound like an elaborate excuse to get out of marching with our mother," says Beata, smiling.

Mariana laughs. "That's a side benefit," she says. "I'm eight years older than you are, and I got dragged to a lot more protests. You know what it's going to be like. She'll be so surrounded by security and admirers that we'll be lucky to see the top of her head in the crowd."

"I'm not saying you're wrong," says Beata. "Anyway, Mom wants to march with Oscar, so I'll be in the fray."

"Perfect. Someone has to get her to the party, so that can be you."

"It's a great idea," says Nina.

"What do we need to do to get the ball rolling?" asks Beata.

"I'll turn my mind to it and send you some ideas later in the week," says Mariana. She hesitates, and then says, "Have you heard from Eloise?"

Beata's smile vanishes. "She asked me to give her time, and said she'd call when she was ready. She hasn't called."

"I'm so sorry," says Nina.

"I don't deserve your sympathy," says Beata. "Your husband died, and you were so brave that you didn't even tell anyone. My girlfriend dumped me because I was being horrible to her, and I'm a disaster. Why can't I be more like you?"

"I'm not sure you want to be like me," says Nina. "To be honest, I'm trying to be less like me. It's not ideal to get hit with a major tragedy and discover that you're alone. I couldn't share Nils's death with people because I hadn't let them share his life."

Mariana wishes she knew what to say, and she's relieved to see the waiter arrive with their food. "Why are we eating salads?" she asks, as the mood around the table lightens. "We deserve fried food and dessert." She stabs at the lettuce with a fork. "I almost forgot to tell you guys. Harmony Delacroix is trying to persuade Mom to be the face of her anti-aging cosmetics line."

"I know," says Nina. "She told me about it this morning. I told her she can't do it."

"Good," says Beata. "Did she agree?"

"She did once I gave her a rundown on FairMarket's product history."

"Ouch," says Mariana. "Look, why didn't you tell me

that you had such a problem with FairMarket before I took a job there?"

"You're a journalist," says Nina. "I trusted that you'd done your research. You have a right to your own opinions."

"When are you going to admit that working at FairMarket doesn't suit you?" says Beata. "You have serious talent, like Mom does. You're brilliant and articulate. You're a leader. Why are you hawking beauty products?"

"It was a stopgap. I needed time to catch my breath, collect a decent paycheque, focus on my kids, and figure out my next step."

"Have you figured it out yet?" says Nina.

"No," says Mariana. "All I've figured out is that I hate doing work that doesn't matter."

"There's no shame in working to collect a paycheque, but you're letting yourself get stuck," says Beata. "I thought you were going to do some freelance writing to keep your name out there."

"I was."

"What happened to that?"

"I don't know. I got distracted. I couldn't come up with a compelling story."

"Get undistracted," says Beata. "There's a compelling story right in front of you. Why don't you write about Nina?"

"Would you let me do that?" Mariana asks Nina.

"Not if it were only about me," says Nina. "But if it were about Nils and the other doctors at my hospital in Syria and Physicians for Peace? I'd let you do that."

"Is it hard to talk about him?" asks Beata.

"Not as hard as I thought it would be. I've been practising. It gets easier the more I do it."

"Who have you been talking to?" asks Mariana. It's a relief to know that Nina has confidantes. She's curious to know who they are.

"Zack, mostly," says Nina.

"You've been talking to Zack? About Nils?" Beata looks astonished. "You can't trust him, Nina."

"Sure I can," says Nina. "Trust is a choice. Zack's a good listener, and he knows what it's like to keep going after your life blows up. I don't feel like I need to pretend to be normal around him. It's relaxing."

"Maybe I should talk to him," says Beata.

"Maybe you should," says Nina. "You could come stargazing with us sometime."

"I could do what?"

"Come stargazing," says Nina. "That's what I do for fun. Nils taught me. He was an amateur astronomer. He started a club at the hospital, and we'd go up on the roof and he'd teach us the names of the stars. That's how I met him."

"I can't decide if that's the dorkiest thing I've ever heard, or the most romantic one," says Mariana.

"It was both. He was both. That was Nils, exactly. His whole family was into stargazing, and they'd take holidays around major astronomical events. We were supposed to meet them in Chile at Christmas this year, to see the solar eclipse." She takes a sip of water. "They're still going, along with some friends from the astronomy club. It's a kind of memorial trip."

"Should you be going too?" asks Mariana.

"I have a ticket," says Nina. "But I can't seem to make a decision. I haven't met Nils's family yet. If I go, it might make the whole experience worse. It could be the worst Christmas of my life, and of theirs. And what if we don't connect? What if it's awkward and sad? On the other hand, I know Nils would have wanted me to go. I could use a sign."

"Do you believe in signs?" says Beata.

"No," says Nina. "But I wish I did."

CHAPTER 27

Zoe

It's late in the morning and Zoe is in bed, Mavis tucked under her arm. Oscar is staying with Will this weekend, and they haven't agreed on how or when to tell him that they are dating. Will has spoken to Beata and managed to calm her down; there's more than enough drama in this blended family with the wedding cancelled and Beata's relationship with Eloise in limbo. Oscar comes first, everyone agrees.

But in the privacy of her own bedroom, Zoe has the audacity to wonder (theoretically) what circumstances might permit her needs to come first. She doesn't need to come first all the time, or even most of the time. She only wants an occasional taste of it. She's not lobbying for parity, even. Children *should* come first, although Oscar isn't her child.

And yet, leaving children aside, it does feel to her, when she reflects on it, that the men in her life have tended to ask for, and receive, more of what they want than she has. She accepts that she is an enabler in this regard. Who wouldn't prefer to be with a contented, satisfied man? Every woman knows that a man's threshold for discomfort is lower. Every woman's radar is set to read the faintest signals of dissatisfaction, triggering an early-warning prevention/intervention system of coddling, jollying, praising, and accommodating.

That was life with Richard. And where did it get her? It's been a year since she realized, lying in bed one Saturday morning like this one, that it was over. A year since she reached out to a lawyer and got the process of disentanglement rolling. Two years since he started cheating on her (this is what she can confirm, but it was probably longer ago than that); eighteen months since she took him back; eleven months since he moved out; nine months since she told her family. The memory of that life exhausts her so much that she can hardly move.

Will Shannon is no Richard. And yet.

There's a knock at the door. "Come in," she says.

"So," says Zack. "Do you want to tell me what's wrong?"

Occasionally, Zoe has a flash of her future, where she and Zack are still bickering, still up in each other's business, still living together. They are so old by this time, so completely devoid of sexuality, that most people assume they are married, and refer to them as "that funny old couple down the street." There are worse fates, she supposes; there are always worse fates. But it isn't the one she'd choose, that's for sure. "Were you abducted by aliens in LA?" she says.

"Not that I remember. Why?"

"When did you become Mr. Emotional Connection?"

"Oh, *those* aliens. The ones who alter your brain to make you more sensitive and emotionally available? Come on, Zoe. You've been down for a few days. Spill."

As much as she wishes for solitude from time to time, she has to admit that having a roommate is healthy. Zack is a valuable safeguard against excessive wallowing. "I'm frustrated with the Will-slash-Oscar situation."

"It's not going the way you wanted?"

"Who would want a part-time semi-secret romantic entanglement?"

"Some people might."

"I'm not one of those people."

"I got that from the amount of time you're spending moping around the house."

"I'm not moping," she says. "I'm waiting for it to resolve itself." Will's a smart guy. Eventually, he's bound to realize how unsustainable it is to keep their relationship under wraps and take steps to resolve it, proving that he loves and understands her.

"How's that going for you so far?"

"Don't play Dr. Phil with me, Zack. It doesn't suit you."

"Lying around in bed feeling sorry for yourself doesn't suit you."

"I'm not here for your entertainment, Zack," she snaps. "Don't you have friends you can harass?"

"Not really," says Zack. "Not anymore. I have followers, but not friends, which is my own fault. I was a shitty friend to people who weren't shiny enough for me when I got famous, and then when I got un-famous, they weren't around anymore. And the shiny ones sold me out to the tabloids, or just disappeared. So no, I don't have friends I can harass. I have you."

Zoe feels her heart clench. "I'm sorry," she says. "I—" Her phone rings. It's Will.

"Answer it," says Zack. "I'll take Mavis out. We'll be back soon."

She watches him go, and then she answers the call. "Hi there," she says. "What's going on?"

"Not much," says Will. "Oscar and I are watching soccer and making Bolognese sauce. I'm passing along my one culinary secret to the next generation. How about you?"

"Oh, you know, errands. Busy day, as usual." Why is she lying to him? Why shouldn't he, her sort-of boyfriend, know she's sad and lonely? Is that so repulsive? Zack, she recognizes, has a compelling point. This isn't who she is. Or rather, it's who she is, but not who she wants to be. She takes a deep breath and says, "Listen, Will, have you given any more thought to telling Oscar about us?"

Will lowers his voice. "I know we decided to tell him once Beata found out, but now that she's calmed down, is it necessary to rock the boat? I feel like Oscar and I are doing some solid father-son bonding. Maybe I shouldn't interfere with that. And you and I are getting to have adult time, like regular people who date. So, thinking out loud here, is this a problem that needs to be fixed? Eventually, obviously, it would, but for the foreseeable future? I'm not sure."

Zoe doesn't try to smother the flash of anger. "I'd point out that you're whispering, and presumably hiding from Oscar right now. So that, to me, seems like a problem if you take the perspective of someone who wants the relationship to evolve. This relationship, the one between you and me, I mean, rather than the one between you and Oscar. If you're asking my opinion, which I'm not sure you were."

"Are you upset?"

"Why would I be upset, Will? Why would I be upset that I never come first with you?"

"Whoa," says Will. "Where is this coming from, Zoe? This is a new relationship, a terrific one, but still, a new one. And I'm learning how to be a father for the first time. I'm trying not to fuck it up. I thought you understood that."

"What I understand is that we've known each other for over twenty years. I'm Oscar's first cousin once removed, apparently. I'm a known quantity. Either you're serious about me or you're not. I'm not here for your convenience. I have my own plans to make."

"What do you want me to do here, Zoe?"

"I want you to tell Oscar about us so that we can be a real couple. I don't want to spend Christmas pretending that I'm single when I'm not. I don't want to feel as though I'm single when I'm not."

"I've said that I'll tell him. I'm waiting for the right time."

"That's not good enough."

"Zoe," says Will, "it's what I can offer right now."

Silence grows on the line between them. She knew that once she opened this conversation, they'd end up exactly here, although she expected it to take longer than it has. But Will, to his credit, doesn't prevaricate. He's a straight-up, unvarnished, almost-perfect guy. This is no surprise; she knows him. She wonders why she, like so many women, is perennially susceptible to the ideal of male perfectibility. She's too old to expect that a man can change, or even to wish for it. She's mature enough to live with flaws. But the deal he's offering isn't one she can accept.

"I deserve to be with someone who puts me at the centre of his life," she says.

"Of course you do," he says. "You deserve nothing but the best. I want that for you."

"Where does that leave us?"

"Zoe," he says, "I could ask you to wait. I could give you a timeline. But I don't know what that would look like. You want certainty and you aren't unreasonable to want that. I think we're at an impasse."

There's nothing more to say, except the truth. "That's extremely disappointing." She hangs up. "Damn it," she says.

She hears the front door open and close, and the tell-tale clatter and jingle of Mavis's return. She climbs out of bed, puts on a bathrobe, and goes down to the kitchen.

"Uh-oh," says Zack. "You don't look good. What happened?"

"We broke up," she says, and bursts into tears.

"Fuck, fuck, fuck. It's my fault, isn't it? Goddammit,

Zoe. You should know not to listen to me when it comes to relationships."

Zoe blows her nose. "Give me credit for making my own mistakes. I didn't ditch the last nice man on earth because you told me to. I did it because I'm an idiot."

"Let's sit down," says Zack. They do. "Would you take it back if you could?"

"I don't know. It depends."

"On what?"

"On how badly my life turns out as a result."

"Okay," says Zack. "What's the worst-case scenario?"

"I never find love and I live with you forever."

"That's mean, but I'll overlook it. So, the worst-case scenario is that you never find love, but you live a full life with a family who loves you, dogs to cuddle, friends to vacation with, and work you enjoy, and from time to time, you feel like you missed out on a great love that might have been."

Zoe is quiet for a moment. "It isn't bad. But I think I'd be disappointed."

"You might. But not all the time, or even all that often. How does that compare to settling for a relationship that doesn't give you want you want? You had that relationship already, so it shouldn't be hard to imagine."

"No," says Zoe. "It isn't."

"Which scenario is more desirable?"

"If I have to choose? The friends and family one. And dogs." She scratches Mavis. "But I hope I don't have to choose."

"I hope that too," says Zack. "In the meantime, go make your bed."

"Why?"

"They teach you that in rehab. You make your bed every day, so that your future self will have an experience of order and comfort."

"I like that."

"It works on a bunch of levels. You want to ask how your future self will feel about having that drink, or eating that unhealthy meal, or settling for that guy who can't love you the way you deserve to be loved. Once you do, you can make better choices, choices that demonstrate you respect yourself."

"How's that working for you?"

"Well, every day I'm putting more distance between my present self and the one who was an insufferable turd, so I consider that a positive. Every day, I get up, I'm nice to the people who love me despite my flaws, I treat my body with care, I recycle, and I fulfill my contractual obligations. I'm kind to animals." He puts food in Mavis's bowl. "And at night I tuck myself into a bed with hospital corners, and then I get up and do it all again. And that means that I'm not creating any new regrets, because I have enough to last me for a very long time already."

Zoe gives her brother a hug. "I love you," she says. "Almost as much as I love Mavis."

Zack kisses the top of her head. "Likewise," he says.

"Zack?"

"Yeah."

"I know you had a bad time in LA, but you seem pretty recovered to me. What am I missing? How serious was your substance problem?"

"Serious enough to make some bad decisions, but not serious enough to compromise my health in any permanent way."

"Does that mean you're an addict, or not?"

Zack smiles. "Everyone's an addict," he says.

OCTOBER

CHAPTER 28

Mariana

It's a crisp, sunny day, ideal for a political uprising. Mariana feels younger today than she has in years. The organizers are expecting thirty thousand marchers, an astonishing number, and with the weather cooperating, it could be even higher.

Tomorrow, she's handing in her resignation at FairMarket. She has no regrets. It's been a learning experience, even if the main thing she's learned is that she isn't the sort of person who can do a job for money alone. Her mother's legacy lives in her, however much she's denied it in the past. She's Lydia Hennessey's daughter. She wants to make a difference in the world. And she'll be able to do that as the new communications director at Physicians for Peace. The piece she wrote last month profiling surgeons in war zones proved click-worthy (take that, MERLIN), and Nina's former employer was so delighted with the increased visibility that they offered her a full-time job. The piece inspired Zack too, apparently: he's working on a pilot for a series about modern war surgeons, with a female lead based on Nina. Zack says it's *M.A.S.H.* meets *Grey's Anatomy*, and that Nina missed her calling as a script doctor.

And then there's Tim. After her behaviour last month, she expected never to see him again, but he is far more mature than she would be in the same circumstances. She apologized, he accepted, and now they are not dating, although they are doing so exclusively. They hang out, and talk at night before bed, and go to movies. They do not refer to each other as boyfriend or girlfriend, nor do they kiss or have sex with each other. If adults can go steady without dating, that is what they are doing. Modern love is extraordinarily confusing, if indeed it is love. Time will tell, says Tim. He's here in the gathering crowd somewhere, and the thought warms her.

She's standing below the stage, waiting for the organizers to lead her to her seat. She and her sisters, and their father, have reserved spots in the front row, behind the podium. After the speeches, Mariana and Nina will race over to her parents' house to meet the caterer and put up the decorations. Marvin, Beata, and Oscar are going to march with Lydia and distract her if she asks where Mariana and Nina are. As far as Mariana can tell, Lydia is oblivious to the party planning that's been happening for weeks.

Beata comes to stand next to her and murmurs in her ear. "The estimates on numbers are rising," she says. "The police liaison says the crowd may be twice what the organizers anticipated. And one of the men's rights groups put out a call on social media for supporters to show up and protest. Apparently, it went viral, and they aren't sure what to expect. They're trying to pull in additional officers to place along the parade route."

"Should we be worried about Mom?" asks Nina, joining the huddle.

"They say not," says Beata. "They're going to have security all around her, on stage and during the march itself. Mom, of course, is fired up and ready for a fight. She loves this stuff."

Mariana shakes her head. "She's something, isn't she?"

An organizer comes up to them. "It's time to take your seats, ladies. Your dad's already up there."

From her seat, Mariana gazes out at a sea of placards and pink hats. One of the organizers is at the microphone, introducing Lydia. The list of her mother's achievements goes on and on, drowned out at points by the applause and cheers of the crowd. Is it impossible, Mariana wonders, or simply very, very hard, to love someone and still manage to see them in their entirety? Can you hold a perspective that includes irritation at your mother's shortcomings in parenting and awe at her contributions to the wider world? Mariana vows to try. At least today, she is going celebrate what her mother has given her, not as a daughter, but as a woman.

Lydia rises and walks to the microphone. The crowd is deafening. She raises her hands. "Friends," she says, "we stand at a crossroads in history. The future is female, and it's glorious."

Mariana's throat is tight. She glances at her sisters and sees tears in their eyes.

"Many of you are angry," Lydia says. "Many of you feel your voices have not been heard for far too long. But history runs forward. It's made every day. And we are part of it. This march, today, is part of it. You must not fear your anger. Anger is energy and fire and passion. Anger is what brings us here, but *it cannot take us further.* It isn't powerful enough to get us where we want to go. To get there, to a world where equality and justice flourish, where the principles of democracy are realized, we need hope. Anger burns down what is rotten, but hope lets us create a new world. Hope lets us imagine what is possible."

Women are screaming and crying, Mariana along with them. "I am proud to stand here today," says Lydia. "Proud to stand with my daughters behind me. Proud to walk alongside each and every one of you. Our work is not done. It continues with every act of resistance, however small. It continues every time we rise up and say what we know is right and what we know is wrong. It continues every time we support our sisters. It continues when we say that we will not be divided, when we recognize that our strength is in our numbers and in the truth of our cause." Lydia spreads her arms. "Walk with anger," she says, "but walk also with hope. Let the Women's March begin!"

She turns away from the microphone and blows a kiss in their direction before she's hustled off the stage by her handlers.

"That's my cue," says Beata. "I'll plan to have her at the party by four, and I'll text you if anything changes. Ready, Dad?"

"Will you look at that," says Marvin, pointing. The crowd is huge, and it's already moving with its own internal logic, serpentine, inexorable. "Look what your mother made."

"She's an amazing woman," says Nina.

"She always was," says Marvin. "See you girls later."

It takes Mariana and Nina forever to push through the stragglers and make their way to the car. There's a huge jam in the parking garage, and by the time they exit, they're running late for the caterer. Mariana hits the gas.

"Wait," says Nina. "Do you hear that?"

"Hear what?" asks Mariana.

"Sirens," she says.

CHAPTER 29

Beata

Beata is relieved to see Oscar exactly where he's said he'll be, and he slides into their group as if he's been there all along. She hugs him harder than is really warranted, and he makes a pretend wheezing noise, but he's smiling.

"Did you hear your grandmother's speech?" she asks. The roar of the crowd is ear-splitting, assaultive.

"What?" he yells.

"The speech! Did you hear it?"

"It was rad," he yells. "Way to go, Grandma."

"Thank you, darling," shouts Lydia. She grabs Oscar's hand. "Your first political protest! I'm so proud!"

Beata pulls Oscar close and speaks directly into his ear. "We need a plan about what to do if we get separated. There are a lot more people here, and it may be hard to stick together. If you get separated from me, jump on the subway at the first stop you see and head for home, okay? When you're clear of the crowd, text me and let me know you're fine."

"Give me some space, please," says Lydia to the female police officers walking beside her. "I want to march with my grandson."

The four of them—Lydia, Beata, Marvin, and Oscar— lock elbows and move as one, exhilarated. All around them, women are singing and chanting and carrying placards. Their causes are urgent and specific: protection for abortion rights, better funding for women's shelters, pay equity, prevention of gender-based violence, improved sex education. Their voices are united in a desire for action. It's beautiful, and Beata is so proud to have her son at her side. "What do you think?" she asks. Oscar shakes his head. He can't hear her. He's smiling, though. On her other side, Lydia is beaming.

As they round the first bend in the parade route, the march hits a sour note. The counter-protesters are here, their predominantly male faces set in angry lines. They chant and wave signs that read FEMINISM = FASCISM and END THE WAR ON MEN.

"What a bunch of assholes," says Oscar.

"It's their right," says Beata, feeling a rush of anger as she looks at their pinched, nasty expressions. "But I don't disagree with you."

"What's the war on men?" asks Oscar.

"There isn't one," says Marvin.

"How dare they ruin our day?" says Lydia. "I'm going to give them a piece of my mind." She steps out of formation and rushes towards the men's rights protesters, her security detail and Marvin in hot pursuit. "You don't belong here!" she shouts. "Go home!" Other women begin flanking Lydia, joining in the chorus of insults, and the men respond in kind.

"Mom!" Beata grabs at Lydia's sleeve as the crowd begins to surge around them. She misses, and Lydia is pushed forward, straight into the conflict. The noise is deafening. She grabs Oscar by his shirt front and screams into his ear. "You need to go! You'll get crushed!" She can see his mouth moving, but she can't hear him. She pulls him towards her again, and yells, "Go home! Not safe!"

"Got it!" he yells back, and she hugs him fiercely and then pushes him away. She turns back to where Lydia has disappeared into the crowd, and steps forward. Where is she? Where is her father? She isn't tall enough to see. Wait? Is that her mother? The crowd is squeezing her on all sides, and it's hard to breathe. She's being jostled, and she nearly loses her balance.

She hears a siren. She needs to find her parents and get out of here before they get crushed. She tries to move sideways through the crowd, the way you swim out of a strong current. She's able to make some headway and finds herself standing on the sidewalk, a few inches higher than the road. She realizes she needs to scan the crowd from above, and she notices a group nearby, standing up on a large concrete planter full of trampled chrysanthemums. She pushes her way to the base of the planter and clambers up, ignoring the shouts of the people she displaces.

She digs in on her corner of the planter, trying to hold her ground. Below, more protesters are trying to climb out of the fray. She ignores them. She's trying to get her bearings. There are placards blocking her view. Where are her parents? Is that her mother's hat? There's a surge in the group, like a wave hitting shore, as several new bodies force their way onto the planter from the other end. There's nothing and no one to brace against. Beata loses her footing, grabs at air, arms windmilling as she falls, blinded by the sun in the blue, blue sky.

CHAPTER 30

Oscar

Oscar sits in the waiting room at the hospital, his phone clutched in his hand. He has blood on his shirt, his mother's blood. He wants to take the shirt off and throw it out, but he's freezing as it is. It was warm when they left this morning, so he only wore a T-shirt. This place smells like disinfectant and sweat and old people, and they should turn the heat on.

He arrived here by ambulance with his mother, which was nothing like on television. It wasn't exciting; it was terrifying and so loud that his ears are still ringing. And they rushed his mom through the doors on a stretcher, and they didn't let him follow her. He doesn't know what's happening to her. He doesn't know if she's okay.

"What should I do?" he asked the paramedics, as they ran past him with his mother. Her eyes were closed.

"Call your dad," said one.

"Wait here," said the other.

That was an hour ago, and he's still in the same crappy

plastic chair. His legs stick to the vinyl when he moves. He has his earbuds in, with the volume high enough to compete with but not entirely eclipse the other sounds in here—monitors beeping and people yelling and crying, and one very scary man thrashing around in handcuffs with tattoos on his face. Oscar won't cry, though, even if his mom says crying is healthy and boys should do more of it.

He closes his eyes and sees her fall again. Go home, she'd said, but he didn't. Why would he leave, when it was getting exciting? What sense did that make, when his mother and grandparents were diving in and he was a head taller than any of them? He waited until he was sure she wasn't watching, and then he slipped into the crowd behind her.

He watched his mom climb up on a concrete planter, and he did the same, but at the other end so she wouldn't catch him. From this vantage point, the protest felt wilder, like a campfire grown too big and hot. He felt a flicker of fear then, and thought about slinking away, but he couldn't see an easy route out. People on the ground were getting nervous—you could tell by the way they were pushing at each other—and more of them were trying to climb up to where he was. A few launched themselves at the planter together, and he was jolted to the side, along with all of the bodies standing around him. He felt the wave move along the row and saw three figures slide off at the other end, one spectacularly, arms circling and feet kicking, like a stunt from an action movie.

Except it was his mother, who hates action movies. There's too much violence in the world without inventing more, she says.

He feels a hand on his shoulder. He opens his eyes and sees Zoe crouched in front of him. The hand belongs to his father, who's sitting in the chair beside him. They must have arrived together, which is surprising. They've been avoiding each other lately, at least around him, which sucks; Oscar hoped they might get married, like his mom and Eloise. He'd rather have Zoe for a stepmom than anyone else. Zoe and his dad are more than friends, you can tell, but he's pretty sure they had a fight. Maybe they've made up now. That would be nice. "Oscar," she says. "Are you hurt, honey?"

"It's not his blood, Zoe," says his dad. "You're okay, right, buddy? It's going to be okay."

Oscar nods. Will puts an arm around Oscar's shoulder. It feels nice. Oscar leans back into it. "I'm so glad you called me," Will says. "I was so worried when I heard about the riot, knowing you were in the middle of it . . ." He clears his throat.

"Zack's on his way," says Zoe. "Should I tell him to go back and get you some clothes? Maybe a clean T-shirt and a sweatshirt?"

Oscar nods again. It's difficult to speak. He's so tired.

"Zoe?" Aunt Mariana appears, with Grandpa Marvin. "What's going on? Where's Mom? Where's Nina? She came ahead of us."

Zoe looks confused. "Lydia's here? Oscar, did you see your grandmother here?"

"I don't know," he says. "I didn't see her after she got in a fight with those men's rights assholes. She went all ninja on them. I saw her break a sign over someone's head. Grandpa was there too."

He closes his eyes. He wants to lie down and sleep for weeks. He hears the adults talking around him.

"Never a dull moment in this family," says Will, looking at Zoe. He leans in to Oscar and says, very quietly, "Let's keep that part about your grandmother to ourselves for now, okay Oscar? I want to make sure she isn't in any trouble. A lot of people were hurt today."

"Okay," says Oscar. "Can you ask about Mom?"

"I'll find out about your mom," says Zoe. "In the meantime, how would you feel about going home to my place with Zack and having a rest?"

"I promise to text you the second we hear anything about your mom," says Will. "You can be back here in fifteen minutes. Does that sound like a decent plan?"

Oscar nods. "Thanks, Dad," he says.

CHAPTER 31

Zoe

How do you get over a guy like Will Shannon? Zoe wonders. How do you purge your romantic feelings for someone who meets you at the hospital in the middle of a family crisis, wraps you in his arms and plants a kiss on the top of your head, and says, "I can't tell you how happy I am to see you"? How do you move on from a man who squeezes your hand as he scans the waiting room for his son, and seeing him, murmurs, "Thank god," and then runs over and folds him in a bear hug? How do you not burst into tears as you see that boy wilt with relief when his father says, "It's going to be okay, Oscar. I'm here with you. I love you"?

With great willpower, it turns out. But Zoe is nothing if not disciplined, and there are distractions: Mariana and Marvin arriving and wanting information about Beata and Lydia; Zack appearing, guilt-stricken and needing reassurance that his aunt and cousin are not going to die hating him; and Oscar providing details about Lydia's clash with protestors, which led Will to suggest that he might be needed in a professional capacity.

"Let's get Oscar out of here," says Will.

"I'll send him home with Zack," Zoe answers.

"You really are the most competent person," says Will. "It's such an attractive quality."

"Let's figure out who's in the building and what state they're in," she says. If he wants competent, she'll show him competent. She walks over to the reception desk and asks for Nina.

"I'll page her," says the nurse.

"Can someone give us an update on Lydia Hennessey?"

"I'll check."

Nina appears, wearing scrubs.

"Oh, thank goodness," says Mariana. "What's happening? Why didn't you call us?"

"I'm sorry," says Nina. "It's absolutely crazy in here, and they needed me to jump in. Beata's in surgery. I had an update half an hour ago, and it's going well, but she was one of the more seriously injured patients to come in. She had some internal bleeding, but they've got it under control." She pauses. "Dad, you should sit down. You're very pale."

"I lost them," says Marvin. "I lost them in the crowd."

Nina sits down next to Marvin and holds his hand. "It's not your fault. Beata's injuries are serious, but her doctors believe that she'll be fine. She hit her head pretty hard, and she broke some ribs, which punctured her lung and caused some other problems. It'll be a little while before she's back on her feet, but she'll get there."

"And Lydia?" says Marvin. "What about your mother? I'll never forgive myself if . . ."

"She's okay, Dad. You can see her. She's on some pain-killers, so she's woozy, but she's conscious. She has a mild concussion and broken leg that is going to need some surgery, but probably not today."

"Thank god," says Marvin.

"I think it might be helpful if I had a quick word with her," says Will, "as her lawyer. Marvin, is it okay if I see her now?"

"Yes," says Marvin. "All right."

Nina leads them into the emergency room. "You might find her confused," she says, opening a curtain to reveal Lydia in a hospital gown.

"I'm not confused," says Lydia.

"Lyddie," says Marvin, sitting down on the bed and clasping her hand in both of his. "I was so worried."

"Why?" says Lydia. "You know I'm unsinkable." They smile at each other.

A nurse stops by the bed. "You're awake," she says. She turns to Nina. "Doctor, the police want to get a better picture of what happened at the protest. Your mother was in the middle of it, and they'd like a word with her. Do you want me to say she's not up to it?"

"Give us a few minutes," Nina says. "I'm not sure how lucid she is."

"I'm perfectly lucid," says Lydia.

Nina's pager goes off. "Damn," she says, "I've got to go. Mom, Dr. Walker is admitting you, and I'll come and see you as soon as I can. As for the rest of you, don't stay too long. Mom needs rest."

They crowd around the bed, and Will closes the protective curtain. "Ms. Hennessey," he says. "How are you feeling?"

"Who are you?" says Lydia.

"He's Oscar's dad," says Mariana.

"Oh, the baby daddy. You're working your way through the Hennessey women, I hear."

"Don't be rude, Lyddie," says Marvin. "He's trying to help."

"I'm not being rude, am I?" she asks Will. "You're very handsome, you know. I bet you have good genes." Her gaze wanders over to Zoe. "Oh, it's Zoe. When did she get here?"

"The whole family's here," says Marvin. "Everyone was worried about you."

"That's so sweet," says Lydia. "But totally unnecessary. I'm completely fine." She tries to sit up, but slumps back down, putting a hand to her head. "I have a headache."

"You hit your head earlier today," says Will. "At the march."

"Oh yes," she says. "I remember now."

"As you know, I'm a friend of the family, but I'm also a lawyer. And if it's okay with you, I'd like to be your lawyer, at least for today."

"Marvin?"

"I think it would be a good idea to talk to him, Lyddie," says Marvin.

"How was my speech?"

"It was amazing," says Mariana. "Everyone loved it. It got a lot of coverage. You made me cry."

"I did?" says Lydia, obviously delighted.

"You did. I was really proud of you. Now, could you answer a few questions for Will?"

"Okay."

"I don't know if you remember," says Will, "but there was a fight during the march."

She closes her eyes. "It was such a beautiful afternoon. The singing, and the chanting . . . I was marching with Oscar, you know. He's getting so grown up. It was his first protest march!"

"He told me," says Will. "Do you remember seeing a group of men's rights activists on the parade route?"

She makes a face. "I did. Such unpleasantness. There's no reason for it. But there are always going to be men who need to blame women for whatever's wrong with their lives. It made me so angry. I told them what they could do with their self-pity. I even grabbed one of their signs, and I—"

"Lydia?" interrupts Will. "Can you listen to me for a second?"

"Yes?"

"Some people were hurt today, and the police are going to be asking questions about how the confrontation started. I think it would be best if you didn't talk to anyone unless I'm with you. If I'm not here, I'd like you to say that your son-in-law is a lawyer and you'd feel more comfortable with him present."

"Didn't anyone tell you? You can't be my son-in-law. Beata likes women."

"He knows, Mom," says Mariana. "He wants you to say he's your son-in-law so the police don't push you around."

"I'd like to see them try," says Lydia. Her face brightens. "Am I getting arrested?"

"No one's getting arrested," says Will.

How do you get over a guy like Will Shannon? Maybe, thinks Zoe, you don't.

"That's too bad," says Lydia. "I haven't been arrested in ages."

CHAPTER 32

Mariana

"Mom?" says Mariana. She pulls the curtain around Lydia's bed to give them privacy. What a nightmare this day has been. Beata is out of surgery, but they haven't been allowed to see her yet. Mariana feels wrung out. "Are you awake?"

Lydia's eyes flutter open. "Where's Marvin?"

Mariana clasps her mother's hand. "You've been asleep for a few hours, Mom. Nina took Dad home. He'll be here in the morning, after he's had some rest."

"That's good," says Lydia, her eyes closing again. "He needs looking after. Not like me."

"No," says Mariana. "Not like you."

Lydia is quiet for a few minutes, and Mariana thinks she's drifted off again, but then she says, "We were supposed to be the women behind the men. They educated us for it. Math for household budgets. Science for cooking. History for . . ." She seems to struggle for a word.

"Don't worry, Mom. It's not important."

"It is," says Lydia, as if it should be obvious to anyone paying attention. "I have to remember. It's going to be on the test."

A nurse opens the curtain. "How's she doing?"

"A little foggy," says Mariana. "She's back in high school, I think."

"That's to be expected, between the bump on her head and the painkillers. It's good that she's communicating, even if she's hard to follow. Are you going to sit with her for a while?"

Mariana nods.

"We just changed shifts, so I'll be here if you need anything. Let me know if she seems uncomfortable."

Lydia opens her eyes again. "Are you married?" she asks the nurse.

"Mom," says Mariana.

The nurse laughs. "Not yet," she says. "But I don't need to be in a hurry, do I?"

"No," says Lydia. "You have to be careful. If you marry the wrong man, you can flush years of your life down the toilet. My daughter did that."

"I'm sorry to hear it," says the nurse.

"Mom," says Mariana, "my life is fine." And it is, she realizes.

"I never thought I'd get married," continues Lydia. "That was never my plan. I wanted to be a professor. I wanted to write books."

"You did write books," says Mariana.

"I wasn't a very good wife. I should have been better." There are tears in her eyes.

The nurse checks Lydia's vitals. "Morphine can make patients quite emotional," she says to Mariana, "but your mother's doing exceptionally well, considering her age. Try not to worry. I'll be out at the nurses' station if you need me."

"Poor Marvin," says Lydia.

"Dad's doing fine, Mom. He's only tired."

"No. He's sad. It's all my fault."

"He's worried about you, that's all. You're going to see him again in the morning." Mariana strokes her mother's hand.

"We had a fight. He wants to help Beata."

"Beata has great doctors looking after her. There's nothing we can do for her right now."

Lydia doesn't seem to hear her. "Why does she want a baby? She's only twenty. She needs to go to school. She's going to ruin her life!"

Mariana sighs. The day is endless. "You don't need to be upset, Mom. That was a long time ago. Oscar's a teenager now."

"She doesn't have to have the baby. I don't want that for her. She can have a baby when she's older." Her mother's agitation is painful to watch, and Mariana considers calling for the nurse. "Marvin says that she can do what she wants, but he doesn't understand."

"What doesn't he understand, Mom?"

"He isn't a woman. He doesn't know what she'll be giving up."

Mariana gives up on trying to separate the present from the past. "It's Beata's choice to make, Mom."

"I fought for her to have the right to choose. But she's choosing wrong. She wants to have the baby and raise it alone."

"She won't be alone, Mom. She has you and Dad and the rest of us to help."

"What will people think?"

"Since when do you care what other people think?"

"She needs to keep it a secret from the baby's father."

"Why should she do that?"

"Because if she doesn't tell him, she can say she went to a sperm bank."

"That was *your* idea?" says Mariana.

"They're going to come after her if they find out."

"Who's going to come after her?"

"The press," says Lydia. "She's my daughter. It's going to be a story. Lydia Hennessey's daughter had an unplanned pregnancy. Lydia Hennessey's daughter doesn't believe in abortion."

"So what?" says Mariana. "So what if they say that?"

"They'll use it to discredit the movement. To hurt me. I can't have that. I've worked too hard. We need to tell a different story." Lydia looks at Mariana, defiant.

"Oh, Mom," says Mariana.

Lydia's face falls. "Marvin is so mad at me," she whispers. "Beata, too. I deserve it."

"No one's mad at you," says Mariana, gently. "Not anymore."

"I need to see Beata. I need to tell her I'm sorry. I shouldn't have asked her to lie. It's my fault that Oscar hates her now." Lydia closes her eyes. "We need to give Beata a nice wedding. I want to make it up to her. I want her to have everything she missed out on."

"I'll take you as soon as she can have visitors, okay?" Mariana strokes her mother's hand. "But you have to let Beata decide what she wants now. She's a grown-up." This doesn't seem like the moment to remind her mother that Beata and Eloise have broken up. "And as for Oscar, he's a teenager. It's his job to hate his mother. Don't you remember how much we used to fight when I was that age?"

"I got in a fight," says Lydia.

"You were just telling me. With Dad, right? About Beata?"

"No," says Lydia, confused. "With the protestors. I hit a man on the head with his own sign."

"At the Women's March?"

"He deserved it."

"I'm sure he did. But Mom? You shouldn't tell anyone you did that, okay? Remember what Will said? The lawyer?"

Lydia looks straight at Mariana, and her eyes are clearer than they've been. "Of course I remember," she says.

"I'm sorry I wasn't at the protest with you," says Mariana.

"I'm sorry too," says her mother. "I always liked taking you to protests with me. My first child. So scrappy. So fierce." She looks sad. "Beata is more like your father."

"Is she?" asks Mariana. "I don't know. It's pretty gutsy to have a baby at twenty and raise him alone, against your mother's wishes. I'd say that Beata's got some fight in her. So does Nina. And so do I." She strokes her mother's hair. "You gave us that."

CHAPTER 33

Beata

Beata opens her eyes. The room is bright with fluorescent light that hurts her head. Where is she? She turns her head to get her bearings, and sharp pain explodes in her skull. "Ouch," she says.

She hears a crash, and Eloise appears at the side of the bed. She looks rumpled and sweaty. "You're awake," she says. "You're in the hospital. I'm going to call the nurse."

"How long have I been here?"

"Three days," says Eloise. "You were hurt at the Women's March, do you remember?"

"Oscar?"

"Oscar's fine. He wasn't hurt."

"My parents?" Her tongue feels thick and pasty.

"Your dad's totally unscathed. Your mom broke her leg, and they're putting a pin in it this morning. I saw her yesterday and she was relishing the prospect of becoming a bionic woman."

The nurse bustles in. "Welcome back," she says. "There are a lot of people who are going to be very happy to see you, starting with this lady right here." She smiles at Eloise. "Eloise has been here the whole time, you know."

"What happened?" croaks Beata. Her whole body hurts.

"You were knocked unconscious," says the nurse. "And you broke three ribs, one of which punctured your lung. But all in all, I'd say you were very lucky." She checks Beata's blood pressure and takes her temperature. "It's going to be a big effort to talk while you have the chest tube in, so try not to do too much of that, okay?" Beata nods. "Are you in pain?"

"Yes," says Eloise. "She is." She squeezes Beata's hand. Beata squeezes back. It's a relief to be understood without having to speak.

"She's going to be fine, Eloise. Her vitals are nice and stable. Her body's been through a lot." The nurse turns to Beata. "I'll bring in some meds for the pain and hook them up to your IV. Sound good?"

"Thank you," says Eloise.

"Tell me everything," Beata says, slowly and with great effort. She remembers being in the crowd, all those bodies pressing in, not being able to see. She remembers not knowing if Oscar was safe.

"You went crowd-surfing and hit concrete. Oscar saw the whole thing." She sees Beata's expression. "I promise, he's fine. I wouldn't lie to you. He got you out of harm's way and into an ambulance. He was in this very room this morning. I don't think he'll be in a hurry to attend any other political protests anytime soon, but otherwise, there's no lasting trauma. Will is keeping a close eye on him. You should be very proud. He was the hero of the hour."

Tears leak out of the corners of Beata's eyes. "I'm sure this is a lot to take in," Eloise tells her. "It's normal to feel emotional. The important thing to remember is that you're going to be fine. Your ribs are healing, and the tube can come out in a couple of days. The concussion will take longer. You need to be prepared for a few months off work and a lot of rest so that you can recover properly." Eloise adjusts Beata's pillow. "But it's not the end of the world. It could have been so much worse."

Yes, thinks Beata. She could have lost this magnificent woman, which she had come terrifyingly close to doing. That would have been the end of the world. And for what? What had she been fighting against? The privilege of growing old with Eloise?

Her anger has burned to ash, and now she chooses to hope. "Marry me," she says.

Eloise's gaze is steady. "I appreciate the sentiment, honey, I do, but I won't hold you to anything you say for the next little while." She smiles. "I've had some free time to read up on brain injuries lately."

Beata's chest hurts, but she forces the words out. "I made a terrible mistake. I miss you all the time. Marry me. Please."

"I'll tell you what," says Eloise. "Why don't we give it a few days? If you still feel the same way once you're on your feet, we can talk more about it."

"You waited for me," says Beata. "I'll wait for you for as long as it takes."

NOVEMBER

CHAPTER 34

Beata

Beata was prepared to wait as long as necessary to persuade Eloise that she was serious. But once Eloise figured out that her head injury wasn't impairing her judgment, events transpired quickly. Her ribs are still tender around the incision, and every so often, she gets a splitting headache, but all in all, her recovery has been easy. She is lucky, she knows.

Eloise and Lydia have planned the whole wedding. Eloise's old law partner, now a judge, is doing the service. They've given Lydia free rein on flowers, music, and outfits for Mariana's girls, and this seems, miraculously, to have satisfied her.

The doorbell rings. "I'll get it," yells Oscar.

She hears the door open and close, voices, footsteps on the stairs. "Beata? Are you ready?"

"Come on in." The door opens, revealing Nina in an emerald-green coatdress with a pillbox hat. "Wow. You look spectacular."

Nina hugs her carefully. "That's my line. Oh my gosh, Beata, look at you. You're perfect. You're like a hippie princess."

"You like the flower crown?"

"I love the flower crown. It's very you."

"I made up with Greta from the bridal shop."

"How did you do that?"

"I gave her my credit card," says Beata. "And as for you, you're a knockout. The look is very Jackie O., as Greta would say."

"Mom decided to dress the whole family so that we'd coordinate in the photos. She wanted jewel tones, and hats."

"The photos are going to be fairly casual. I mean, we didn't hire a professional. We asked my friend Abby to take some documentary-style shots."

"I think plans may have changed on that front," says Nina. "But don't worry about it. Just focus on enjoying your day."

"What did you do on your wedding day?"

"It's not very romantic."

"Tell me anyway."

"We took the day off, which we rarely did. We slept in, and cooked breakfast, and ate in bed. And then at noon, we washed up, went to the chaplain's office at the hospital. There was a lull in the fighting, so our friends were able to come, and we all squeezed into this tiny room. And then we went to a restaurant around the corner and had dinner."

"A restaurant?"

"It's funny, even in a war zone, there are these little corners of normalcy and comfort. For us it was Naranj. We had our first date there, and we'd treat ourselves with a dinner out whenever we had a particularly bad day in surgery. There were six who celebrated our wedding with us, and the owner treated us like royalty, and it was magical."

Beata smiles. "That sounds beautiful."

"It was. I loved every minute of it. And I wish the same for you today."

"Thank you." Beata's eyes are wet.

"Don't cry!" Nina dabs at her face with a tissue. "Your makeup is perfect!"

"Okay." Beata breathes. "I'm ready. Let's get this show on the road."

"Oscar?" calls Nina. "Come and escort your mom downstairs." Beata hears him take the stairs two at a time. "I told him he looks devastatingly handsome and shockingly old."

Nina speaks the truth. Oscar is wearing a tie and jacket, like a more-than-respectable citizen. He looks sheepish and proud and awkward all at the same time, and her chest aches with love for him. She makes a choking sound and reaches for the tissue box.

"Mom," says Oscar. "Don't freak out, okay? Everyone told me not to upset you today, and they'll think I did if you're all snotty and red."

Beata laughs through tears, and stands. "Crisis averted," she says. "Come and give me a hug." He towers over her now; he's grown visibly over the past few months. He lets her hold on to him for several seconds without squirming.

"Time to go," says Nina. "Oscar?" Oscar holds out his elbow and Beata takes it, and they make their way down the stairs and into the car without incident.

Nina pulls the car up in front of the local restaurant where they're holding the ceremony and reception. Two valets spring into action, one taking Nina's key, the other holding the door open for Beata, and then Oscar.

"I didn't realize they had a valet service," says Beata. "And they've landscaped since I visited last month. Those ornamental trees with the fairy lights weren't here."

"Roll with it," says Nina. "Oscar, go find your grandmother and tell her we're here and headed downstairs. She should tell Eloise that we can start the ceremony in fifteen minutes."

"So soon?" says Beata. "I thought we were going to mill around and visit before the ceremony."

"It's been determined that no one should see you before the ceremony," says Nina, directing her around the side of the building, through a door, and down a flight of stairs. "So we're going to do that part right away and then you can enjoy yourself."

"Was that the original plan?" Beata isn't completely confident in her memory. She's forgotten many of the details from the march and from her subsequent hospital stay; she doesn't remember her accident at all. It's unsettling, and she's vigilant about identifying other gaps in her recall.

"It's not your brain." It's so reassuring to have a doctor in the family. "You're recovering really well, Beata. There have been some changes that weren't discussed with you. But maybe try to focus on the big picture. At the end of it, you'll be married and there will be a nice dinner with cake."

"I like cake," says Beata. The room in the basement is comfortable and warm. Beata sits on a sofa, and Nina hands her a glass of champagne. "Is it a good idea to start drinking now?"

"I think definitely," says Nina. "Do you want to look over your vows for a few minutes? Oscar will come and get us when it's time."

"That's okay," says Beata. "I know them. I'll get nervous if I read them again. Let's have a toast instead."

Nina sits beside her. "What are we toasting?"

"Love," says Beata. "In all its messy, glorious, heartbreaking, crazy-making, necessary beauty."

Nina nods. "To love," she says. They clink their glasses.

"Did you decide what to do about Christmas?" asks Beata.

"I'm going to go," says Nina.

"Did you get a sign?"

"No. But I decided I'd rather go and have a bad time than stay here and wonder if I might have had a good time."

Oscar appears. "They're ready," he says. "Grandma says we have to go back outside and around the front so that you can make a proper entrance."

"Then that's what we'll do," says Nina.

They retrace their steps. Nina opens the front door to the restaurant, and Beata glides in on Oscar's arm.

The space is utterly transformed. Once a rustic Italian trattoria, it is now a winter garden. The walls are covered with trellises, and the trellises with flowers. Vines (artificial, Beata assumes) hang from the chandeliers, vases with fresh arrangements sit atop each table, and there are petals strewn across the floor. "Good grief," says Beata.

"Don't you just love it?" says Lydia, appearing in front of them amid applause. She has not slowed down, despite her reliance on crutches. "The colour combination in the table arrangements isn't exactly what I wanted, but overall, I'm very pleased."

"It's overwhelming," says Beata.

"Didn't I tell you?" says Lydia to Nina. "I said she'd love it when she saw it."

"Mom," says Nina, "go and sit down for the ceremony. We're doing the procession now, right?"

"Right," says Lydia. "I'll cue the musicians."

"What musicians?" says Beata, as a photographer appears and begins to snap pictures. "Who is that?" She hears the opening bars of Pachelbel's Canon. "Is that a string quartet? Is Eloise processing?"

"Smile," says Nina. "And start walking when I get halfway down the aisle."

"The aisle?"

"Where the petals are. Ready? Here we go."

"Don't let me fall, Oscar," says Beata. "Petals can be slippery."

"I won't," he says. "I promise. Now?"

"Now."

One step, and then two, and she catches sight of Eloise in a spectacular satin gown in winter white with jewelled combs in her dark hair. "My god," she says, as she reaches Eloise's side, "you're breathtaking. But why weren't you in the procession?"

Eloise takes her hand. "Because I wanted to be able to watch you coming towards me."

"Good answer," says Beata.

"Friends," says the judge. "We are gathered together today to witness the union of two people who have made the joyous discovery that they belong together, and who have decided to formalize their relationship in marriage. Beata and Eloise have written vows to each other that reflect their intentions. Before I invite them to speak, is there anyone here who can offer an objection to this marriage?" He pauses. Hearing none, he continues, "Beata, please make your vows to Eloise."

Beata squares her shoulders. She is ready. "Eloise," she says, "for many years before I met you, I had a good life. I had a family who loved and supported me, and friends all over the world, and interesting work, and a son. I needed nothing else. And then I met you, and you pushed me to imagine a bigger life. You challenged me to believe that I could replace *or*s with *and*s, that I could be connected and independent, a mother and a partner, true to you and to myself.

"Life is fragile. We don't always have as much time as

we would like. Windows of possibility open, and they close. I don't want to miss another moment of the time that's been given to us to be here, now, together. And so I make these vows to you today: I promise to love and support you for all the days of our lives together. I will celebrate with you, grieve with you, care for you in times of trouble, and cheer for you in times of success. I will remember that it is as important to receive love as it is to give it, and I will receive your love each day with gratitude.

"I promise to live with purpose, integrity, and authenticity, both in our relationship and in the world outside our home, so that you can be proud to call me your wife, and so that my contribution to our shared community is a positive one.

"I promise to appreciate and celebrate all of the beautiful aspects of our life together, so that we never lose today's sense of wonder at having found each other."

Eloise squeezes her hands. There are tears in her eyes, but when she speaks, her voice is clear. "Beata," she says, "I promise to love you unreservedly, as the woman you are today and the woman you will become in the future. I will honour our differences as strengths. My love will never depend on a static conception of who you are or who we are. I recognize the inevitability of change and will strive to welcome it with grace. I will make space in our marriage for evolution, risk, creativity, and growth.

"I promise to put our family at the centre of my life. I promise to love Oscar and to embrace my role in his life with energy, compassion, wisdom, and love. I promise to honour your family, in all their rich and varied differ-ences, and find a place for myself within it."

The judge beams. "Beata and Eloise, having witnessed your declaration of love for one another, it is my sincere pleasure to pronounce that you are now married, and to invite you to seal your vows with a kiss."

DECEMBER

CHAPTER 35

Zoe

It isn't Zoe Hennessey's usual habit to take a boyfriend to Christmas dinner at her mother's house, but habits are a relic of the past. How can it be a year since she told her parents that Richard had left? It feels like only a few months and also a decade ago.

Will puts a hand on her knee. "Everything okay?"

"Everything's wonderful. You're sure it's not too much pressure, spending Christmas with my family?"

"Your family includes my son, his mother, and her wife, who are all my family. I might ask you the same question. I have every confidence that we can roll with it."

"What did you do last year?"

"I went to my friends Matt and Avery's house, and deflected questions from their relatives all night about how I could possibly be single. How about you?"

"I did the same thing we're doing tonight, except that I told my parents I was getting a divorce."

"It shouldn't be too hard to improve on that, then," says Will, parking in front of her parents' house. "Zoe?"

"Yes?"

"Have I told you how happy I am with you?"

"You have," she says. "But I never get tired of hearing it."

"Thank you for giving me another chance."

"You're worth it," she says, leaning in for a kiss.

After a few minutes, Will says, "We should probably go in."

"If we must." They get out of the car and walk to the door, holding hands. She knocks, and Zack opens the door.

"I wondered if you were going to come in or just make out in the car all night," he says.

"Zack!" says Judy, coming into the hallway. "Don't embarrass them. They're in love."

"Please stop talking," says Zoe.

"Why don't you get Zoe to help you in the kitchen?" suggests Zack. "You can ask her all about her new boyfriend."

"You know, Judy," says Will, "I'm quite an experienced sous-chef."

"You don't say," says Judy.

"Save yourself!" hisses Zoe. "You know not what you do."

"I guarantee that I can survive an hour in the kitchen with your mother better than you can."

"Bold words," says Zoe.

Will raises his voice. "I'm at your service, Judy. Put me to work."

"I'm so glad you could join us this year," Judy says, leading the way to the kitchen. "Larry and I were delighted to hear that Zoe had a lovely new man in her life. And Oscar's dad, too! What a coincidence!"

"That's not exactly the word I'd use," says Zack to Zoe. "Where's Mavis, by the way?"

"She was looking extremely relaxed at home," says Zoe.

"When is she not?"

"And I promised to bring her turkey leftovers. I thought it might add to the chaos to have a dog underfoot."

On cue, Mariana's girls dash past, screaming. It's unclear whether they are happy or angry. Maybe they are both.

"Girls!" Mariana pokes her head into the hallway from the living room. "Lower your voices. Santa is watching! If you want to chase each other, go down to the basement." The girls open the basement door and descend. Mariana shuts the door and leans against it.

"Does the Santa threat work?" asks Zack.

"Not to the naked eye," says Mariana. "But I still use it on the off chance that it has some small internal effect."

"Rumour has it that you're dating," he says.

"I'm pre-dating," she says. "We're taking it extremely slowly."

"Since when are you the type to take anything slowly?"

"Since I met a therapist who has his shit together and insists that the people he dates have their shit together as well."

"No kidding," says Zack. "And? What's the report?"

"I'm terrible at it, but he's worth it. I'll see him tomorrow, when the girls are with their dad."

"Are they upset to be moving around at Christmas?" asks Zoe.

"Not that I can tell," says Mariana. "They've been told they'll get more presents."

The door to the basement opens, and Oscar emerges. "Jesus, those kids are loud," he says.

"Tell me about it," says Mariana.

"Oh, shit," says Oscar. "No offence, Aunt Mariana."

"None taken."

"Is my dad here?"

"He's in the kitchen," says Zoe.

"Cool." Oscar wanders down the hall.

"Come and sit down," Lydia calls from the living room. "We're going to call Nina on the computer."

Zoe finds Lydia on the sofa, her leg in a cast and extended on an ottoman. Marvin is next to her and they appear to be . . . cuddling. She realizes she's staring and deliberately shifts her gaze to Beata, who's fiddling with a laptop. "Are we calling her, or is she calling us?" asks Beata. "Hi, Zoe."

"Hi. Is Eloise here?"

Beata smiles. "She disappeared upstairs. I think she wanted a few minutes of quiet. She'll be back soon."

"Does anyone want a drink?" Zack asks.

"I'll take one. Thanks, Zack," says Marvin.

"Mariana, can you come and help Beata?" says Lydia. "I don't want to miss Nina."

"I'll come with you and check on the sous-chef," Zoe says to Zack.

At the bar, Zack fills two glasses with club soda.

"What about Marvin?" asks Zoe. "No double Scotches this year?"

"Nope," says Zack. "He's cutting back."

"Really?"

"Really. And he and Lydia are going to marriage counselling with Ben Jackson."

"Who's he?"

"You know. The celebrity therapist with the TED Talk. Beata knows him."

"Huh," says Zoe. "It's a Christmas miracle."

"They're everywhere," says Zack. "You just have to pay attention. For example, your boyfriend is managing our mother beautifully. She's thirty minutes from turkey launch, and—knock wood—there's no sign of a meltdown. I like that guy. You should keep him around."

"That's the plan," she says. She walks over to where Will is stirring gravy, resplendent in a floral apron. She wraps her arms around his waist. "How's it going in here?"

"Aren't you supposed to ask if you can kiss the cook?" says Will.

"Can I—" Zoe begins, but Will stops her with a long kiss.

"You don't really have to ask," he says. "And to answer your question, Judy and I are an unbeatable team. Larry is pinch-hitting, Oscar's in the bullpen warming up, and we're going to bring this dinner home with no extra innings."

"So, you don't need any help in here."

"Correct," says Will. "Go chill out with your cousins and keep your aunt out of here. Although the broken leg is fairly effective, am I right, Judy?"

"He's very naughty," says Judy to Zoe, laughing.

"She knows," says Will, winking.

"Getting uncomfortable," says Zack. "Leaving now."

"Coming with you," says Zoe.

In the living room, Mariana has taken control of the laptop. "The connection's bad, Mom. We're trying again now. We'll get her, I promise."

She taps on the keyboard. "There," she says. "I think we've got a connection now."

Nina's image pops up, waving. "Merry Christmas!" she says.

"Where are you?" asks Lydia.

"I'm in the Atacama Desert, in Chile. The sky here is unbelievable. We're going stargazing tonight after our Christmas dinner."

"How was the solar eclipse?" asks Beata.

"Incredible," says Nina. "And a bunch of our friends from the hospital in Syria were able to make the trip. It was an amazing reunion. Nils would have adored it."

"Who's with you now?" asks Lydia. "I still wish you'd come home for Christmas."

"I know," says Nina. "But I wanted to spend some time with Nils's family. I never got to meet them when he was alive, and this was a perfect opportunity." Nina looks away from the camera, and Zoe wonders if she's crying. But when she turns back, her face is bright and clear. "I have a surprise for you, Mom," she says.

"No more surprises!" says Lydia, but she's laughing.

"You'll like this one," says Nina. She gestures to someone off screen, and a second face appears, a woman with silver hair cut in a stylish bob.

The woman waves. "Lydia Hennessey," she says. "I cannot believe it."

"Sigrid?" says Lydia. "Oh my god. Sigrid Larsen?"

"Sigrid is Nils's mother," says Nina. "It turns out that she knows you."

"Nils's mother," says Lydia faintly. "How is that possible? Sigrid, my god. Your son! I have no words."

"How do they know each other?" Zoe asks Mariana, who shrugs and shakes her head.

Lydia wipes her streaming eyes. "Sigrid was part of the European delegation at the 1985 World Conference on Women in Nairobi, and I was in the American delegation. We drafted a women's manifesto together. Such a mind! She coined the term 'all issues are women's issues.'"

"I believe you came up with it, dear friend," says Sigrid. "But certainly it was an exceptional moment in the global feminist movement. I was always sorry that we didn't keep in touch. But now we share a daughter, and you are my family."

"Oh, Nina," says Lydia. "I'm overwhelmed."

"Do you like your surprise?" asks Nina.

"I love it," says Lydia. "Marvin, come and wave to Sigrid."

Additional faces appear on the screen, all smiling and waving. "This is Linas, my husband," says Sigrid, "and these are my sons, Patric and Milo. Nils was my oldest child."

"I am so sorry for your loss," says Lydia. "I'm heartbroken."

"As we are," says Sigrid. "But having Nina with us for Christmas this year has made such a difference. It has been so joyous." Her images wavers and then resolves. "I'm afraid that we may lose our connection. I will call you again soon, but you must make plans to visit us. We have a holiday house in Lapland. The aurora is magnificent there. You are welcome, all of you." Her image freezes and then disappears. Nina's voice emerges from the machine. "We're losing the connection. Merry Christmas, everyone! I'll call again soo—" And she's gone.

"Nina looks happy," says Lydia, wiping her eyes.

Marvin puts an arm around her shoulder. "She does," he says.

"She wanted a sign," says Beata to Mariana. "I'd say that counts."

"Dinner!" calls Judy.

"Can you help me up, dear?" Lydia asks.

"Always," says Marvin, with great tenderness.

The clan gathers around the dining table.

"How wonderful to see everyone here," says Judy. "Welcome to Will and Eloise, who join us this year for the first time. We have an annual tradition, which provokes some mixed feelings, I know, but which is very important to me."

"Mom?" says Zack. "I have an idea about that."

"You do?" says Judy.

"I do. I'm going to propose an update to the tradition for this year. Hear me out, okay?"

"Okay," says Judy, in a tone of nervous encouragement.

"We're going to do an experiment. We're all going to take one minute to reflect on the past year and come up with one word that captures your sense of gratitude."

"One word?" says Judy.

"Only one word," says Zack. "It could be a person, or a thing, or a feeling, or a mantra, whatever. It's personal. It's not for public consumption. We're all going to scream the word out loud at the same time, so don't be shy. Everyone's going to be concentrating on their own word so they won't hear yours."

"Santa!" shrieks Iona, while Siobhan yells, "Presents!"

"Exactly, girls. Just like that, but all together. I'm going to ask what we're grateful for, and then I'm going to count to three, and *then* we're all going to call out our answers at the same time. Yes?"

The twins nod, solemnly.

"Any questions?" asks Zack. "All right, you have one minute to find your word. Go."

Zoe closes her eyes, and she's flooded with possibilities. She's grateful for Nina's resilience in the face of tragedy. For her brother's health and brilliance. For Oscar's steely determination. For Mavis's soft fur. For her mother's unyielding commitment to family. For her father's gentle heart. For her aunt and uncle's renewed affection.

"Everyone ready?" asks Zack.

"I need another minute!" says Zoe.

"You have twenty seconds."

For Mariana's fire and Beata's grace. For her thriving business. For Will's readiness and ability to love. For Richard, the crack in her life that let the light come in. For heartbreak. For healing. For suffering. For courage. For longing. For belonging. For love.

"Do you all have your words? All right then, here we go. What are we grateful for? One, two, three!"

It's deafening and joyous, and over too soon. The girls are giggling hysterically, and Mariana is laughing with them, and Oscar is giving Will a high-five, and Judy is hugging Larry, and Marvin is wiping his brow, and Lydia is toasting him with champagne, and Beata and Eloise are embracing, and Zack is grinning from ear to ear.

It's over too soon, but it's enough. It's more than enough.

THE END

Acknowledgements

Whken I tell people that I wrote a divorce comedy, they invariably ask how such an oxymoron is possible. The truth is that time and reflection can transform even the most painful experience into a good story. For giving me time and the space to reflect, I thank Laurie Pawlitza and Heanda Radomski, women of great brilliance, professionalism, and compassion.

A variety of people assisted with research for this book, including Elizabeth Renzetti and Marsha Lederman, two exceptional journalists who answered my questions about the challenges of working in print media while female and feminist; Amy Stuart, who filled me in on the logistics involved in a Women's March; and Cris Martin, who gave me the dirt on running a small but mighty advertising agency.

As usual, my Canadian editor, Jennifer Lambert, brought out the best in my work. I am truly fortunate. I'm grateful as well to the rest of the team at HarperCollins

Canada, including Iris Tupholme, Cory Beatty, Catherine Dorton, Helen Reeves, Noelle Zitzer, Lauren Morocco, Leo MacDonald, and Michael Guy-Haddock.

My sincere thanks go out to Beverley Slopen of the Beverley Slopen Agency and Samantha Haywood of the Transatlantic Agency, excellent agents both, for their efforts in finding loving homes for this book in various territories around the world.

I am lucky indeed to have a supportive community of writer friends, including the now-notorious Coven consisting of Karma Brown (who provided the most extraordinarily helpful notes on my draft), Kerry Clare, Chantel Guertin, Liz Renzetti, Jennifer Robson, and Marissa Stapley. These women are my first readers and most loyal fans, and I love them madly. I am also grateful to Uzma Jalaluddin, Roz Nay, Laurie Petrou, and Kathleen Tucker for catching errors and providing generous blurbs, and for being lovely humans.

My mother is my most reliable beta reader and has been following the progress of this book through every single draft, as she does with all of my writing projects. I'm grateful to her for every phone call and check-in, and for her love of books in general and of my books in particular. Other faithful beta readers who are not mentioned elsewhere in these acknowledgements include Marie Campbell, Todd Ducharme, Leah Eichler, Bonnie Goldberg, Ana-Maria Hobrough, and Amreen Omar.

Thank you to the following Facebook pals for sharing their most irritating examples of work jargon:

Travis Allison, Anita Anand, Vanessa AvRuskin, Andrew Bernstein, Sandra Block, Marie Budworth, Claire Cameron, Janie Chang, Amanda Clark, Caroline Conacher, Claudio Crespi, Bindu Cudjoe, Rebecca Cutler, Mike D'Abramo, Adriana De Marco, Madeline Duke, Jean-François Gaudreault-DesBiens, Ana Ines Ferrer, Amy Fisher, Jon Friedman, Stephanie Fulford, Anne Hilton, Betsy Hilton, Julie Kibler, Scott Lanaway, Krista Lucenti, Shelley Macbeth, Amulya Malladi, Stephanie Marshall, Kerry Owen, Allison Rogers Sinclair, Patricia Smith, David Spiro, Archana Sridhar, Lisa Stam, Lisa Steinke Dannenfeldt, Christina Wendel, Kevin Wilson, and Jeff Ulster. I hope Harmony Delacroix annoys you in the best possible way.

This book is not dedicated to my beloved children, Jack and Charlie, who are in truth more of an obstacle than an advantage when it comes to writing. It's a good thing I love them to distraction. Shelby, the Canine Assistant, on the other hand, deserves substantial recognition for her gentle snores, which are the background music of my writing days. Most of the time I think she rescued me and not the other way around.

This book got shunted aside for a time while other priorities (see children, above) took over. My ability to manage those other priorities improved exponentially when I married Sasha Akhavi, to whom this book is rightfully dedicated.